TEMPTING Him

BESTSELLING AUTHOR
ISABEL LUCERO

SOUTH RIVER UNIVERSITY #4
BY
ISABEL LUCERO

One

JAYDEN

SPRING BREAK—THE week off from school where students let loose and enjoy not having to worry about assignments, projects, or anything education related. Everyone dips out and spends most of their time getting drunk, whether that be locally, or flocking to major beaches to get drunk there.

For me, I'm sticking close by, but that doesn't mean I won't be fully enjoying myself. Quite a few people don't travel for the break, leaving me with plenty of options. Unfortunately for me, most of my closest friends are all in relationships, so I've lost several wingmen, but I'm recognized as the guy who knows pretty much everybody, so I don't doubt I'll find someone to hang out with.

As soon as I'm finished with my last class of the day and heading toward my car, my phone rings with a call from my dad.

"Hey, Dad," I answer.

"Hey. How's everything going?"

"Can't complain. I'm done for the day and ready for spring break. What's up with you and Mom?"

"We're good," he says. "I want to talk to you about something."

I roll my eyes, grateful he can't see me. Based on his tone, I know this is going to be something I'm probably not ready to hear.

"What is it?"

"Well, I know you've been enjoying your college years, which I can appreciate. You've done well in school, you've succeeded in athletics, and I know your fraternity is important to you. However, based on all the photos your sister's shown me from your Facebooks and Instaphotos, it's obvious you're partying a lot. Why do you kids feel the need to post pictures of you drinking? Anyway," he says, clearing his throat. "It's time to get ready for life after college. Son, you graduate in just a few short months. A job at a restaurant is not going to prepare you for what you're studying to become. I've set up an internship for you."

Ignoring the fact that he got Instagram's name wrong, not wanting to answer why we post drunken photos, and making a mental note to ask my sister why she'd even show him in the first place, I focus on the last thing he said. "What? An internship where?"

"My company has expanded and they've actually set up a new location not far from you. Your old man's got a connection, and I was able to get you a spot working with the man who can teach you the most about marketing."

"Really? Wow, that's awesome."

"It's going to be hard work. You'll lose out on a lot of free time, but at least sports are done for the year."

"When does it start?" I ask, worried I'm about to miss out on spring break.

"Next Monday."

"Nice. Thanks, Dad."

"Thank me by succeeding. Don't mess this up. The boss is pretty stern, and doesn't tolerate any goofing off."

"Yes, sir. I'll be on my best behavior."

He harrumphs. "Good."

"Why is Janae snitching on me, though?" I ask with a laugh, talking about my fifteen-year-old sister.

Dad chuckles. "That's what younger siblings do."

I stay on the phone with my dad for another fifteen minutes before we end the call and I start my drive back to the frat house.

I talk to my parents at least once a week, but sometimes it's been pushed to once every two weeks. I stay pretty busy, and they work a lot, but my sister, Janae, will text me fairly often and I'm sure she tells them I'm alive and well. While also letting them know about all my partying. Brat. I'll have to remember to text her about this later.

While Dad is right, my part-time job as a host and waiter at a restaurant isn't going to teach me much about a career in marketing, I will miss the laid back atmosphere and being able to talk to everyone who comes in. My extroverted self enjoys socializing. Hopefully there will be some cool people in the internship program with me who I can talk to. I don't want to be stuck alone with this uptight boss.

My friend, Ivy Montego, texts me as I'm entering my room. She graduated last year, but we've stayed fairly close. She was basically a friend with benefits for a while, but we've moved on to just being friends.

Hey! Spring break plans?

You know we'll have a party or two at the frat. Other than that, whatever I can get myself into.

Well, I have an invite for you. My friend/boss is having a bachelorette/bachelor party at Three Sheets on Saturday.

Three Sheets? Gross.

Oh stop. It's not that bad.

So the bride and groom are partying together? Aren't they supposed to be separate?

We don't have to stick to the old traditions, you know? Everyone will be partying together and it'll be fun. Come on!

Fine. Luckily, my friend works there, so if anything, I'll just annoy him all night.

You'll have fun. There's a lot of cute and single guys and girls coming. ;)

Well, say no more.

Ha! I'll talk to you later.

~

Later that night, the frat house is booming with people and music. We organized a beach themed party for the first day of spring break for everyone who stayed behind and didn't go to an actual beach, so almost everyone is in their bathing suits. We have a beach backdrop on one wall that people take photos in front of, and a small plastic kiddie pool that's filled with ice and drinks.

Our cups are shaped like beach balls and pineapples, and there's inflatable palm trees in almost every corner. And we're not gonna mention the ridiculous straw hats that Liam wanted to have.

Renzo and Ronan approach me, wearing nearly identical, bright orange board shorts.

"Do people in relationships have to dress like twins, or what?"

Zo smacks me in the arm. "It was a complete accident."

"I bought mine first," Ronan says.

"Mine are a little less orange," Zo chimes in. "And you don't have room to talk. Are you really wearing shorts with roosters on them?"

"They're my cock shorts."

Ronan barks out a laugh.

Dom and Trevor saunter up—Trev wearing a teal pair of swim trunks with banana bunches on them, and Dominic sporting bright blue shorts with black palm trees across them.

"Bananas?" I ask.

Trev rolls his eyes. "Dom said my plain black ones weren't good enough."

"They had a hole near the crotch," Dom exclaims. "I wasn't about to have your cock playing peek-a-boo."

Trevor laughs.

"But bananas?" Renzo questions, an eyebrow arched.

"The store didn't have much left in my size," Trev answers. "And also, fuck off."

Everyone laughs before heading to the kitchen for drinks, where Dex and Violet find us several minutes later.

"So, my dad got me an internship," I announce. "Starting next Monday."

"Where?" Dex asks, his arm slung around Vi's shoulders.

"I guess the company he works for expanded and has an office here now."

"You're wanting to become a marketer, right?," Ronan asks. "Your dad does that too?"

"Yeah, I wanna get into marketing. My dad is a communication specialist but he said he got me in with the guy who can teach me the most. I'm assuming some sort of brand manager."

"Well, that's convenient," Dom says.

"I know. It's like a form of nepotism. Don't judge me, but an internship will help me when it's time to graduate. Maybe I can secure a job at the end of this."

"Well, at least you didn't have to work during spring break," Renzo offers. "I'll be back in the doctor's office this week."

Dom takes a sip. "I only have today and Sunday off. It's about time you join the workforce."

I flip him off. "Please, your boyfriend doesn't even work."

Trevor narrows his eyes at me. "No need to throw me under the bus. It's not my fault my grandparents died and left me money."

Dex, the richest one of all of us, takes a gulp of his beer. "I know, I know. I'm a privileged shit, but I will be working with my dad once I graduate."

"Not that you have to," Ronan says. "If I was the son of a billionaire, I'd travel the world for at least five years."

Dex shakes his head and the topic of work, money, and our future as adults is put on hold, and we allow ourselves to enjoy the short time we have to be slightly irresponsible and relish in tonight.

Most of our lives are spent working to be able to live. We work to pay bills and eat, and maybe afford small luxuries. Childhood isn't nearly long enough, but I suppose I've had my fair share of fun. Well, after this week.

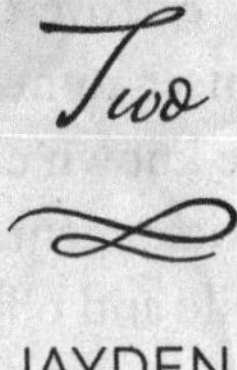

Two

JAYDEN

DAY two of spring break begins with me having to let my job know that I'm quitting. There's no way I'll be able to continue college, an internship, and a job at the restaurant. The internship is paid, so at least I won't be missing out on any money.

A group of us from the frat house go to Nicola's Pizza for lunch, then me and Luke split off and head to the mall to do some shopping before we head back home and I have to start getting ready for this bachelor party Ivy invited me to.

I've never been to one before, so I'm hoping I'll have a good time, regardless of the fact that it's being held at Three Sheets. Not sure if there's much else to these types of parties besides getting trashed.

It's nearly eight-fifteen when I arrive at the bar, dressed in a pair of dark denim jeans, a maroon polo shirt with shoes to match. Normally, this place stays pretty empty. The sign near the road actually boasts about its quiet atmosphere, but when I walk in, it's packed. They must've rented the entire place out.

This sort of situation isn't for everyone. I know plenty of

people who would rather stay in bed than go to a bar where a large group of people you've never met are hanging out, and you have to introduce yourself to them. Luckily for me, this is right up my alley.

I've always been an extrovert. I love socializing and talking to people. I can meet someone and hold a conversation for an hour like we've known each other our whole lives. I thrive in this type of environment, so when I stroll through the crowd of people, I smile and offer friendly greetings until I spot Ivy.

"Hey! You made it!"

"Did you think I wouldn't show? Come on now."

She laughs. "I guess you're right. You're not one to turn down a good time."

"No, ma'am. Now who's the bride and groom? I should introduce myself."

She grabs me by the arm and tugs me behind her until we reach a long table decorated with penis cutouts, balloons shaped like diamond rings, and a jar full of lollipops that look like tits. The bride-to-be sits next to the groom-to-be, wearing a headband with cocks bouncing around with each shake of her head, while the guy has a sash on that says, *Same Vag Forever*.

I laugh, and Ivy gets their attention.

"Tiff, this is my friend, Jay. Jay, this is the beautiful bride, Tiffany, and this is her soon-to-be husband, Curtis."

"Hey, nice to meet you guys. Thanks for letting me crash the party. Congrats," I say, shaking each of their hands. "I like the decorations."

Tiffany laughs. "Thank you. There's more littered around the other tables."

"She chose the decorations," Curtis offers. "I had nothing to do with all the dicks and tits."

"Oh shush," Tiffany says with a giggle, playfully hitting

him in the arm. "Jay, don't mind him. He's mad we couldn't get strippers in here."

Ivy hands me a cup with a penis shaped straw. "Here."

After inspecting the cup, I realize it says, *cheers to beer and bad decisions*. I lift it in their direction, "Well, seems like a good plan to me."

"You don't have to suck out of the dick straw, man," Curtis says.

"Well, it wouldn't be the first time there's been a dick in my mouth, but I appreciate it," I say with a laugh. "I don't normally drink beer with straws anyway."

"We have to use the straws," Ivy complains. "I bought them."

I humor her by taking a huge sip out of the straw while staring into her eyes. "There. Used."

She smacks my shoulder before spinning around and rushing off to talk to someone else, so I maneuver through the tables and say hi to people, stopping to talk to a guy in a South River University football tee. Turns out he played for my team five years ago. The engaged couple look to be in their thirties, but the guests range from early twenties to maybe early fifties.

After I finish my beer, I travel to the bar to harass Ash, the bartender I've gotten to know since coming here to visit Dom from time to time.

"Hey, Ash. Penis straw?" I ask, holding it in his direction.

He laughs. "No thanks. Want something else? They have a keg, but I know you like your shots."

"Sure. Surprise me. Dom back there?"

"Yeah. I'll grab him in a minute."

Ash pours me a shot of dark liquid before disappearing in the back. I swallow it down, making a face as Dominic struts through the black curtain that blocks the kitchen area from the rest of the place.

"Drinking alone?"

"For now," I say with a shrug, holding out my fist to knock with his. "I'll find someone to drink with soon."

"You with this wedding party?" he questions.

"I'm friends with a girl who's friends with the bride."

He snorts. "Of course you are."

"Don't hate on the fact that everybody likes me."

He rolls his eyes. "So, you planning on partying every day of spring break, or what?"

"It's likely. I might as well take advantage. I redownloaded this dating app not that long ago. I may log back in and see if I get lucky."

Dominic chuckles. "Dating app or one-night stand app? And since when do you need an app?"

"Actually, it *is* called One Night Finder," I say with a laugh. "And I don't *need* an app, but when you're just looking for a no strings situation, it works. If I find someone here, for example, they may be under the impression it could turn into something serious."

"And you're not about that?"

I shrug. "Not yet. I don't know. I'm still young."

"You just haven't allowed yourself the time to find someone who may be worth more than one night."

"You fall in love for the first time in your life and now you're giving me advice?" I say with a laugh. "I know Trev made you feel differently about relationships, but yeah, I'm not there yet. I'm twenty-two. I have at least ten years before I have to worry about settling down. Y'all just started early."

Dom shakes his head. "You do you, man. I'm not gonna lecture."

"Yeah, yeah." I turn my head to the right and spot a guy sitting alone at a table in the corner. "Tell Ash to pour me a couple shots, yeah? I'll be over there." I jerk my head in the direction of the attractive man at the table.

Dominic follows my gaze and then looks back at me with raised brows. "Older than you usually go for."

"I'm checking this off my list."

"What's left on your list?" he jokes.

"Not much," I answer with a laugh. "He's hot though. You gotta admit."

Dom studies the man again. He's wearing a suit, but the jacket is hanging from the back of his chair as he holds a highball glass in one hand and types into his phone with the other.

"Yeah, I'll give you that. Doesn't seem like much fun, though. He probably only fucks in the missionary position."

I bark out a laugh. "I'll teach him more positions then. See ya later."

"Good luck."

Starting toward the table, I wonder if he's one of the guests who's just too introverted to mingle. I slide into the chair across from him and give him a smile.

"Hey, I'm Jay. Are you with the wedding party?"

His head snaps up and his piercing blue-green eyes find mine, his brows knitted in the center, confusion and surprise written on his face.

"Sorry?"

I point toward the large group of people. "It's a bachelor/bachelorette party. I thought you might be a guest."

"Oh. No. Just the unfortunate luck of choosing what I thought would be a quiet place when they decided to party here."

"Ah. Yeah, that is unfortunate." I pause, drinking him in. "Or, maybe a blessing in disguise. Maybe what you need is to loosen up and have a little fun."

He peels his eyes from his phone and stares at me. "You think I need to loosen up? Do you know me well enough to make that assessment?"

"I'd like to get to know you a little more," I flirt.

He puts his phone down and rubs his thumb across his bottom lip as he studies me. He's definitely more attractive up close. His skin is flawless and bronze—the color people attempt to get via tanning beds, but his is natural. I can tell. His hair is an inky black, and his thick eyebrows and dark lashes make the blue of his eyes stand out even more. The color is mesmerizing. I'm not sure if they're actually blue or green. They seem to be a good mix of both.

Before he can say anything, Ash appears at the table and drops off two shot glasses before he returns to the bar.

The man in front of me raises a questioning brow.

"Care for a shot?" I ask, handing him one.

He's slow to take it from me, but he does.

"To what?" he asks.

"New friends?"

He shakes his head. "I don't have friends."

"Then you have room for one."

"I don't have room for anything," he counters.

"To tonight?" I question.

He nods once. "Okay."

We clink our glasses together before drinking down the liquor.

"Can I get your name?"

"Aleksander."

I smile. "Aleksander. That'll sound good later." I give him a wink, and for the first time since I sat down, his stern face twitches in what is almost a grin.

Three

JAYDEN

"YOU DON'T FEEL bad for leaving your friends?" he asks.

"Not my friends," I say with a shrug. "Well, one of them is. I don't know the others."

"So, you don't know the people who are getting married?"

"Nope."

"Then why are you here?"

I laugh. "My friend invited me, and I'm not really one to turn down a night out."

He takes a sip of his bourbon, his eyes trained on me. "And yet you've resigned yourself to this table with me. As far away from the fun as possible."

"Oh, I don't know. I think we could have some fun if we wanted."

"What makes you think I'm into men?"

"If you weren't you'd have sent me on my way by now."

"Hmm."

"So, why are you here all alone?" I ask, leaning forward.

"Just trying to relax after a long day at work."

"You came straight here after you got off?" I ask, eyeing the tie around his neck. I could use that later.

"Yeah."

I finish my second drink and get right to it. "You got a place we can go back to?"

He rotates his wrist, the remaining liquid in his glass swirling around as he pins me in place with an intense gaze. "You seem like you're used to getting your way."

I give him a smirk. "I guess I am."

"Well, I'm used to getting my way, too. And I have a feeling I've been on this earth a lot longer than you, so we're going to need to get something straight." I stare back at him, anxious and somewhat eager to hear what he has to say. "What happens tonight will only be what I allow. You'll get what you want, with my permission. You'll do what I say. And when the sun comes up, you'll never see me again."

A thrill of excitement runs through me. I've never been with someone so authoritative, and though I never gave it much thought, I think I might like it. He's right, I'm used to getting my way. I typically control everything that happens in the bedroom. I'm the alpha in the situation, always. In this case, we may have a war of wills between us, but if it's just one night, I guess I can relent.

"Got it."

"Good. Let's go."

He stands up and snatches his suit jacket off the chair, then reaches for his wallet and drops a hundred dollar bill on the table before marching to the door.

With a glance back at the bar, I spot Dom and give him a wink. He shakes his head, a grin on his lips.

~

I don't pay attention to where we're going until we're standing in front of a sky high hotel building.

"You live in a hotel?" I question as we walk through the glass doors. "Or is this what you do for your one-night stands, because you actually have a wife and kid back home?"

He makes a noise I can't quite decipher—something between a huff and snort. It's probably as close as he gets to a laugh. "I definitely don't have a family. I don't have time for it."

"So, you live here?"

"For the time being," he states as we enter the elevator.

"When I was a kid, I always wanted to live in a hotel. It was so much fun to wander the halls late at night, and I would always offer to go to the vending and ice machines." I laugh. "I don't know why I thought it was so much fun."

He stares straight ahead. "It's just a place to sleep at night."

This guy has a hard shell, and he's difficult to crack, but I keep talking, hoping to get him to open up a little bit.

When we enter his hotel room, I let out a low whistle. "A little more than a place to sleep at night. This is like a penthouse. You're living my fucking dream."

As he drapes his jacket over the back of a chair, I run straight for the floor-to-ceiling windows that overlook the city.

"It's probably more than I need, but—"

"But you want the best," I say, angling my head over my shoulder and winking at him.

The hotel room, if you can even call it that, is massive. The living room consists of a giant, creamy white sectional with a glass top coffee table in the center, all of it resting on an oversized white and blue rug that covers the glossy tile floor.

There's a small bar, a dining room table, and a kitchen

made for a chef. The decorations are modern and sleek, making it look both simple and elegant.

"Drink?" he offers, pouring a small amount of dark liquid into a crystal glass.

"I don't really sip on straight alcohol, but I'll take a shot."

He doesn't say anything, but pours more of the same liquor in another glass and extends his arm in my direction. "They don't supply shot glasses, but here you go."

I make a point to let my fingers touch his when I take the glass. "Thank you." I drink it all down in one gulp and place it back on the bar before spinning back around to the windows. "Please tell me you have a balcony."

"Bedroom."

I point in one direction, and he points in the opposite, letting me know where to go. I peek inside and then snap my head back toward him. "My guy," I say with a laugh. "Are you kidding me? I'd never leave. You sure you don't want me for more than one night?"

For only the second time tonight, his lips twitch like he wants to smile. "Don't make it sound like you're a prostitute."

He follows me through his room and onto the balcony. I let my hands run along the metal railing as I gaze down at the view below. "The things I'd do on this balcony."

I sense him at my back before he even touches me. His presence is immense, and the power he radiates permeates my skin, spreading through every vein in an attempt to bring me to my knees. When his breath dances across the back of my neck, goosebumps break out across my arms.

"The things I'm going to do to you on this balcony," he says in a husky whisper.

He barricades me between his arms, pressing himself into my back. My eyes close on their own accord, a soft moan rumbling in the back of my throat.

"I can't wait."

"Do you switch?" he asks, his hands resting on my hips.

"Mm. Yeah."

"How long has it been?"

"A few months," I reply, my breath quivering slightly as his hand travels across my abdomen before sliding over the front of my jeans.

With dexterous fingers, he easily unsnaps my button and drags the zipper down. "Clean?"

"Of course." I moan when he squeezes my growing erection. "You?"

"Yep."

He pushes my jeans down my thighs, and I quickly step out of my shoes so I can remove the pants completely.

Aleksander spins me around to face him before lifting my shirt from the hem and pulling it over my head. His eyes skate over every muscle in my chest, arms, and stomach before traveling up to my face.

"Can anyone see us?" I ask. "Like other guests from rooms nearby?"

"Would that bother you?"

"Not really."

"Good." He undoes his belt and pants, the material opening up and showing me a glimpse of dark fabric underneath.

I reach out to touch him, but he steps back, his eyes on me. "Did you get my permission?"

My teeth sink into my lip briefly. "Ah, right. Only what you allow," I say, remembering his words from the bar. "But that doesn't seem fair."

He isn't fast enough to keep me from touching him when I reach out again. My fingers graze the hard shaft hiding behind a pair of boxer briefs, before I gently cup his balls in my hand. The flutter of his eyelashes lets me know he enjoyed the contact regardless of whether he told me I could do it or not.

When he removes his tie, he says, "Don't make me restrain you."

"I might like it."

Aleksander puts space between us while he finishes removing his clothes—everything but his underwear.

I don't know how old he is, but I'd guess early forties at most, late thirties at least, but regardless of his age, his body is fucking perfect. Sculpted like the most beautiful piece of artwork you could find. There are a few thick scars on his torso that don't look like they came from the hands of a skilled surgeon. A smattering of hair covers his chest and creates a small trail down his stomach, leading to the thing I'm dying to lay my eyes on. Hell, my hands and mouth, too.

My cock twitches and I run my palm across it, squeezing at the tip while I study him.

"Do I have your permission to suck your cock?" I ask in a teasing tone. "Or do I need to continue to wait?"

His eyes narrow on me before he shoves his boxer-briefs down, leaving him completely naked on the balcony, his large, beautiful dick pointing right at me. He sits on the couch, one arm outstretched along the back while his right hand grips the base of his shaft.

"You can wait."

Fuck. I wasn't expecting that.

With torturously slow strokes, his fist moves up and down his erection as his eyes peruse my nearly naked body. He's using me as his own personal porn, and I can't say I hate it.

"Take off your underwear," he states, eyes focused on my crotch already.

"What do you say?" I goad, wondering if I can get him to say please.

"Now," he says instead.

I push them down and start walking toward him. His gaze is frozen on my cock until my foot nearly touches his, then those hypnotizing eyes find mine.

"What do I have to do to get your dick in my mouth?" I ask, my tongue wetting my bottom lip.

He gives me a mocking smirk. "Say please."

I drop to my knees between his parted thighs, my hands on his legs. "If you think me saying please is a hard task, you're wrong. It's only polite to respect your elders." His nostrils flare slightly and I grin. "Can I suck your cock?" I whisper, hands traveling up his legs while the tip of my nose drags up his shaft. "Please."

Aleksander growls, his hand flying to the back of my head. "Do it."

I don't bother wasting time teasing him with gentle licks and kisses, it doesn't seem his style. Instead, I lower my mouth all the way down his shaft, not stopping until I feel his crown kissing the back of my throat.

I suck and slurp, gag and nearly choke, but I put a crack in that hard shell of his, because I have him cursing and gasping, giving me praise and begging for more. It's the most he's talked at one time since I met him.

"Fuck," he says, pulling me off of him. "Get up. Come over here."

He takes me back to the railing, and with his hands on top of mine, he places them where he wants, his cock poking me in the ass.

His lips touch the shell of my ear before he speaks. "Stay here. I'll be back."

"Right back? You're not gonna have me waiting out here for hours with my dick hanging over the balcony, right?"

A sharp smack against my ass cheek has me shutting up. "Stay here."

I watch cars driving in front of the building, people

walking around the block, and I wonder if anybody focused their attention up here if they'd know what was going on. We're ten stories high, but it's pretty dark. If it was the middle of the afternoon, it might be more obvious. My head swivels, checking out the nearby windows. When I spot Aleksander's naked body moving in front of one of them, I know all the closest windows belong to his suite, so we shouldn't have to worry about any neighbors spying on us.

The sound of footsteps approaching has my pulse spiking.

"Look at that. You *can* follow directions."

"Sometimes."

He makes a *tsk* noise before warm slick fingers slide between my cheeks, ripping a gasp from my throat.

"Relax," he says in a soft tone, his fingers gently pressing against my hole.

"Nnuaahh," is the noise I make as he pushes a digit inside.

"That's it," he croons, one hand on my neck as he rotates his finger.

I squeeze the metal in my fists, my head dropping down, chin touching my chest. "Oh God."

"Not here there's not," he retorts. "There's no higher being that'll save you from the devastating pleasure I'm about to fill you with."

"Ahh."

He takes his time stretching me, adding an additional finger after another squirt of lube until he's three fingers in and I'm fucking myself on his hand, begging for more.

"Fuck me," I groan.

Without uttering a word, he removes his fingers, rips open a condom wrapper, and seconds later a hand lands on my back, forcing me to bend at the waist. All I see are cars and twinkling lights as I stare at the view ten stories down, and then his cock slides inside me in a single forceful thrust.

"Ah shit!" I yell as he releases a throaty roar.

Aleksander fucks me like it's the first time he's had sex in years, or like it might be the last time he ever will. His fingers dig into me as he holds me tight, fucking me with such force that he very well could fuck me over the balcony. The fear of that happening never hits me, because all I can think about is wanting more.

"Yes," I cry. "God, yes."

He buries himself to the hilt and stops, his hand coming up around my throat and forcing me into a standing position.

"If you're gonna call out someone's name, make sure it's mine."

I angle my head to try to get a better look at him. "If you're gonna boss me around, don't stop fucking me," I say, moving my hips in an attempt to continue what he put a pause to.

He squeezes my throat and I moan, biting down on my lip.

"You're not in charge here," he says. "If I wanted to stop right now, we'd stop."

"But you know you don't want that," I breathe, pushing my ass against him again. "You want to fuck me until I come over this fucking balcony. You want to shoot your load while you're what...six inches deep?" I tease with a grin.

His eyes narrow again as his jaw clenches. "Try adding a few more to that number and you might be close."

"Prove it. Make me feel every fucking inch."

Aleksander releases my throat and shoves me back down, his fingertips once again imbedding themselves in my skin as he uses my body like a fucking sex doll.

When I drop an arm and slide my hand through the bars, I grab a hold of my cock, grateful for the wide spaces so I'm not being hurt by the metal.

He slows down just as I start stroking myself.

"Don't stop," I demand.

Of course he doesn't listen. Ever so slowly he eases out of me until I can only feel his crown, and then leisurely moves back in. It's fucking torture.

"Fuck me!"

He doesn't say anything, he just continues these languid movements, pulling almost all the way out just to bury himself again.

"Do you feel them?" he asks.

"What?" I reply, still stroking myself, ready to explode.

"Every inch. Do you feel them?"

"Oh shit." I moan as he gives me a little more force with his next thrust. "Yes. I fucking feel them."

"Good."

He doesn't speed up though. The teasing strokes are driving me insane, filling me up, but not giving me the full effect.

"Come on," I all but whimper. "Fuck me. Please."

"Mm," he moans. "I like that."

"I'd like it more if you'd fuck me harder."

The asshole pulls out completely, running a hand over the curve of my ass. "I told you you'd get what you wanted. Don't worry."

"I want your dick in my ass so I can come. My balls are gonna fucking explode."

I think he chuckles. Mr. Serious actually laughed, but the fact that he's finding humor in denying me an orgasm is a little frustrating.

Standing up, I turn around and take a step toward the couch.

"What're you doing?" he questions.

"I'm gonna sit on this couch and get myself off."

"You're trying to provoke me."

I smirk and move past him. "I'm just trying to get off. Isn't that the whole point of this?" I say, gesturing between us.

"No," he says simply, shaking his head.

"No?" I question, arching a brow as I sit down.

"I mean, no. Get up."

I stroke my cock and watch him. "I'm up," I say with a glance at my erection.

He gives me a look that a parent gives their stubborn child. "Get. Up."

"What're you gonna give me?"

His patience snaps and he rushes over. I allow him to manhandle me into a position on my knees as I grin.

"Don't get cocky," he says. "We're still doing this my way."

"Okay," I say with amusement.

He shuts me up when he spreads my thighs and fucks me with furious passion. I grip the arm of the couch as he pummels me with thrusts meant to rip me apart. My cock is shoved up against a pillow, getting friction with each movement.

"Fuck," I gasp, shifting enough to be able to stroke my dick. "I'm so close."

Aleksander grunts. "You know what to say when you come."

I release a loud moan followed by a guttural roar as an overwhelming amount of pleasure travels throughout my body, hitting every nerve ending and igniting an intense euphoria that swallows me whole.

"Aleksander."

His name leaves my lips with a whimpering moan I might be ashamed of later, but right now, with my muscles weak and skin sweat-slicked, and as my body shakes with my release, he definitely earned the right to hear me completely wrecked.

A gratified groan leaves his throat before the slam of his hips into my ass has me gasping. A minute later, his breath stutters and the moans and gasps coming from him let me know he's nearly as wrecked as me.

His forehead falls to my back as he sucks in deep breaths, his hands moving softly over my hips and down my thighs.

When he pulls away, I carefully turn over and watch him as he spins around and removes the condom before walking inside to dispose of it. I close my eyes for a few seconds, trying to compose myself before getting up. They snap open when something soft and heavy falls on me.

Aleksander returned wearing a robe and tossed me a spare.

"Sleepover?" I question with a grin and hopeful gleam in my eyes.

"I have until sunrise."

"Then what? You turn into a pumpkin or something?"

He's not amused by my jokes. "Until you leave and I never see you again."

"I see." I stand up, grimacing as I do. It's his turn to smirk at me. "Let's shower, eat, then I get to fuck you."

Aleksander turns around, shaking his head as he walks back inside. "Funny that you still think you can call the shots."

"Fine. You say it now and we'll do it and pretend it was your idea."

"Maybe I need to shove my cock down your throat again to shut you up."

I rush up and push him against the wall before we get to the bathroom. "Maybe I'll let you, but not until you taste mine."

His surprise fades into something else as we stare each other down. I can't fully decipher the expression, but I'd like to think it's interest.

Four

JAYDEN

EVEN AFTER RAILING me over the railing of his balcony, pun intended, the man is still fairly quiet. Clearly the opposite of me, because I can't keep quiet to save my life. I pull every response out of him like a dentist pulling teeth.

"So, are you gay or bi?" I ask after we've both showered and sit in the living room with a couple of sandwiches from room service.

His eyes slide to mine like he doesn't want to answer. He's gotta be one or the other considering how deep in my ass he was half an hour ago. Not sure why he's acting like it's a hard question to answer.

I huff. "So, I'm bi. I don't mind switching, but I've topped more than I've bottomed. Have you ever bottomed?"

Aleksander wipes his mouth with a napkin, his eyes roaming my face, and then he takes another bite.

"I'm going to assume you're an exclusive top. You got that top energy. Which is a little disappointing, because I'd love to fuck you as hard as you fucked me out there." I grin at him, but get nothing in response.

25

I shake my head and take a bite, focusing on the TV for a couple minutes. "How old are you? Can I guess?"

His brows raise marginally, my only clue that he's saying *go ahead.*

"Hmm." I sit back and study him. He's got a couple lines in his forehead and around his mouth. I thought they called those laugh lines, but I'm not sure this man has laughed enough in his life to have them. They're far from wrinkles however. His skin looks smooth and well taken care of. Looking at him, you can tell he's seasoned, but yet still holds a youthful glow. "Thirty-nine?"

Once again, his eyebrows go up, but I can't tell if it's surprise that I'm right, disbelief that I thought he was that old, or shock because he's actually older.

"Does it matter?" he finally says.

"I guess not. I'd fuck you if you were fifty. You're pretty fucking sexy."

His lips twitch. "And you? Can I guess?"

I swipe my thumb over my bottom lip after taking a bite. Once I'm done chewing, I smile at him. "Please do. I'd love to hear it."

After a brief onceover, he says, "Twenty-six."

I cough out a laugh. "Nope."

"Are you going to tell me?"

"Once you tell me how old you are."

"You're stubborn," he says, reaching for his glass of water.

"Me?" I laugh. "Pot, meet kettle."

He shakes his head. "I'm not stubborn."

"I beg to differ."

"I'm strong-willed."

"Uh, sir, I believe that's a synonym of stubborn. Just like uncompromising and bull-headed."

He sits back on the couch, the robe exposing his thigh. I

have to rip my gaze away because I could definitely go for another round.

"So, Aleksander," I say. "Do you go by Alex?"

"No. Alek. It's Bulgarian, so it's not Alexander with an x, but with a ks."

"I see. So, you're Bulgarian?"

"And Greek."

I nod my head. "Cool." After a pause, I say, " I'm Black."

He smirks, the tiniest of laughs slipping between his lips.

With a chuckle, I say, "I know I probably didn't have to say that, but you shared, so I felt I should share."

"Want to share your age?" he asks again.

"Do you?"

With a sigh, he says, "I guess it doesn't matter."

"You're right. It doesn't. But what does matter is that the sun will come up in," I pause to look at the time on my phone, "about four and a half hours, and since you plan on kicking me out, we shouldn't waste any time. Unless you want to change your mind," I say, waggling my brows.

He shakes his head, his lips fighting off a grin. "One night only."

I sigh. "If you insist." I open up my robe and lean back into the couch cushions, draping an arm across the back as I watch him. "You gonna..." I trail off, my eyes flickering down to my cock and back to him. "Or should I do it myself?" I say, sliding my hand into my boxer-briefs.

He mimics my pose, calling my bluff. Little does he know, I live for these kinds of games. Sure, having someone give in to you is nice, but someone who forces you to work for it makes it a little more exciting.

I tug my underwear down to my knees and start stroking myself, my eyes never leaving him. As my dick grows harder and longer in my hand, his breathing changes and I can spot the erection pushing against his own boxer-briefs.

"It would be a shame to come like this," I say, taking a moment to spit in my hand and slowly tug on my cock again. With a moan, I say, "Especially since I'm sure your hand would feel so much better."

"I wouldn't come like that if I were you," he warns.

My movements slow, but don't stop. "Why?"

"Because I wouldn't like it."

"What would you like?" I ask between moans. "Ah, God."

"I'd like to fuck your mouth again."

"Then come touch me." I study him again, his hand palming his cock. "Looks like you need some relief."

"Come give it to me."

"When you touch me, I will." He doesn't move, but I'll be damned if he doesn't wrap his hand or mouth around my cock, considering this will likely be the last time we'll do anything.

"I don't like being told what to do," he says, adjusting his cock.

"What if I ask?" I moan, my body writhing as I stroke. "Will you come touch me, Alek? Hmm?"

"You're teasing."

"Then come make me beg." I put one hand on my balls while the other curves around my crown. "Oh God. Mm."

Alek rushes over, and as much as I want to grin victoriously, I'm too desperate for his touch to be smug.

"Stop," he says, knocking my hands away as he sits next to me.

He doesn't touch me right away, leaving my cock throbbing as he stares at me with those bright and intense eyes.

"Alek," I say, trying to keep the desperation from my voice.

"Need something?" he questions, an eyebrow arched.

"I hate you."

"Hmm," he hums, a hand skating up my right thigh.

His hand dances across my lower abdomen, his knuckles brushing my cock. I turn my head to look at him, wanting his lips on me. He eases back, letting me know a kiss is not in the cards. As his hand travels up my stomach, he leans in close, his lips ghosting over the shell of my ear.

"Spit in my hand," he demands, and my stomach clenches with desire.

Not one to back down from almost anything, and definitely someone who's willing to do nearly everything at least once, I lean forward slightly and with a quick glance into his eyes, I spit into his waiting palm.

His lips draw up a little on one side, loving that he's able to get me to obey. Before I can open my mouth to say anything, his hand wraps around my cock.

"Oh, God," I say on an exhale.

Aleksander strokes me with slow and steady movements, making my stomach quiver with each breath I pull in. He focuses on my crown for several seconds, teasing the most sensitive part of my cock by swirling his thumb and forefinger around the tip.

"Fuck, that feels good. Let me touch you," I say, reaching for the waistband of his boxer-briefs.

"Later," he says simply, keeping me from touching him by holding onto my wrist. He lets go of my cock and brings his hand back up. "Again."

I spit in it immediately, and he goes back to stroking my length, but I want more.

"Fuck me again," I tell him.

He gives me a look like he isn't sure. Yeah, I'm feeling sore from the assault on my ass earlier, but I don't care.

"Got another condom?" I ask.

"Follow me," he responds.

We move through the living room and back into the master suite. I lay down on the oversized bed with a view of the balcony we were on earlier. After disrobing and removing his underwear, he grabs a condom and a small bottle of lube from the nightstand, and covers his cock with the latex.

Between my legs, he pushes them up, exposing me to him. He takes a few moments to press two lubed fingers inside me before slathering his erection with the liquid.

When he pushes in slowly, I grunt and moan as I feel the ache and slight pain of his reentrance. He never lays over me, choosing to stay on his knees, his hands holding my legs up by the underside of my thighs.

He rocks in and out, his pace unchanging and composed. I can tell he's holding back, but why he's doing that is unknown. Is he afraid of hurting me? Or is he simply teasing me? Keeping me just out of reach of a climax.

"Alek." I breathe his name and his eyes snap to mine. "Give it to me. All of it."

"You may not be able to sit for the next few days," he says with a smirk as he begins pushing in deeper.

"Ah," I moan. "A temporary souvenir. I'll take it."

He wraps his arms around my legs and yanks me into him, eliciting a gasp from my throat before he begins to absolutely ravish me. He fucks hard and deep at the perfect pace, and begins to push my legs farther back, bringing us into a position that easily allows him to hit my prostate.

"Oh fuck," I curse. "Shit, oh...my fuck. Yeah. Oh."

I'm a mess of words and sounds that don't make any sense together, but it spurs him on. I reach for my cock and stroke it with fervor.

Alek grunts and moans, cussing as he goes deeper and deeper. "You feel so good," he murmurs.

"That's it," I tell him. "Right there. Oh fuck."

I explode, my release erupting suddenly as I yell into the room. My entire body feels ablaze as heat spreads through me, and every ounce of energy I have is expelled as I finish coming.

Aleksander finds his peak shortly after me, pummeling into me harder until his body tenses and his back bows.

"Fuck yes," he growls, his body convulsing with aftershocks of pleasure before he pulls out.

"Oh my God," I say as I attempt to catch my breath. "That. That was... Yes. Just what I needed."

My eyes close until a couple minutes later when Alek is back with a warm washcloth. "Figured you'd need this as I don't see you getting up anytime soon."

I grin up at him, feeling almost drunk with exhaustion. "Thanks."

I don't remember much after that. I cleaned myself up and probably passed out shortly after. It had been a long day, but one of the best I had in a while. I sleep peacefully for eight hours, and wake up to an empty bed with a note.

Five

JAYDEN

Last night was fun. Thanks for that.
-Aleksander

I DROP the paper and roll back over. No need to wonder if he's still here, the note makes it clear he left to allow me time to get my shit together and get out.

With a full body stretch that showcases all the places I'm sore, I push myself up and get out of his bed to search for my clothes. I find most of them on the balcony, the only exception being my underwear in the living room. After gathering them up, I rush to the bathroom for the quickest shower possible.

I think briefly to leave my number somewhere, but he made it clear he was in this for one night only. No need to give myself hope for something that won't happen again. Which really is a shame, because Alek is unlike anyone I've ever been with. Maybe it's his age and his experience. Maybe it's the push and pull between us, both of us used to running things and getting our way.

Damn. Guess, I'll get on my app later and try to find someone older than me. Maybe I've been doing myself a disservice by only messing around with people in my age group.

I leave his room and travel down the elevator until I hit the lobby. Outside, I have an Uber waiting for me, taking me back to Three Sheets so I can get my car.

Once I get back to the frat house, I strip out of my clothes and sprawl across the bed, falling asleep for another two hours.

When I wake up, it's because my phone is ringing off the hook. With a glance at the screen, I see it's Dom.

"What's up?" I answer.

"You still with Mr. Missionary?"

I laugh. "No, I'm in my bed, and he was anything but Mr. Missionary."

"Oh, the old guy had some tricks up his sleeve, huh? Nice."

"I don't think he's that old, but I never found out. He left me a nice note letting me know he had a good time but there's obviously no plans to meet up again."

"At least you can mark that off your college hook-up bucket list."

"True. So, what's up?"

"Not much. Me and Trev are gonna head to the movies in a little bit, but I wanted to make sure you weren't abducted and taken to some creepy ass dungeon to be kept as a sexual servant."

"A sexual servant doesn't sound too bad," I say with a laugh. "And he had this fucking penthouse suite. I'd love to be held captive there."

"He took you to a hotel? He have a wife or something?"

"That's what I said." I chuckle. "He said he doesn't have time for a family and that the hotel is temporary."

"Weird. Anyway, did you get your car? I saw it when I left work and had to make sure the other workers knew not to have it towed."

"Yeah, I got it. Thanks."

"Cool. Well, I guess I'll talk to you later."

"All right, man."

After I end the call, I get some new clothes on and make plans for the rest of the day. I arrange to meet up with Ivy since I bailed on her friend's party, and want to make it up to her with lunch. After that, I'll get with my friend, Bryant, who's been wanting to hit the gym with me. After that, who knows? But I'm sure I'll find something to get into.

Spring break went by way too fast, but I definitely had a good time, so now it's time to hold up my end of the bargain with my dad and start the internship today.

He called yesterday with strict instructions to not be late, and to take it seriously, reiterating that the man I'll be working with isn't the most easy going guy, but assuring me he's a good man.

I leave campus around two-thirty, giving me a half hour to get to the new building north of town. I'm due to work from three to six, Monday thru Friday, for two months. It's not too bad, considering I worked more hours at the restaurant, and didn't always have weekends off. Plus, this will earn me credits.

I show up at five to three, but have to change in the parking lot, because I didn't think to go to class dressed in the clothes I need to be in for this job. Apparently, you can't just wear anything. The boss wants everyone in the internship to be in solid colored Polos. So once I'm out of the car, I strip out of my striped T-shirt and grab the Polo I had to stop at the frat house for. Once I pull it on, I lock my car and jog toward the tall, modern building with the words MGD Advertising plastered on top in a sleek font .

When I first enter, I spot a couple people behind the largest desk in the center of the lobby, so I go there right away.

"Hi, I'm Jayden Brooks. I'm here for the marketing internship. Can you tell me which way to go?"

The guy behind the desk glances at his watch. "You're gonna be late. Head up to the fourth floor, they'll tell you where to go from there."

"Thanks."

I rush toward the elevators, which of course are both in use and at the top floor. By the time I get inside one and reach the fourth floor, my watch lets me know it's already three o'clock.

The doors open, and after glancing side to side, I approach a woman who's walking past me.

"Excuse me. I'm here for the marketing internship. Can you tell me where to go?"

She purses her lips slightly, as if she's annoyed I'd ask her for directions. "They're in conference room two."

I grant her my best smile, trying not to come off rude. "Can you tell me where that is? I'm new. First time here."

With a sigh, she turns and points down a hallway. "Go down there. Second door on the right."

"Thank you."

When I get to the room, the door is already closed, but through the blinds of the glass window, I can see everyone seated around a table, focused on someone in the front of the room. Shit. Late is late, even if it's just two minutes.

I try to slip in as quietly as possible, closing the door behind me with a soft click before rushing to an empty chair between two guys at the far end. The man speaking has his back turned as he writes on the whiteboard, so hopefully he won't notice I came in late.

I scan the table, noticing everybody already has folders in front of them, so he'll definitely realize I was late when he sees I don't have anything in front of me. Great.

Any hope of him not looking closely enough to find a new face in the crowd is instantly shot and killed when he slowly spins around, and I see the face of the man who nearly fucked me to death over the balcony of his hotel suite.

"Oh my God."

His beautiful piercing eyes zero in on me as soon as the whispered words leave my lips. He's got a damn good poker face, because he doesn't show an ounce of shock or concern after recognizing me. Aleksander simply picks up a paper and scans it before focusing on me again.

"Mr. Brooks. You're late. I'd advise you to not let it happen again or you'll find yourself looking for another internship."

I swallow, ignoring the eyes of every other person staring at me, concerned only with the uniquely colored ones at the front of the room. "Yes, sir."

ALEKSANDER

HAVING Jay show up as an intern in my program is one thing, considering I'm the one in charge. Had he just been a one-night stand under regular circumstances, maybe it wouldn't feel so bad, but Jayden Brooks is a name I was already vaguely familiar with.

His father, Calvin Brooks, works with me in Chicago at the marketing firm downtown. Not only that, these past couple of years we've gotten pretty close, even having drinks after work, or enjoying dinner with his wife at the restaurant she works at. I'd consider him a friend, and the fact that he'd probably say the same thing, even though I'm his boss, says a lot. He's a hard worker, a good man, and when he asked if I had a position for his son here, I didn't hesitate to say yes.

However, after meeting Jay at the bar, not once did I consider he was Jayden, the son of my friend and the man who's in charge of the public image of the company. That makes this a little more awkward, and probably the number one reason why I shouldn't feel this tinge of excitement of having him working here with me.

"In a minute, I will bring in a few of the marketing

managers you'll be working for. You'll be expected to be self-motivated. Don't wait until someone has to ask you for something. You need to assess the situation and figure out what needs and can be done by you. We don't like for our employees to do the bare minimum. You will prepare promotional presentations and monitor social platforms. Organizational skills and the ability to multitask are needed. If you don't have a passion for marketing, this will not work out for you. There will be marketing events that you will plan and host, amongst many other things. You will speak to the person you'll be working under for more details." I pick up the phone and press a button to connect me with Linda. "Send them in. Thank you."

A minute later, Ivan, Zola, Luther, and Micah stroll in and I send two interns with each of them. Once they've stood up and followed the marketing managers out of the room, I'm left with Jay.

"Mr. Brooks, you'll be working with me today. Come on, my office is upstairs."

"Hey, umm, this is weird, right?" he says from behind me. "Did you...oh shit."

I angle my head over my shoulder to see his wide eyes bounce around as if he's just figuring something out.

"What's that, Mr. Brooks?"

"Sorry. Uhh, so you're the guy my dad knows?"

"I do know him, yes."

I move through the room, heading for the elevators. Next to us, Zola and her two interns wait as well.

"So, does that mean you knew?" Jay asks.

I ignore him, not willing to have this conversation right now.

"Mr. Brooks, are you aware there's a—"

"No, wait. Ale—"

I cut him off with a stern glare as Zola's head swings in our direction.

"Sorry, I mean, Mr. uhh," his eyes give him away. He has no idea what my last name is. Why would he? Obviously his father didn't tell him my name, and Jay didn't look into this job at all to be able to find out on his own.

"Mr. Drakos," Zola says with a bite in her tone.

"Right," Jay offers, pretending like he forgot. "Drakos. Yes, Mr. Drakos."

The elevators open and I gesture for Zola and her interns to go in first. The second elevator dings, informing us it'll be ready. "We'll take this one," I say with a smile. She nods, her eyes roaming to Jay once more before we step into the neighboring car.

Jay exhales as soon as we're alone. "Shit, I'm sorry."

"This is a place of business, Mr. Brooks, and I am in charge. I will never be Alek or Aleksander in this building."

"And I clearly won't be Jay."

"No, you won't."

"Did you know? Who I was, I mean."

"I did not, and had I known, it never would've happened."

"No?" he questions, moving into a position where I can see him.

I meet his gaze. "No. You are Calvin's son, and not only am I your boss, but I'm his, and more importantly, your father and I are friends."

His shoulders drop. "Friends? You're *friends* with my dad?"

"Is it so unbelievable that either of us would have friends?"

He laughs. "Kind of, yes. Also, I thought you said you didn't have friends."

"I don't have any here."

"You never saw any photos of me?"

"No, I never saw any pictures , but don't worry, I'm sure your father dotes on you."

"This is so crazy," he muses, mostly to himself.

I focus on the doors as they open up and then make my way to my office with Jay on my heels.

Once behind my desk, I say, "Okay, are you aware there's a music festival coming this summer?"

"Wait. Well, no, but hold on, can we talk about this?"

He sits in a chair across from me, his dark eyes focused on mine. He looks worried.

With a soft sigh, I sit back in my chair. "What are you concerned about?"

His hands go up. "This whole thing. I'm working for you, but we slept together, which I'm sure there will be some rules about. I could get disqualified from the program, you could lose your job, and what the fuck are we gonna do about my dad?"

I lean forward and cross my arms on my desk. "First of all, your dad doesn't have to know anything about this. He doesn't know about any of your other hookups, does he? Secondly, you will not be disqualified. I'll make sure of it. Unless, of course, you show up late again."

He bites back a grin. "So, nobody will know anything?"

"Who would know? I don't necessarily go around telling my employees that I slept with someone over the weekend."

"Well, I told people," he says with a nervous grin. "Only a couple, but they don't know who you are."

"Then it's in your hands. As long as you don't tell them that your boss is the same person you slept with, then nobody will know."

He exhales, his body relaxing slightly. "Okay."

"So, let's talk about this music festival," I state, clicking a button on my keyboard.

"Wait."

I sigh and look at him. "Yes?"

"Are you gonna pretend nothing happened? You don't feel weird having to work with me with the knowledge that you were balls deep into my ass ten days ago?"

I clear my throat as I adjust my tie, not prepared for the blunt reminder of what we did. "It was only meant to be for one night, so us working together means nothing. You're my intern, plain and simple."

He appraises me. "I see. Business as usual, then."

"Yes. Now, let's discuss how we can advertise this music festival. It's geared more toward people your age, but it is technically a family friendly event. The company in charge has hosted a couple of festivals in Indiana, but this is their first time in Michigan. We'll be working with local companies for sponsorships and advertising."

We spend the next two and a half hours discussing strategies on marketing the event. I let him come up with ideas, and then I touch on how for a festival like this, it's best to cast a wide net, and not solely focus on the locals. A lot of people will travel for music festivals.

Jay knows his way around social media, and jotted down plans to get word out via those platforms, ads, and giveaways. We'll expand more on this over the next few days, because with an event like this, there's quite a few things we can use to our advantage.

"Well, we can pick up on this tomorrow. We have fifteen minutes left, so I'd like for you to tell me why you're interested in marketing. Is it because of your dad?"

He grimaces. "Can we not touch on the fact that you know my dad, or that my dad exists, or anything like that?"

I grin. "Sure. Please, tell me why this is for you."

"Okay, maybe the idea was planted when I saw a *certain somebody* working on how to advertise for this pizza company. Chicago is known for several sports teams and deep dish pizza, you know? Anyway, all I remember is he was able to get this pizza franchise's logo up on a billboard at the baseball field. I don't know the details of how it all worked out, but I know that when we went to a game and I saw that pizza logo up, that my dad had made it possible. And I'm pretty sure the pizza place had the baseball logo on their takeout products and such." He exhales. "That planted the seed, but I'm a very social person. I'm outgoing, talkative, and love meeting new people. Dad always told me it was a very social career and you'd need outstanding communications skills. Besides that, I'm a creative person, and I like the fact that not everyday will be the same. You'll end up working on a new project and the vibe will change. I wouldn't want to walk into an office and do the same, I don't know, like accounting every day. No offense to accountants, but that's not for me."

I nod. "Sounds good."

He grins. "Sounds good? That's it? It takes a lot to get high praise from you, huh?"

I drag my teeth along my bottom lip. "I give praise when it's earned."

"Mm." His eyebrows go up. "Like, 'Last night was fun. Thanks for that.'?"

I level him with a look. "I didn't have to leave a note at all."

A laugh emerges from his lips. "In that case, thank you." He stands up. "Am I good to leave, Mr. Drakos?"

My eyes travel up his tall frame until they land on his. "You have five minutes left."

He coughs out a chuckle. "What would you like me to do for the next five minutes?"

"It should be seven, considering you were late."

Jay's thick arms cross in front of his chest. "You heard of

the game seven minutes in heaven? Was that a thing in your day?"

My jaw clenches as I roll my chair back from the desk. His gaze takes a journey from my face, down to my chest, and then landing on my crotch.

"I'm aware of the game, but I'm not a child and would require a lot more than seven minutes."

He takes a few steps toward my desk. "The game doesn't have to include sex. It could be kissing, touching, maybe a little tasting."

"It could also be nothing at all."

He bites down on his lip as he grins, coming around to the side of my desk. "You know, I was sore for two days after I left your hotel room."

"Only two? I may have to up my game a little then."

His lips pull into a smirk as he rests his ass on my desk in front of me. "Right now?"

I shake my head once. "I don't do repeats."

"No repeats, huh? Why's that?"

"I have reasons."

"Is it the typical, cliché reason like you don't want to give anyone the opportunity to catch feelings?" When I don't answer, he continues. "Because I don't catch feelings. I throw those bitches back. I'm too young to settle down. My friends are all loved up with people, and now they're boring. Who wants that?"

His smile is saccharine, but his eyes twinkle with mischief.

"What happened to you having a panic attack over me knowing your dad?"

"Like you said, he doesn't have to know."

"Seems like you're awfully interested in me, Mr. Brooks." I arch a brow in his direction, stretching my leg out while I run my palm down to my knee.

"Interested in sex, sir," he teases with a wink. "I don't do the love thing. I can tell you that right now— me and probably about ten people from my past. But, your cock interests me, and I like the idea of attempting to get you under me. Maybe make you sore for a couple days."

I run a finger over the scruff on my chin. "Hmm."

"So, what do you say?" he questions.

Pushing up from my black leather chair, I reach over to my coat hanger and grab my suit jacket from the hook. After pushing my arms through the sleeves and fastening the buttons, I step up to Jay who stands from the chair, watching me with a triumphant grin.

"I say, your seven minutes are up. You can go home now, Mr. Brooks."

He's shocked silent for a few moments before he laughs. "I see. Okay, Mr. Drakos," he says, emphasizing the last two words. "I'll see you tomorrow."

"On time."

"Yes, sir."

Seven

ALEKSANDER

WHEN I WALK BACK into my office Tuesday afternoon, I stop short when I find Jay sitting in the chair opposite mine.

With a glance at my watch, I note he's early.

"Making up for yesterday, I see."

"Your secretary let me in, but only after I charmed her with my smile and a free coffee."

"Sometimes bribery will get you places."

"I think she likes me," he says. "Kinda hot."

"Is she?" I ask, removing my jacket and hanging it up.

"So, not bi, then," Jay says with a grin.

I ignore him. "Any new thoughts regarding the festival?"

He places his coffee down and opens up a notebook. "Yeah, so I was thinking, this is about music, so obviously getting spots on some of the local radio stations would make sense. The DJ's can talk about it, host a giveaway or something. Would a billboard be too expensive? Anyway, flyers are easy, and I can get them on campus no problem."

"Have you thought about getting clips of the bands performing, and broadcasting those on social media, so people know what they'll be buying tickets for? The clips don't have to be long, and I have a list of the performers."

"Yeah, that would be dope. Let me get that list. The contact info is there, too, right?"

"Of course."

"Maybe we could get a local TV station to play them along with info about the festival."

I nod, and we continue working and fleshing out his plans.

The three hours that he's here go by quickly, and before I know it, he's minutes away from having to leave. He doesn't attempt to flirt this time around, which makes it easier for me, because I don't have to turn him down once again.

"All right, so we're doing pretty good, I think," he says as he gathers his stuff.

"Yeah. Tomorrow, I'll introduce you to Luther. He's working on this, as well as a couple other seasoned employees. Luther will help with the ins and outs of digital marketing, showcasing the difference in social media management versus social media marketing. Soon, you'll start to create and coordinate campaigns, and use social media apps to build, track, and engage with people who fit the music festival demographic."

"Luther? I thought I was working with you?"

"For me."

"Oh, boss man."

"That's right."

He shakes his head, a grin on his lips as if he doesn't believe me. "This Luther? He hot?"

I flatten my lips and send him a look. "He's probably not your type."

"I don't know. I like them in all shapes, sizes, colors, genders." He pauses. "Ages," he finishes with a wink.

"Well, we'll see about that."

"Jealous?" he teases.

I grab my suit jacket and give him a slight chuckle. "No."

"What if I flirted with your secretary out there?"

"I'd advise against that."

"Why?" he asks, amusement in his tone.

"Not for the reason you think."

"Then, I can?"

I face him. "You can do whatever you like, as long as it doesn't put your position at risk."

"I thought you said you'd make sure I didn't lose my spot."

"Yeah, for sleeping with me. Not for any other reason."

He chuckles. "So, I take it you're on the boss's good side if you're confident in that promise."

My lips pull up slightly as I study him. "I guess you could say that."

"Then maybe we can get away with a little more."

"You're incorrigible."

"I'd say persistent."

A knock on my door breaks up our banter. "Come in."

It's Linda Thompson, my secretary. "Sorry, Mr. Drakos. I'm heading out, but Mr. Lewis called and had to change your meeting from two to three tomorrow. Is that okay?"

"That's fine. Thank you."

"Hey, Linda," Jay says, walking toward her. "Let me walk you to your car. You never know what kind of people might be lurking around."

"Ms. Thompson is how you should address her," I admonish.

"It's fine," she says with a grin, pushing her blond hair behind her shoulder. "I don't think I have anything to worry about, Mr. Brooks, but you can join me."

"Oh, you gonna protect me? Do you work out?" he flirts, knowing damn well he's the size of a professional football player and doesn't need any protection. Linda is five foot six at best and fairly slim.

"Have a good night, Mr. Drakos," she says before stepping back through the door.

"Yes, goodnight, Mr. Drakos," Jay offers. "See you tomorrow."

"Oh, sir?" Linda adds, popping next to Jay. "I meant to give you this."

"Let me," Jay says, taking the card. "Rest your feet. Those heels look killer."

Linda shakes her head, but hands the card to Jay. He glances at it before handing it to me. "Oh yeah, I wanted to ask. What does MGD stand for?"

"Oh, you don't know?" Linda muses from the doorway. "M and G are his parents initials. D is, well, his last name."

I take the card and study his face. He glances back at Linda. "Whose?"

She laughs, a little disbelieving. "Mr. Drakos, of course. This is his company."

His dark eyes find mine, his lips parting slightly.

I smirk. "Have a good evening, you two."

Eight

ALEKSANDER

ON WEDNESDAY AND THURSDAY, I don't see much of Jay. He's been with Luther and a couple other team members, learning the ropes, and working on this new campaign. When we've passed each other in the hall, he's given me his usual grin. The one that looks like he's always thinking something filthy, and who knows? Maybe he is.

I've stopped in Luther's office, observing his progress. Do I need to do that? No. Luther will tell me everything I need to know. I'd rather not get into why I feel the need to check on him, but I've also watched him interact with not only the seasoned employees, but the other interns. He's clearly well-liked by almost everybody he comes in contact with. He always has them laughing or smiling, and during the breaks, he's the center of attention, always with a story at the ready that will entrance everybody in the vicinity.

Today, an hour before the interns are set to leave, I enter the break room and linger near the doorway. The permanent employees are used to me, but I've noticed the interns tense up when I'm around, all of them aware of my position. So, I keep back and listen to Jay tell them a story.

"No, I'll tell you an embarrassing story. I was maybe ten or eleven, I don't remember, but my class took this field trip to some ranch. I was excited, not because I really cared about cows or pigs, but because it was a bit of a drive and we spent most of the day on the bus and not in class. Anyway, it's not the best day. It had been raining, so it was muddy, and we're all trekking through this filth while smelling the scent of cow shit. Honestly, I don't know why we took this trip. So, we're in the barn where the cows are in their stalls, just chillin'. I'm at the end of the line. Thank God. I'm just looking around at these massive animals that you never think you'll see up close, and this fucking cow. This bitch ass cow has her ass to me, and shoots shit at me! It wasn't a massive amount, but enough that it got on me. On my face! I'm pretty sure she was annoyed with all the kids ahead of me being loud and annoying, and she took it out on me. It felt personal, not gonna lie." Everybody laughs. "Like, it was a warning shot. She was telling me to get out. So, I freak out but don't want anybody to know because I'll be *cow shit boy* for the rest of my life, and my friends will never let me live it down, so I wipe it off." He pauses, looking at everyone. "I. Wiped. It. Off. With my hand. Again, it wasn't a lot, but now I got shit on my hand and nowhere to wipe it, so I bend down and try to wipe it off in the mud." He shakes his head, chuckling. "This girl in front of me turned around and gave me a weird look, and all I said was, 'mud.'" He laughs some more. "It was so dumb. I used the sleeve of my jacket to wipe my face again to make sure it was gone, but I felt so embarrassed and annoyed. Which is why I'll never be a vegetarian. Fuck them cows."

I laugh louder than I meant to, and everyone spins around to see who's eavesdropping. When Jay realizes it's me, his smile grows. "Hey, boss. We're just shootin' the shit," he jokes, making people laugh again.

I nod, a small smile still on my lips before I turn and head back to my office. Ten minutes to six, I hear Linda laugh outside my door before my phone buzzes.

"Sir, Mr. Brooks is wondering if he can talk to you."

Jay says something in the background that I can't quite hear, but through the door, I hear Linda giggle again.

"Send him in," I reply.

Seconds later, Jay struts in. "If you're still willing to protect me, you can walk me to my car in ten minutes," he tells her with a grin before shutting the door behind him.

"Do you want to lose your position here, Mr. Brooks?" I ask.

"What'd I do?"

"The flirting. I warned you about that."

"Did you?" he asks, sitting down. "I thought you said you'd advise against it. Is that a warning?"

I shoot him a look that says I'm not amused. "Did you need something?"

"You were right. Luther is not my type. He's a good guy, though. Didn't expect him to be seventy-three, but you know."

"I thought you liked all ages?"

He smirks. "Well, I do have limits. For one, they have to be adults, and I guess they can't be much older than however old you are."

I shake my head. "I'm assuming women with boyfriends are also your type."

"What? You talkin' about Linda?" I nod. "Oh. She told me they broke up."

"Fantastic," I murmur, gathering some papers to put into my briefcase. When I look up, he's grinning at me. "What?"

"Nothing," he says with a shake of his head. "So, any weekend plans?"

"Probably working, as usual." I hesitate, then ask, "And you?"

"I never know till I know."

"Sounds adventurous."

He shrugs. "Only way to live."

"If you say so. I like things to be a little more controlled. Organized."

"Oh, controlled fun? Sounds like a blast."

My eyes flicker back to him. "You might be surprised."

His eyes narrow slightly. "Give me an example."

"I shouldn't."

"Because you're the boss or because of your no repeats rule?"

"Both."

"You know what they say about rules, right?" he asks with a flirty grin.

"They're put in place for a reason."

He laughs. "I don't know why I like you. You're so boring."

I grin before I tamp it down. "If you say so."

"Well, not for any specific reason or anything, but I may stop by Three Sheets tonight. I have a friend I can harass there."

"So, it's not just me you like to bother?"

"I'm not bothering you and you know it, but maybe someone else might show up there, too. Then I can transfer my harassment to them, and then maybe I can be taught about controlled fun."

"Jay," I warn.

"Mm." He arches a brow. "I guess I could invite Linda. She'd probably have a good time."

"I know what you're attempting to do."

He smiles. "I'm not doing anything. There's also this really hot intern I've noticed looking at me. Joel? You know him? He's cute, right? And not technically an employee."

"Jayden."

He moans. "Ooh. I like when you say my name like that."

"Cut it out."

He stands up. "I'll be there around nine."

"I don't care."

"Okay," he replies with a shrug. "Have a good weekend, Mr. Drakos." Jay pulls open the door. "Don't work too hard. You know what they say about all work and no play."

He winks before closing the door behind him. Soon after, he and Linda are laughing again, and I hate that it bothers me so much. Why should it grate on my nerves that they like each other?

Nine

ALEKSANDER

DON'T ASK me why I'm parked outside Three Sheets at a quarter to nine. I have no fucking clue. Well, that may be a tiny lie. The clue is a tall, muscular, attractive man that I want to pretend irritates me with his incessant flirting. The man who doesn't really know how to listen or obey rules, but who ignites a spark, regardless of how small it is, in my gut, that tells me I'm not as bothered by his persistence as I act like I am.

As I'm debating with myself about whether I should just reverse out of here and leave it alone or stay and see what happens, a light knock on my window gets my attention.

In black jeans and a T-shirt to match—and one that squeezes his biceps, highlighting how in shape he is—Jay bends down and flashes me a bright smile.

I roll my eyes as I roll the window down. "Don't start."

"Whatcha doin' here, boss?"

"How'd you even know this was my car?"

He chuckles. "Not many Teslas around here. Plus, I recognized it from work."

I glance past him. "Where's Linda or Joel?"

Jay leans into the car, arms braced in the window frame. "I didn't invite anybody. Was hoping a certain brooding, bossy, boring man would show up."

"Funny."

"And here you are. I knew I'd get you to come."

"First of all, you didn't get me to come." He opens his mouth like he's about to have some smart remark, but I hold my hand up. "I came because I wanted to, and I'm not staying."

"No?" he questions.

"No. Get in the car."

"No drinks?" He faux pouts.

"I have drinks at my place."

His perfect white teeth flash between his lips as he smiles before jogging toward his vehicle and pulling something from the back. When he gets to my car, he tosses a backpack in the back.

"Wishful thinking."

I shake my head. "Don't be smug."

"Never."

"So," Jay muses, dropping his bag on the couch before he sits next to it. "Aleksander Drakos. CEO and CMO of MGD Advertising. You've been in charge for a few years now. Sorry to hear about your parents."

I pour some liquor into a couple of highball glasses before pulling a Coke out of the fridge to add to Jay's. "I see you've done some research."

"Just a little."

"Hmm. What would I find if I Googled you?" I ask, handing him a drink.

"Jayden Brooks, best wide receiver to ever grace South

River University's football team, and the winner of a couple national wrestling championships. That's probably it."

"Best ever, huh?"

He grins. "I like to think so." After a pause, he says, "I may have found out your age."

"Yeah? And you're still here?" I question, sitting on the couch opposite him.

"Forty-one isn't that old."

"How old are you?"

He chuckles. "I'll be twenty-three soon."

"Makes me feel ancient," I say with a grin before taking a sip.

"Younger than my parents," he offers in an attempt to make me feel better.

"Bringing your parents up doesn't help."

Jay laughs again. "Sorry. So, did you always want to do this, or did it fall into your lap?"

"I guess you could say it was expected of me. I didn't really have a chance to find anything else that brought me interest. I got into some trouble as a kid. Typical teenage shit. I was rebellious, got in some fights, and hated authority. My dad got sick of having to bail me out of trouble and really put his foot down. We moved and he started bringing me to work and teaching me everything I needed to know. Just so happened that I fell in love with it." I take another sip of the bourbon before continuing. "Their deaths happened a lot sooner than expected, so being in charge came quicker than I thought it would, but I was prepared nonetheless."

He nods, probably unsure where to go with the conversation after I mentioned their deaths. Death makes people uncomfortable. They don't know how to treat you when they know you've been affected by it. They assume you'll turn into an emotional mess.

"I don't struggle with the fact that they died," I tell him.

"It was an accident, plain and simple. It could've happened to anybody and there was nothing that would've been able to prevent it. Bad weather created conditions where people couldn't see and the roads were slippery. They weren't the only ones who died that day."

Jay watches me with a strange look, and I can tell he wants to question me about something. He opens his mouth, closes it, then takes a drink before asking something else. "You don't have any siblings?"

"No."

"So, who will you pass the company to when you no longer want to run it? If your parents created it, I imagine they wanted it to stay a family business."

I shift, gulping down the rest of the drink before standing up to refill it. "It doesn't really matter, does it? They'll never know who runs it."

He spins around, his eyes full of shock as he studies me. I stare back at him as I pour the liquor, and he must see something in my gaze that tells him not to question it any further. And he'd be right. I'm never in the mood to have the discussion me and my parents had way too many times.

Jay stands up and walks over to me, taking my glass and swallowing down two shots' worth of bourbon. "Let's get drunk and fuck."

I pour more into the glass and drink it down. "I like that plan."

He rounds the small bar and starts undoing my tie. "I wonder if I can get you on your knees for me."

"Probably not."

His tongue dances across his bottom lip as he smiles. He starts unbuttoning my shirt. "I wonder if I can get you to bend over for me." His eyes flicker up, amusement flashing in them.

"Definitely not."

He slides his hands into my shirt, pushing it off my shoulders. "But I'd make you feel so good."

"Your ass feels good enough."

"Good enough? Now you're just trying to offend me."

My lips twitch. "That's not what I meant."

"No? Want to make it up to me by sucking my dick?"

"Funny."

"It wasn't a joke," he says, unbuttoning his pants. "I didn't get to feel your mouth at all last time. No kiss. No blowjob. That doesn't seem fair considering the abuse you inflicted on my throat."

"You seemed to enjoy it."

"Oh, I did," he says with a grin, kicking off his shoes before pushing his jeans down.

"I don't kiss," I tell him. "You should know that now."

He looks slightly disappointed and a little curious, but shrugs. "Okay. Sucking dick isn't kissing."

After removing his shirt, he stands before me in only a pair of white boxer-briefs that do nothing to hide the monster that's trying to escape its cage.

"I think your original plan was to get drunk and fuck."

He swipes a bottle off the bar and takes a swig, staring at me the entire time. "Your turn."

I swallow a mouthful before replacing the bottle. "Let me show you a little bit about controlled fun," I say, walking away.

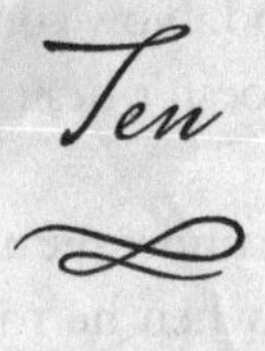

Ten

ALEKSANDER

IN MY BEDROOM, I finish undressing until I'm only in my underwear. Jay strips out of his, lying across the bed naked.

I pull the lube and condoms out and toss them onto the bed. With a few pumps of the liquid into my hand, I inch toward Jay and wrap my hand around his erection.

"Oh fuck."

"Mm," I moan, enjoying the feel of him in my hand.

I start off slow, teasing him with small amounts of pleasure before I lean down and swipe one of his nipples with my tongue before gently biting on the hardened tip.

"Oh shit," he says with a gasp, his hand caressing my back. "Yeah, that's good."

I stroke a bit faster, my mouth moving to his other nipple to inflict the same painful pleasure.

"Fuck yes," he hisses, his back arching.

When I move away, I bring my other hand to his erection and stroke and twist his cock, making him gasp and cuss, desperate and needy.

"Alek. Oh fuck. Alek. Shit, that's so good. Oh, oh, yes."

His shaft hardens in my palm, his hands gripping the covers as his muscles flex, so I stop.

"No," he whines, his eyes finding mine. "Fuck, why'd you stop?"

"I didn't stop for good. Now come touch me."

I lay down and he doesn't hesitate to get up and straddle my hips.

"Looks like I got you under me after all."

I'm about to retort when he rocks into me, his erection sliding against mine, pulling a low moan from my throat.

He keeps moving. "God." His head drops back and his eyes close. "Fucking you would be amazing. I know it."

Jay lowers himself across me, his mouth touching my neck. "I know you said no kissing, but can I kiss other parts of you?"

I swallow, nodding. "Yeah."

His soft lips brush against my throat before he peppers kisses across both sides of my neck, all while grinding himself against me.

"Sit up," I tell him.

He listens, sitting up straight, his muscled thighs trapping me between him. His cock stands at attention and I reach out and grab it.

Jay pushes his hips forward, thrusting into my fist, his chiseled body flexing with each movement. I lick my lips as my eyes are trained on his glistening crown.

"Alek," he breathes. "Fuck, you're so good."

"You like my hands on you?" I ask.

"Yes. I fucking love it."

He keeps thrusting, fucking my hand and seeking a release. I reach for the lube, and with both hands, I stroke his length.

"Yes, I love that," he exclaims.

When I notice him getting closer to an orgasm, I stop.

He growls. "Alek, I swear."

I chuckle, flipping us over until I'm kneeling between his spread thighs. With another pump of lube, I begin rubbing my fingers around his tight hole. "I'm controlling the pleasure."

"Yeah, well I fucking hate it."

"You won't once you have the best orgasm of your life."

I push a finger in and cut off whatever he was about to say. "Oh God."

"I prefer Alek."

"I prefer..." he gasps when I push a second finger in. "I don't know what I prefer. Just keep going."

With one hand on his cock and two fingers in his ass, I quickly bring him close to bliss again. I curl my fingers, seeking his prostate.

"Oh shit. Alek. Oh my God. If you don't want me to come, you need to stop."

"You better not come," I tell him, squeezing the tip of his cock with my hand while my fingers continue to thrust into his ass.

"It's so good. Please," he begs, his head back, veins protruding from his neck as he pants.

"Look at me," I command, slowing my movements. When his eyes finally find mine, I say, "Do not come. You hear me?"

His hand flies to mine, squeezing his cock and halting my motion. "Okay, hold on," he grunts, eyes closing while he wills away his orgasm. "It's not gonna take much," he breathes. "Don't touch me for a minute or I'll blow."

I chuckle, getting off the bed and removing my boxer-briefs. "I'll give you a minute."

"What're you doing?" he asks, watching my every movement.

"Putting a condom on. Want to help?"

"Mm. I'm afraid even that will make me come, but yeah, I do."

He sits up and I stand in front of him, handing him the condom. Before opening the package, he wraps his fingers around my cock, tugging on it with languid strokes. His free hand cups my balls, and his gaze finds mine.

"I love your cock. This vein right here," he says, touching it with his fingertip, "begs to be traced with my tongue."

"Do it," I tell him, wanting to feel his mouth on me again.

He ignores me, holding my shaft in his hand, inspecting every inch of me. "This right here," he says softly, brushing his thumb over my glistening slit, "makes my mouth water."

"Taste it," I say, feeling myself becoming more desperate. My stomach clenches while my pulse picks up.

Jay looks up at me, his lips pulled into a lopsided grin. "When you taste me, I'll do whatever you want."

"Don't play with me, Jay."

He bites his lip. "Fair's fair, right?"

I reach for the condom but he snatches it out of my hand, opening it up before slowly rolling the latex down my shaft. He gives me a squeeze at the base before scooting back on the bed.

"Turn over."

He hesitates briefly before getting on his hands and knees. After another minute of lubed up fingers penetrating his hole, I coat my cock in the slick substance and guide myself in.

"Oh fuck," he breathes, the muscles in his back flexing as he squeezes the covers.

God, he's perfect. I want to run my hands and tongue over every inch of his body. I want to familiarize myself with each beauty mark and scar. I want so much more than I can allow myself to have.

I thrust in hard and deep. "Yes!" I cry out, loving the tightness of his ass around my cock.

I push his upper body down, keeping his hips up in the air as I tighten my grip on them and push in and out of him.

"You feel so fucking good," I tell him.

"God, Alek. I'm so close."

"Don't touch yourself yet."

He whimpers.

I get lost in the euphoria of him, fucking hard and fast, wanting to meld my body to his and never know what it's like to not be inside him.

It had been a long time since I'd been with anybody before my first night with Jay. I've come to find out that Jay is like a drug, and I'm already becoming an addict.

Which is why I have the rules I do. He's made me break the no repeats one. I have to hold onto the rest.

"Turn over. I want to see you."

I pull out, allowing him to roll onto his back before I slowly push back inside. Both of us release a moan as he clenches around me.

"Alek." My name is a desperate plea on his lips.

"Tell me what you want."

"I want what you won't give me," he says, eyeing my mouth. "But let me come and I may forgive you."

I lean over him, my face rubbing against his as I move inside his ass. He turns his head and his lips touch my cheek.

"You make me feel so good," he whispers. "Your cock..." he gasps. "God, your fucking cock is perfect."

When I ease away, my eyes land on the pre-cum dripping from his head and smearing on his stomach. I push his legs up, bringing his ass off the bed slightly, giving me the perfect angle to hit his prostate.

"Oh shit," he cries, eyes squeezing closed briefly before they lock onto mine in a frenzied panic. "What...oh fuck...that's it. That feels incredible. Don't stop. Don't stop. Don't fucking stop."

I don't. I keep going. Hitting it a little harder but never slowing down.

"I can't wait to see that cum shoot out of your cock," I say, not taking my eyes off of his erection as it lays against his stomach. "I want to see just how much you loved my controlled fun."

"Oh shit," he breathes, body tense.

I let loose, moving as fast and going as deep as I can. I should worry that I'll hurt him, but it never crosses my mind. His face lets me know he's enjoying it. His noises and mumbled words demand I keep going.

"Alek," he gasps, eyes flying open. "Oh fuck, I'm gonna come."

"Come for me."

White ribbons shoot from his slit, landing on his chest and stomach, and Jay cries out before finally reaching down and grabbing his dick.

Coming hands free is rare, but not impossible, and it's one of my favorite things to do to someone.

Cum keeps erupting even as he's just holding himself.

"Holy fuck," he cries. "Oh my God, I...I...oh God."

"That's it. Fuck, you look so good right now."

It only takes another two minutes before my balls draw up and inexplicable pleasure floods me. My voice bellows into the room, deep and low, scratching my throat as my own release pours out of me.

"Fucking hell," I cry, my body shaking.

Jay's nothing but moans and whimpers below me, muttering words I can't quite hear. It takes a minute before I'm able to pull out of him, holding onto the condom. I don't have the energy for much right now, so after tying it off and tossing it in the trash next to the nightstand, I fall into bed next to him and we catch our breath together.

Eleven

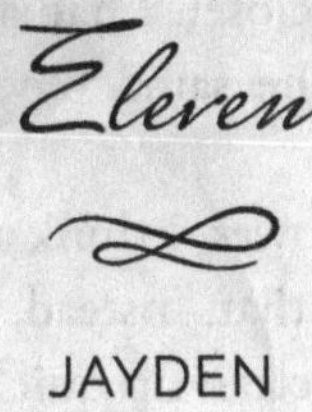

JAYDEN

AFTER ALLOWING himself a couple minutes to get his breathing under control, Aleksander gets up and hops in the shower without any parting words. The man is an enigma. I truly don't understand why I'm so drawn to him. Maybe it's the fact that he's a mystery—a puzzle. I want to find all the pieces and put them together to figure him out.

I got a hint that the relationship he had with his parents might've been a little rocky. He hardly seemed affected by their deaths, but I know some people can handle their emotions better than others. It's not like he's the best at showing any emotion anyway.

There have been brief moments where I'll catch him grinning or laughing, and I find myself waiting for those, wanting to be the one who creates the crack in his wall.

When we fuck, he does it without emotion. There are never times where he's gentle or soft. He doesn't kiss, and apparently doesn't suck dick, but I'm determined to get him to break that last rule. But the fact that he's so anti-intimacy sparks curiosity. How can you be with men and yet not want to perform blowjobs?

Regardless of all that, I still enjoy our time together. It's not like I require whispered love declarations while in the midst of getting fucked. I've only felt close to being in love once before, but that didn't work out because he was never gonna come out of the closet. I had a girlfriend say she loved me, but I didn't feel the same way, and she ended things shortly after.

While he's in the shower, I think about joining him, but I doubt he's interested in that. Instead, I go to the bathroom in the other bedroom and clean up quickly, grabbing my lounge clothes from my backpack to change into.

When I emerge into the living room area of the suite, I find him standing over a table littered with papers and an open laptop, talking on the phone to someone about business.

He looks sexy as fuck, all business but wearing a plain white T-shirt and a pair of navy colored pants. It's the least dressed up he's ever been around me, well, besides when he's naked.

His eyes flicker over to me as I take a seat that allows me to keep him in my line of sight. He calls me over with two fingers, and when I get there he hands me the room service menu.

I slide into the chair as he keeps talking, and look over the options for food.

Aleksander ends the call. "Sorry about that. Know what you want?"

"You don't have to apologize. Are you actually ever off?"

He grants me a small grin. "No, not really."

I hand him the menu. "The chicken marsala sounds good."

He nods, grabbing the phone on the table and placing our order. "Drink?" he asks me.

"I'll go to the vending machine."

He shakes his head slightly before finishing up and hanging up the phone. "I forgot you get your joy from taking trips to the vending machines."

I laugh, remembering what I told him my first night here. "Don't forget the ice. I'll grab us a bucket of ice, too."

"I think there's ice in the freezer."

"There's also a fridge, oven, stove, and microwave, and yet we're ordering room service."

"I don't have time to shop."

"You can now order your groceries online and have them delivered to you, you know?"

"Well, I don't have time to cook."

"You have time to fuck," I say with a grin.

"Priorities."

I laugh before having a sobering thought. "Do you...never mind."

His eyes meet mine. "What?"

"Nothing. Doesn't matter."

I don't want to ask if he's fucking anyone else. It would force us to have a conversation about what we're doing. Is this the second and last time? Or is this going to be ongoing until one of us gets tired of it? Are we being monogamous? Isn't monogamy only for people in relationships? Thinking about it all makes my head spin, so I move on.

"Want to join me on my ice and drink trip?"

He moves like he's about to start walking with me, but stops. "Maybe next time."

I shrug. "Okay."

Sliding my feet into my Nike sandals, I leave the room and follow the signs until I find what I'm looking for. There isn't one on this floor, because the suites don't need them I guess, but on the floor below, I find an abandoned ice bucket and a box of liners. After lining it with the small plastic bag, I fill the bucket with ice and then grab too many drinks and snacks from the vending machines.

When I get back to the room, Alek opens the door and arches a brow. "You know I just ordered food, right?"

I lift my arms, full of chips and candies, and grin. "I'm a big guy, in case you didn't notice. It takes a lot to keep me satiated."

His piercing eyes look me up and down. "Mm. I noticed, and I'll keep that in mind."

I start taking the drinks and putting them in the fridge. "I got Gatorade. We may need to get our electrolytes up later."

He grunts in response. "How can you eat all that junk and stay so fit?"

"Oh, you think I'm fit?"

He gives me a look. "I'm not blind."

"No cataracts yet?"

"Funny."

I laugh and lean against the counter in the kitchen. "Well, I'm pretty active, and I try to keep from eating too much crap when I'm actively playing sports. But, you know, I'm young. Got that good metabolism."

"I see."

"You look good, too. You know, for a guy your age."

"Are you trying to piss me off?" he says, narrowing his eyes at me.

"Maybe. Could be hot."

He shakes his head and goes back to work at the table, so I grab my phone and reply to several texts. As soon as I respond to Trevor's message, he calls me.

"Hello?" Alek's eyes snap to mine, but I shrug. "Hey, what's goin' on?"

"Where the hell are you? We've had four different people trying to get in touch with you."

"I'm...with someone right now."

"Oh." Trevor laughs. "He's hooking up," he tells someone in the background.

"Who you tellin' my business to?"

"Dom."

"Of course. Couple's tell each other everything."

"Well, that's the way it should be. Anyway, you gonna be held up all night, or you gonna be able to come out later?"

I eye Alek. "Uh, I think I'm stuck for tonight. I'll meet up with you tomorrow."

"Ooh, I think it's serious," Trevor tells Dom with a laugh.

"Since when have I been serious with anyone?" I ask, walking to the balcony.

"There's always a first time. Is it a guy or girl?"

I glance over my shoulder and find Alek watching me. "A man," I answer.

"A man," Trevor says, chuckling again.

"Are y'all drunk?"

"Maybe. Your ass should be here. Everyone's asking about you."

"I *am* the life of the party," I joke. "Y'all will be fine without me tonight."

"Whatever. Go get laid."

"If you insist."

Once I end the call, I spin around and find Alek back at work. Without looking up, he says, "If you're needed elsewhere, you can go."

"I wouldn't say I'm needed. More like, wanted."

"Either way."

As I make my way closer, I ask, "Do you want me to leave and this is your way of saying it without saying it?"

"If I wanted you to leave, you'd know."

I grin. "Then I'm staying. You don't have to beg, you know?"

I watch as his lips start to draw up, his head shaking.

When I'm up close, I reach down, putting a finger under his chin. When he gazes up at me, there's a brief moment where something passes between us. But it doesn't last. There's a knock on the door and he shoots up from his seat and pushes past me.

Twelve

JAYDEN

RIGHT AROUND THE time we're finishing our relatively quiet, late night dinner, I decide to speak up. "Wanna play a game?"

He shoots me a curious look. "Game?"

"I'll ask you some questions, and you answer."

"Doesn't really sound like a game."

"Rapid fire. You can't think. Just answer."

He exhales, putting his fork down. "Okay."

"Favorite color?"

"Gray."

I snort. "Favorite drink?"

"Bourbon."

"Favorite hobby?"

He hesitates and I gesture for him to hurry.

"Sex."

I laugh. "Really?"

He shrugs, a grin pulling on his lips.

"Okay. Favorite guilty pleasure?"

Once again he pauses. "Butterfingers."

"The candy?"

He nods. "They're good."

"I'm not into chocolate. I like Skittles and Starburst."

"You gonna answer the other questions, too?"

"Not yet. Okay, favorite movie?"

"Scarface."

"Dogs or cats?"

"Dogs, I guess."

"Books or movies?"

"Books."

"Men, women, or both?"

He levels me with a look, but then sighs. "Men."

"Had your heart broken before?"

"No."

"Been in love?"

"No."

"Really?"

"I don't like where this game is going," he says, standing up.

"Okay, I'm sorry. Ask me anything you want."

He stops at the bar where he pours himself a drink. I shift under his intense gaze as his eyes swallow me up.

"Does our age difference bother you?"

"No," I answer honestly. "Does it bother you?"

His head moves marginally, like he isn't really sure.

"Are you fucking anybody else?"

My brows nearly reach my hairline, shocked by his question. I was curious about this exact thing earlier, but didn't think for a second he'd ask.

"Not currently."

"If we're fucking, I don't want have to worry about catching anything. If we're doing this, I don't want you with anybody else."

I sink my teeth into my lip. "I love this possessiveness, Mr. Drakos."

"I'm not playing, Jayden."

"Okay, okay," I say, holding my hands up. "I haven't been with anyone since I've been with you, and before you, there had been a bit of a break. I'm going to assume you aren't fucking anyone either?"

He takes a drink. "I don't know anybody but the employees."

"Clearly employees aren't off limits."

"You aren't official yet."

"Semantics."

"I'm not fucking anyone," he bites. "Only you."

"Good."

"Just because I'm breaking one of my rules, doesn't mean I don't have other ones in place."

I sigh. "What are the other rules, besides denying me the pleasure of exploring your mouth with my tongue."

His nostrils flare slightly as his chest expands with a deep breath. "This is short-term. No kissing, no intimacy, no romance. Sex is sex."

"I don't need rose petals or candles," I say. "And I agree, sex doesn't have to come with emotions, but I'd like to discuss something."

"What's that?"

"You sucking my dick. Why won't you do it? It's not kissing."

"It's a form of intimacy."

"You let me suck your dick."

"You don't have my rules."

I huff. "Sex is a form of intimacy."

"Not the way I do it."

"You're a pain in my ass." His smile makes me smile in return. "In more ways than one. I'm guessing another rule is I can't ever fuck you."

He watches me but doesn't respond.

"Have you ever bottomed?"

"Why does it matter?"

"Why do you seem afraid to talk about the sexual acts men do together if you're gay?"

"Jayden," he growls. A warning.

"Fine. You say short-term. How short? You already have an end date in mind?"

"When I go back to Chicago."

I sit up straight, my back coming off the couch cushions. "You're going back to Chicago? When?"

"The beginning of July."

For some reason, my body reacts to the news as if I'm unhappy about this. Disappointment swirling in my stomach. But I shouldn't care. That's still a good amount of time, and since when do I go past that time frame with anyone?

"Okay."

"Now come here." He reaches into his pants, stroking his dick, and my feet take me to him before I drop to my knees.

Thirteen

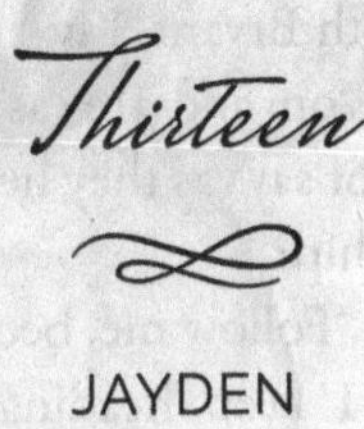

JAYDEN

THE WEEKEND FLEW BY, and I stayed with Alek the entire time. We fucked, ate, showered, and watched TV. Well, I watched TV while he worked and made phone calls, and the showers were always separate. We slept in the same bed, but there was no spooning or cuddling. Regardless of his rules, we had a good time. He's opened up a little more, but he's still very guarded, and I'm starting to think it's rooted deep and probably stems from something in his past.

I didn't see him at all on Monday, and wondered if he was avoiding me because he regretted all the time we spent together over the weekend, but he's back at work Tuesday, saying he had to leave early on Monday for a meeting.

On Wednesday, I check in with him before I'm set to leave, and he lets me know he's happy with the work I've done so far. He doesn't flirt or act like he knows me better than anybody else in that building, and sometimes I'm not sure if I should be offended or praise him for his professionalism, because I've thought numerous times about how I'd love to hide under his desk and suck his dick while he's on the phone, or how he could lock the door and bend me over that same desk. I'm down for it all, but it's almost like he doesn't think about sex until we're locked away in his suite.

Thursday comes and is anything but typical .

It all starts after my last class of the day. I stupidly got caught up in a conversation with Bryant, Liv, and Ronan. Once I pull myself away, I run into Dom and Trev as I'm heading to my car.

"There he is," Trevor says as they head toward me.

"How's the internship?"

"It's good," I reply. "Follow me, because I can't be late."

They trail me as I keep heading for the parking lot. "How's the boss? You said your dad warned you he didn't fuck around."

I laugh. "Yeah. He doesn't. Which is why I can't be late. He already warned me after I was late on the first day."

"Who's this guy you're hanging out with?" Dom asks.

"Nobody. Just a guy. Nothing serious."

I take off my shirt and put on the white Polo. "Gotta go guys. I'll talk to you later, yeah?"

"Party this weekend? Dex is having people over."

"Oh cool. Yeah, text me the details."

Dom drapes his arm over Trevor's shoulder before they head to Trev's car, and I peel out of the lot. I hit every red light in the city, and then on the highway that heads to MGD Advertising, an accident brings me to a halt for ten minutes.

I keep tapping my hands on the steering wheel as the time gets closer and closer to three o'clock. I pull out my phone and call the company, hoping to reach Linda to explain what's happening, but the line stays busy.

I don't even have Alek's number to be able to get in touch with him, however, I doubt he'd want to hear it.

When I finally pull into the company parking lot, it's eight past three. I run to the elevators and rush to Alek's office where Linda's on the phone, holding a finger up to me.

I decide to just head to Luther's office, hoping he won't tell on me for being late, but I know Alek is pretty on top of when all the interns arrive.

I step into his office and find Alek standing inside, talking to him.

His eyes find mine, bounce to the clock on the wall next to me, then land back on my face. "Mr. Brooks. You're just now getting here?"

"Yes, sir. There was an accident, and traffic was slow."

Alek spins back toward Luther and finishes his conversation before walking past me. "Come to my office at the end of the day."

"Okay. Yes, sir," I say, looking at Luther and avoiding the green-blue eyes burning holes into the side of my face.

"Come on, kid," Luther says with a sigh. "We got work to do."

The three hours I spend here each weekday usually go by fast, but today they seem to drag, keeping me on edge. I continuously glance at the time, thinking at least a half hour has passed, only to find it's been five minutes since I last looked. I wonder what Alek will say. Will he actually try to dismiss me from the program? How does our...*relationship* factor into this? He doesn't seem the type to give special favors, and I guess that's why they say you shouldn't fraternize. I shouldn't expect him to take it easy on me simply because he fucks me, but there's a tiny part that thinks I'll get off easier than I should.

I almost want him to call me into his office early and just get this over with. Instead, I stay focused on the work with Luther and the other guy who's been working on this campaign with us—Phillip. When six o'clock comes around, Luther dismisses me with a job well done clap on the back.

In front of Linda's desk, I wait and hope she'll say he left, but when she hangs up the phone, she says, "Have a seat. I'll let you know when he's ready for you." She smiles, unaware of my nerves.

"Okay."

Minutes tick by, feeling like hours. My legs bounce as I wait for Alek to call me in. My mind wanders with all the possibilities.

Linda calls my name, and my head snaps up. "You can go in now."

"Okay. Thanks."

I close the door behind me as I keep my eyes trained on Alek behind his desk, rifling through papers and putting them in folders. I sit down in front of him and he spins toward his computer, typing and clicking the mouse, never acknowledging that I came in.

After another few minutes, he finally faces me, leaning back in his chair with his hands steepled in front of him.

"I told you on your first day that you couldn't be late again."

"I know. I'm sorry."

He holds a finger up, cutting me off. "As much as you may not agree, there are rules for a reason."

"It was ten minutes," I say, trying to defend myself.

"Ten minutes can turn into thirty, and thirty can turn into an hour. Next thing I know, you won't show up at all."

"I wouldn't do that."

"Maybe you think you can get away with it because of our situation."

"It's not like that. Honestly."

A hint of fear burrows itself in my gut, worried he'll want to end things.

"As a consequence, you'll come in on Saturday and work."

I nod. "Okay."

"And you will not let this happen again. Several other people travel from distances farther than you and still manage to make it when they're supposed to. You need to manage your time better."

"I will."

"Good. You may leave."

I stand up, not really wanting to leave. "Alek."

His eyes stay on his work. "Not in this building, Mr. Brooks."

"Mr. Drakos." He looks up at me. "I really am sorry. I don't want you to think I'm taking advantage. I'll do better."

He studies me for several seconds before nodding. "Okay."

Fourteen

JAYDEN

I MAKE it to work early on Friday, not willing to piss off the boss again. I bring a coffee for him, Linda, and Luther, leaving Alek's with Linda before going to Luther's office.

"Trying to suck up?" Luther asks with a grin, the wrinkles around his eyes deepening.

"No, I'm being nice. Everybody needs a little pick-me-up in the afternoon."

"I saw you dropping off goodies at Ms. Thompson's desk."

I grin. "Think it'll work?"

"Mr. Drakos is too hard of a man to soften with coffee and cookies."

"Do you have any tips?"

Luther chuckles. "No."

"How long have you known him?" I ask, knowing it's risky to try to inquire too much.

"A long time. I came over with him from Chicago to get this branch started. He's a good man, and though he's pretty young, he knows what he's doing."

I almost laugh at Luther calling him young, when Alek

has been acting like he's ancient around me. "Seems like it," I say.

"He can come off pretty aloof, but he's been through a lot."

"His parents?" I ask. Luther's eyes flick to mine. "I Googled a little about the company before I started," I say. It's only sort of a lie. I didn't do it before I started, but he doesn't need to know why I was interested.

"That's only the most recent thing. Don't worry about it, kid. Just do your job, do it well, and you'll be fine." Luther runs a hand through his white hair and calls me over. "Now, let's get started."

The first two hours fly by. I've been in contact with customers and clients about sponsorships and cross promotion. Most of what I've done has been traditional marketing, and under Alek's orders, Luther's taken me to the digital marketing department to learn more about leveraging digital channels. I've also spent time with social media marketing, since I've needed to use all aspects to market this festival.

Thirty minutes before the end of my day, I'm in the break room chatting with the other interns while eating a glazed donut.

Joel knocks his arm into mine, lifting up a donut. "Heard you brought these in today."

"I did. Feeling generous, I guess."

"Heard it was because you were late and trying to kiss up to the boss," he says with a grin.

"Is this middle school all over again?"

He laughs. "We never grow up. Everyone loves gossip."

I shake my head. "Turns out the boss isn't a fan of cookies and donuts. So, I failed."

"But we win," he says with another smile, his eyes dropping to my mouth briefly.

Joel is definitely attractive. The epitome of tall, dark, and handsome. He's lean, and his hair is cut so short he's nearly bald. He's someone I'd spend some time with for sure.

"Got any plans this weekend?" he asks.

"Well, besides working on Saturday? I'm not sure. My friends are having a pool party, I think."

"Oh, Mr. Drakos is making you work Saturday? That sucks."

I shrug. "Guess I deserve it."

"Well, let me know when you're free. I'd love to hang out sometime. You know, outside these break room moments." He flashes me his perfect white teeth.

Joel hands me his phone, and I put my name and number in there without thinking about it. "Definitely need to get some more socialization. I feel like I haven't been out in forever and it's probably only been a week."

Once he has his phone back, he sends me a text. "That's me. Text whenever."

"Okay."

When I turn around to grab a napkin from the table behind me, I find Alek in the corner of the break room talking to a couple of guys, but his eyes are trained on me.

I give him a friendly smile, but it isn't returned.

After wiping my mouth and hands, I head for the door with the plan to go to Luther's office for the next twenty minutes.

"Excuse me," Alek tells the guy who's speaking to him. "Mr. Brooks," he says as I'm passing. "Meet me in my office, please."

"Right now?"

"Right now."

"Oh. Yes, sir."

As I'm leaving the room, I hear him continue his conversation, obviously not in a rush to meet me.

I sit in the chair for the first couple minutes before getting up and walking to the window. It's floor-to-ceiling and over-looks the parking lot. Past that, you can see the buildings of downtown South River. Lost in thought, I don't realize he's in the room until he's right behind me.

"Not quite the view from my hotel room, but good enough."

I jerk slightly, angling my head to the side before staring back out the window. "Just like my ass, right?"

He chuckles. "Speaking of which."

"My ass?"

"Yes. I just want to make sure you still remember our conversation about...safety."

"You mean sleeping around?" I ask, turning to face him while I lean against the window.

"Looks like you might've forgotten that you and your ass are mine for the time being."

I can't help the grin that stretches across my face as I shove my hands in my pockets. "Oh, is that right?"

"You're aware of our situation, and until one of us says otherwise, you are mine and you aren't to be dating or leading certain interns on."

My teeth sink into my bottom lip, my joy hardly able to be contained. "Sir, I have to admit, I like you like this."

He narrows those piercing eyes at me. "It's about safety."

"I think it's about jealousy."

Alek sighs. "Maybe I have a sharing problem. I am an only child, after all."

I laugh, crossing my arms over my chest. "You can admit you like me, you know? I won't tell anyone."

His face remains emotionless. "I hope you won't be texting Mr. Grenald anytime soon."

"Who?"

"Joel."

"Oh. Well, he might text me."

His jaw clenches as he gets more annoyed. "Then I expect you to let him down easy."

"If me and my ass belong to you, then that must mean that you and your cock belong to me, yes?"

He hesitates. "If that's how you want to look at it, yes."

"No, that's how it is."

My phone vibrates in my pocket, so I reach for it and read the screen. It's a message from Joel. I look up and smirk at Alek.

"It's Joel."

"And?"

"He said he thinks I'm sexy. He was too afraid to tell me to my face. Wants to take me to dinner tonight."

Alek's chest expands as he inhales. "And your response will be?"

"Maybe I should say yes. It's not like you're taking me to dinner or saying I'm sexy. Maybe I am a romantic, after all."

I'm just talking shit to piss him off, hoping it'll push him to open up a little more. I assume he likes me enough if he wants me to himself, but he doesn't voice that. I could very well just be a hole for him to use.

I move past him and head to the chair at his desk, typing a response.

"Jayden," he says huskily.

"Not in this building, Mr. Drakos."

His inhale and subsequent exhale is loud as he marches toward me. "Stop playing these childish games."

"Oh." I look down at my phone. "Dinner invitation just turned into dinner at his place. He'll cook for me. That's sweet."

Aleksander stops in front of me, reaching down and pulling me up by my collar. His hand snakes around my throat as his eyes focus on my lips. He stares at them so long I think he'll kiss me. Instead, his other hand goes to my button and zipper, undoing them with ease.

"What're you—"

"You don't want *sweet* and you know it."

I attempt to think straight as his hand slips into my pants, palming my cock through my boxer-briefs. "I know what I want."

"What is it then?"

With a moan, I say, "Your mouth on my cock."

"What else?"

"Your cock in my ass."

"And?"

He reaches into my boxers, his palm running down my shaft. I suck in a shaky breath. "My cock in your ass."

"You know what I heard? *Mine* and *yours*. Nothing including Joel or anyone else."

"Yeah," I moan. "Me and you."

"Good. Now tell him you can't make it," he says, wrapping his fingers around me and stroking.

"Okay, but don't stop," I breathe.

He stops. "Tell him."

"I was just joking. He didn't invite me to dinner. I was messing with you."

"You were joking?"

I meet his gaze, my lips quirking up on one side. "I just hoped you'd show me you wanted me."

He grabs my hand and places it on his hard cock. "You don't already know? I have to avoid seeing you during the day because otherwise I'd rip you away from your work and fuck you over my desk."

"Oh," I say, gripping him in my hand.

Alek grins slightly. "Yeah. Oh."

"Wanna hang out this weekend?"

He steps back, removing his hand from my pants and

letting my hand fall to my side. "I overhead you earlier. You want to socialize, and hanging out in my hotel room isn't that. You should be with your friends."

"I didn't mean for it to sound like I wasn't happy with what we did last weekend. I enjoyed every second of it."

"But you're young and there are parties to attend, right?" he says with a fraction of amusement on his face as he sits behind his desk.

I shrug. "I'm an extrovert. I thrive on being around people. Do *you* want to take me out?"

"We're fucking, not dating."

I try not to let the sting of that statement show on my face. He's right, and if I'm being honest, I'm pretty sure I've said the same thing to others. The medicine is bitter.

"I can do both—hang out with them first, meet up with you later."

"We'll see. Be here at eight sharp tomorrow morning."

"Okay." I hesitate, not sure how to leave.

I've always been the one in his position—calling the shots. I've slept with people and controlled how it all went down. If I wasn't interested again, I'd let them know. If we fucked and I was ready to leave, I'd dismiss them without a second thought, without caring about how they felt. It was all very mechanical, and being on the other side is a little jarring.

I'm not saying I have feelings for this guy. I guess I have sexual feelings, but just because I want to fuck him doesn't mean I care deeply about him. I don't even know why I feel this way. I should be used to this, it's what I do.

"Bye," I say before walking out.

He doesn't respond, and I hate that I feel a tinge of disappointment that he didn't want me to stay.

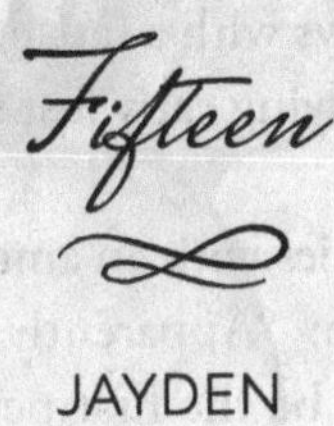

JAYDEN

FRIDAY NIGHT there was a party at my frat, and as I'm usually front and center, coming up with drinking games and forcing people to take shots of weird and random shit, it was hard to pull myself away. I definitely spent a few hours talking and drinking, but by one o'clock, I was in my room, trying to get some sleep even though the party ran until at least three or four.

Renzo was there to harass me over the new guy I was fucking, obviously having heard something from the gossips—Dom and Trevor. Little does anybody know, I'm not fucking anyone, and the guy is a man I work for...who knows my dad.

One of my past hookups was there, and after mulling over how I treated a good majority of them, I went out of my way to talk to her and apologize for all the times I was an ass who made her feel like shit.

She laughed and accepted the apology, happily in a relationship, but I hope that even if she acted like it wasn't a big deal, the apology makes her feel a little better.

I roll up to the building at seven forty-five, positive I'll be waiting for whoever else is supposed to be here to unlock the door. However, I spot Alek's car parked in the lot, and once I arrive at his floor, I find him behind his desk, on the phone.

He gestures for me to come in, and I sit patiently while he finishes his call.

"You're early," he says with a satisfied smile.

"I even stopped partying early just to go to bed to be ready for today."

"Good boy," he replies with an amused grin.

I try not to beam. "Apparently, not early enough. I thought I was going to be the first person here. I also didn't know I'd be working with you."

"Well, I've only been here half an hour or so, and I don't typically make my employees work on the weekends, but sometimes, when we're on a deadline, people will be in here working around the clock."

"Gotcha. Where do you want me?"

His eyes flash with desire before he straightens up. "Later, I'll go over a couple of websites you'll need to learn your way around. It takes some time, but I'm sure you'll figure it out. Until then, you can pick a desk out there in the hub and work. He hands me a folder. "Luther told me you already came up with keyword combinations?"

"Yeah," I say with a nod.

"Good. Now I want you to write a blog on one of those topics. This will help me get a good look at your written communications skills, as well as expanding brand awareness. The point here is to form an incisive narrative of your understanding between the keyword research and the company. Later, you'll track blog hits and that'll help you with your experience with SEO analytics."

I stand up and nod. "Okay."

~

Since starting here, I've learned I haven't learned nearly enough in college, but I'm thankful for everyone who's allowed us interns to ask questions. Apparently, the company only has a few positions available once the internship is over, but between each of us working with our own group for a new campaign, we're learning the ropes about the marketing business in general and splitting the work between handling the company's social platforms, answering customer emails, blogging, sending out newsletters, ordering office supplies, and fifty other things.

I stay at my desk until Alek appears at my side. "Doing okay?"

"Yes, sir. Need me to do something else?"

"Want to have lunch?"

"Is it lunchtime already?"

I look at the clock and see that it's nearing noon.

"Want me to order something in or would you like to join me somewhere?" he asks, his uncharacteristic unease evident in the way his eyes bounce around.

I decide not to tease him about this being a date. "We can order in. Pizza? I know a place."

"Okay," he replies before turning around and heading back to his office.

I follow him in and we decide on what we want before I place the order.

"It'll be twenty-five minutes," I tell him.

He nods, focusing on his computer. I get on my phone to pass time, but he speaks up, stealing my attention.

"What are your plans for today?"

"Once you free me? I'm not sure. I'll probably head back home, take a nap, then later I'll go to my friend's house. He's having a pool party."

"A nap? Are you sure you're not the old one?"

I laugh. "An age joke? From you?"

He tries to stop from smiling. "So, a pool party, huh?"

"Yeah, he's got a hell of a house. Well, his dad. You heard of Owen Anderson? Tech billionaire?"

"Oh, yeah. Of course. That's your friend's dad?"

"Yep. His dad works a lot, so he basically has the house to himself. Pool parties are pretty frequent when the weather's nice."

"Sounds fun."

"Wish you could come," I say with a wink. "I'd love to see you naked and wet."

His lips draw up. "I don't swim naked."

"Well, mostly naked, then."

"Hmm."

"What about you? Plans?"

"I have business calls to make, emails to send, then maybe I'll journey out to find a nice place to eat. Getting tired of room service."

"Why don't you go grocery shopping?"

He makes a face like the idea of it disgusts him.

"How long have you been here? Dad said this branch is new, but you seem pretty established here."

"We've been running for nine months. I've made a few trips out here while it was getting started, but I've been here this time around for a couple months. Maybe three. What month is it?"

I snort. "April."

"Okay, closer to three."

"And you just wanted to make sure things were running smoothly?"

"Something like that. If you haven't noticed, I like to be in control, and I wanted to make sure we were doing everything we needed to do to the best of our ability. I trust Luther, which is why I brought him this time around. He'll stay here once I leave to keep things in order. I also brought over a couple other of the more experienced personnel from Chicago."

"You? Controlling? Weird." He rolls his eyes. "So, Luther. I really like him."

"Oh? Is he your type after all?"

A laugh bursts from my throat. "Stop. No. I mean, he's a good guy. Seems to like you a lot."

A genuine smile forms on his lips. "He's been a mentor to me. The closest thing I have to a father figure now."

"Does he know…" I pause. "Wait. Are you out? Like, do people know you're gay?"

His lips flatten as he stares at me. He's always gotten weird when I've inquired about his sexuality. Maybe he's not out.

"Not many people know," he answers.

"You've never had a boyfriend serious enough to show up to work for lunch or to take to work events?"

His brows furrow slightly as he chuckles. "No, definitely not."

"I have a question, but I'm afraid of how you'll take it."

"Oh, great," he says, sitting back. "Go for it."

With a laugh, I say, "It's not too bad. I'm just curious. Am I the youngest person you've been with or do you have a penchant for younger guys?"

Alek grimaces. "I hate how that sounds. It makes me sound like some sort of pervert, but no, I don't have a *penchant* for younger guys. You're the youngest."

"Ah, a first." I grin. "You're the first older guy I've been with."

"Oh, so you're not out seeking sugar daddies on the regular?"

"Mm," I teasingly moan, shifting in my seat. "You wanna be my sugar daddy?"

He laughs. "No, you're probably too expensive."

"Hey, I know my worth."

Alek shakes his head, a grin playing on his lips. "So, when did you come out?"

"Right before I left for college," I say with a laugh. "I figured if my parents ended up being pissed, then I'd be living in another state soon and wouldn't have to worry about it. But I was tired of not living my truth."

He nods. "And how did they react?"

"Oh, they were surprised," I say with a smile. "I'll never get the looks on their faces out of my head. They were wide eyed and silent."

"But they weren't angry?"

"No. They questioned me a lot. 'Are you sure? Are you confused? Are you curious?' Stuff like that. But they accepted it and never acted weird again. Then again, I've been living here, so it's not like they see me with guys or anything. I'm not sure how they'd act if I introduced them to a boyfriend."

He soaks in the information with another nod. "And your friends? I'd think it would be hard to come out as a young person in school. People can be cruel."

"Definitely. I didn't come out right away. It's not like I ever had to pretend to like girls, because I do. So for a while, they saw me with girls and assumed I was straight and I never said anything to suggest otherwise. It wasn't until I found a guy I was attracted to and started hooking up with that I knew I'd have to tell them. Even then, it was only the people I was closest to. As far as everybody else, I just adopted the I-don't-give-a-fuck-what-you-think attitude. If they saw me with a guy, then they'd know I also liked guys. A few people from the frat or the football team questioned me, but even then the answer was simply, *I like both* with a shrug."

Alek chuckles. "Well, I'm glad you didn't have a lot of issues others have had."

The way he says—with a certain degree of pain in his

voice, makes me wonder if he had issues. It would explain a few things.

"What about you? Did your parents ever know?"

The silence that follows and a face full of resentment while his body bristles with anger tells me everything I need to know.

Sixteen

ALEKSANDER

"THEY KNEW."

I mean to leave it there, not wanting to go into detail about how they found out, and subsequently how they felt about it. But there's something in Jay's eyes that makes me want to say a little more. After all, he told me his story.

"Neither of them were very thrilled about the news."

His lips draw down into a frown. "Damn. I'm sorry. Did they ever get to the point of acceptance?"

I straighten stacks of papers that don't need straightening. "Uh, no. They didn't."

"Unfortunately, the unconditional love you're supposed to get from your parents comes with conditions sometimes, huh?"

The laugh that bubbles out of me is laced with anger. "Oh, definitely. One of them being I wouldn't be in a long-term relationship with a man, because I was to marry a woman and have children."

"What?" he exclaims, his eyes wide. "Even after finding out you were gay they wanted you to have a family with a woman?"

"My parents were quite old, Jay. Very traditional."

"Fuck that. Traditional is typically some antiquated way of thinking, because it keeps getting passed down. Lots of awful things were *traditional*, and it doesn't make them right."

I nod, agreeing with him. "Our relationship was rocky, to say the least. They got to a point where they acted like they never knew. They introduced me to women, and if they ever questioned whether I liked someone, it was in direct reference to a woman they tried to force on me."

He makes a face, a look between disgust and anger. "That's fucked up."

I shrug. "They had a plan in mind, and I was deviating from it."

"Your plan and their plan doesn't have to be the same."

"I know."

I watch as he chews on his bottom lip, his brows knitted as he contemplates his next words. "Is that why you're a little..." My eyes narrow as I wait to hear what he's going to say. He hesitates briefly. "I mean, you didn't seem to want to tell me you were gay. Is it because they didn't accept you?"

I exhale, shaking my head as I stand up. "It's nothing you need to worry about."

I don't intend for it to come off rude, and I hope he doesn't take it that way, but it's true. Knowing the dirty details won't fix or change anything, and the last thing I want is someone's pity. Especially his. I don't allow myself to be vulnerable with people. I don't like for anyone to know the dark secrets I keep in my closet.

"Pizza's here," I announce, watching the delivery guy get out of his car.

He stands up. "I'll go get it."

Once he's gone, I push a hand through my hair and blow out a breath. Talking about my parents always puts me on edge. Just because they're dead doesn't mean I'm free of them. Their words and threats live inside me, constantly reminding me of how I'm *supposed* to be and what I'm expected to do. Them dying didn't release me, instead it left me with a lack of closure.

My parents beat into me the need for having a kid. I needed someone to take over the company. It needed to stay in our family since they worked so hard making it what it is.

The fights were constant, especially in the beginning. My dad actually caught me with a guy, and I thought he was going to kill me. After a while, I allowed them to think what they wanted. I didn't have it in me to keep arguing and trying to get them to understand. It was never going to work. Eventually, I believe they tricked themselves into thinking they had changed me.

Jay's not far off the mark when he asks if I'm the way I am because of my parents. Typically, children are shaped by their families and people close to them. That's why things like homophobia and racism still run strong today. Children are being taught to be hateful. Nobody's born knowing to hate a certain group, someone teaches them to, through words and actions.

On rare occasions, a child will grow up and realize the way they were brought up was wrong, and it is possible for them to break the cycle, but it doesn't happen enough.

My parents never spoke about gay people until they found out about me. That's when I learned their feelings on homosexuality. Regardless of how different we are, what they said has stayed with me, and affects me in my relationships to this day.

"I went to the break room and got some paper plates. They're pretty flimsy, though," Jay says, walking in with two boxes—one holding pizza and one holding pasta."

I walk back to my desk and clear it off. "That's fine. Thanks."

He watches me with curious eyes, perhaps trying to gauge my mood. "I also got some napkins and plastic forks for the pasta."

I sit down across from him and grin. "Thank you."

He smiles, and we break into the boxes and start eating. The conversation is no longer heavy, instead we discuss toppings we don't like on pizza, and debate on the best drink to have with it. I say water, and he claims you have to have a carbonated drink.

"Come on, drink some of this Sprite. I'm telling you, it enhances the flavor."

I shake my head, chuckling, but grab his bottle of Sprite and take a sip before taking another bite of my pizza. "It tastes the same."

"No way," he says with a laugh. "I'm gonna train you to only drink sodas when you have pizza and you'll realize you've been wrong your whole life."

"Sure," I say with a snort, taking another bite.

"Okay, what about this? I swear to God, you better answer right. Do you season your popcorn?"

I make a face. "You mean, besides butter?"

He throws his arms up, letting them drop to his sides, looking up at the ceiling in disbelief. "You know they make actual seasonings for popcorn, right? It's to *enhance* the flavor."

"You and your enhancements."

"Luckily I don't need enhancements in certain areas," he flirts with a wink.

"No, definitely not."

His eyebrows raise. "Oh, a compliment?"

I shake my head, my lips forming a smile while I chew. "Just stating a fact."

"That I'm well-endowed and probably the best dick you've ever had, right?" His grin falls. "Wait. Shit. You haven't even had my dick." With a shake of his head, he looks me in the eye and says, "Sir, let me explain something." I nearly laugh at how serious he gets. "If you allow me to, how should I say this...gift you with my...gifts, then I can assure you it will *enhance* the pleasure when we're together."

"Stop," I say with a chuckle, grabbing a napkin to wipe my mouth.

His smile grows as he watches me laugh, his eyes bright with glee. "Come on, Mr. Drakos. Let me make you feel good," he says in a sultry voice that he might've intended to be playful, but stirs something inside me.

I clear my throat, attempting to keep things light as I stand up with my trash in hand. "Your ass always feels good. Good enough, anyway." I wink, letting him know I'm teasing.

He gives me an unamused look before pushing his chair back and standing up. My pulse spikes as he rounds the table, coming up behind me.

Our height is nearly identical, and I feel the heat of his body at my back before the warmth of his hands seep through the material of my shirt as he grabs my waist, his breath on my neck.

His lips touch my skin, brushing across the goosebumped flesh until reaching my ear. With one hand gripping my hip, the other travels up my torso before journeying back down to run a palm over my crotch.

"I'd make sure you felt every ounce of pleasure possible," he whispers before the tip of his tongue dances under my ear. "There would be nothing to worry about, except that you'd probably become addicted after having a taste of me. But I'll happily be your supplier, baby."

He sucks on a patch of skin, his hand groping my growing erection while his pushes into my ass.

I groan, dropping the plate and bottle of water on my desk, ready to spin around and do more. But my phone rings, the sound blaring through the room, killing the moment and drawing us apart. He steps to the side, watching me carefully. I want to throw myself against him. I want to toss him over my desk. I want to feel his skin against mine, and I'm even curious about his proposition. I want too much, especially when I know I won't be able to keep it.

I pick up the cell. "Hello?"

Jay's shoulders drop as he makes his way to the other side and gathers his trash.

"Oh. Calvin. How are you?"

Jay's bulging eyes find mine, his lips parting as he realizes his dad is on the phone.

Seventeen

ALEKSANDER

"SORRY TO BOTHER you on the weekend, but I figured this would be the best time since you like to work yourself to the bone during the week," Calvin says with a jovial chuckle.

"You'd be right, but I happen to be at work now."

"Jesus, Alek, you need to learn to relax a little."

My brow arches as I watch Jay bend over to pick up a napkin. "I'm relaxing a little."

Jay spins around and shakes his head, amusement in his eyes.

"That's good. I just wanted to check in about Jayden. Make sure he's doing what he's supposed to."

"He appears to be well-liked, and he's not slacking off. He's a good worker, Cal."

"Good, good. I'm glad to hear it. I can't thank you enough for letting him get a spot. The kid is smart, but he loves to party. I just want him to be prepared for adulthood. Sometimes I'm not sure he's aware his college days are almost up."

Something akin to defensiveness rears up. I feel the need

to stick up for Jay to his own dad, when clearly, his father should know more about him than I do.

"Regardless of what he does in his free time, he's giving a hundred percent here. I wouldn't worry."

Jay shakes his head a little, a small smile on his lips like he's used to his dad being this way.

"All right, then. I don't want to take too much of your time. Go home. Take a nap. Have a drink. Enjoy your weekend, Alek."

I chuckle. "I'll try."

Calvin laughs. "I'll take it. Talk to you later."

"Bye."

"Well, talk about a boner killer," Jay says from his seat. "He worried about me not taking this seriously?"

"He's just being a good dad, I suppose."

"Guess I'll get back to work."

"No, it's fine. You can leave. I didn't intend on you staying the whole day."

"You sure?" he asks.

"Yeah. I'll stick around for a little while but I'll be heading home soon."

"Okay then." He pauses, his eyes flickering to me. "I guess I'll see you Monday."

He doesn't form it like a question, but it is one. I can sense he doesn't know how to treat our situation. We've never embraced or kissed, so there's no need to do that as we go our separate ways, but I have a feeling it's an alien thing to Jay. He itches to be affectionate.

I reach into my desk and pull out a card. I scribble my cell number on it and hand it to him. "Text me after your pool party."

His face lights up with a wide smile that reaches his eyes. "Yeah? Okay."

I grin as I watch him walk out, not entirely sure that was

the smartest decision I've made, but excited to see him later nonetheless.

At five o'clock, I get a text from an unknown number.

> I've only been here two hours and I'm ready to leave. Is that bad?

I program Jay's name in my phone before I reply.

> Are you not having fun?

> I just know I could be having more fun. ;)

> Enjoy the day with your friends, Jay. I'll be here all night.

Two hours later, my phone dings with another message.

> Okay, I enjoyed myself.

I laugh when I read it.

Did you? Or have you been watching the clock the entire time?

Are you spying on me? Haha! But no, I've had fun. There's plenty to do and quite a few people.

That's good.

But I would rather be with you.

His message has me freezing up. I hate texting, because you can never read the tone, but his words hit me in the chest and make me feel...something I'm not used to. Do I tell him I've also been watching the clock, wondering when he might show up?

I don't want to monopolize all of your time.

It takes him a while before he responds again, and I worry I've offended him or made him think I'm not interested in spending time with him. The opposite is true. I want to spend more time with him than I should want to. Not only is he so much younger than me, he's the son of a friend and employee, and I'm leaving Michigan soon. Besides all of that, I'm not sure I'm wired to give him what he wants or deserves.

Sorry. I got pulled away. Someone else is trying to monopolize my time.

. . .

Jealousy licks up my spine and the uncharacteristic trait boggles my mind. I told him to have fun with his friends, but based on the last part of his message, it sounds like a specific person is trying to spend time with him rather than him just having a good time with the group.

Oh yeah?

Yeah, just this guy I know.

Remember what I said.

What's that?

Are you being obtuse on purpose? Trying to rile me up?

You've said lots of things.

Jayden.

I can almost hear your growl from here. Hold on. This guy is calling me over.

I call his number and he picks up right away. "Hello?"
"Stop fucking around and bring your ass over here."
He chuckles. "I didn't expect you to call."
"Were you just trying to make me jealous?"
"Are you?"

I'm saved from having to answer, because someone on his end starts talking. Based on what I can hear, he wasn't lying.

"Sorry. So, what were you saying?"

"You know where I am. See you soon."

His laugh is the last thing I hear before I end the call.

Eighteen

ALEKSANDER

ALMOST AN HOUR LATER, and I'm pacing through the hotel suite, anxious in a way I've never been. I begin to worry he won't show. Maybe he got caught up with his friends...with this guy. I want to smack myself for being so out of control.

I'm starting to wonder if only being with him on the weekend is enough. Five days without him already has me on edge. It had been a long time since I was with anybody, and that was fine. I wasn't struggling with the lack of sex. I was used to it. It was nothing I couldn't solve with a little solo stroke action, but now that I've had a taste, I find myself constantly starving.

I do my best to control myself around him, not wanting to lead him to believe this can be anything serious, but I'm struggling to hold onto the reins.

When a knock sounds on the door, I have to force myself from jogging toward it. Yanking it open, Jayden stands there with a cocky grin. I want to attack his mouth and plunder it with my tongue.

I inhale deeply, trying to keep my cool. "You finally made it."

He walks in, his hand gently touching my stomach. "I had to go shower and prepare myself for tonight."

Closing the door, I spin around and follow him inside. "Oh? Not too busy with *certain* guys?" I clench my jaw, hating that I sound like a jealous teenager. I forge on, hoping to move past that. "That's good. I'm glad you're ready for me."

He turns and watches me, sitting on the arm of the couch. "I told you I wouldn't see anyone else while we do this. I meant it."

"It's just about—"

"Safety," he finishes for me, not sounding at all like he believes it. "Right."

I shove my hands in my pockets to keep from reaching out to him. "So."

"Do you know how to swim?" he asks.

"Yes."

"Good. Come on," he says, standing up and walking back toward me.

"What?"

He grabs a hold of my wrist as he passes me, spinning me around and tugging me along for a couple seconds before letting go. "Just come with me. Live a little."

"I don't even have shoes on," I complain. "And I'm not really dressed—"

"You don't need to wear a suit to go to a pool. What you're wearing is fine."

I'm wearing a dark T-shirt and a pair of lounge pants, with only socks on my feet. "Jay."

"Alek," he says, mimicking my tone before laughing.

I manage to swipe the extra key from the counter before we leave the room. I follow him as we make our way down to the first floor, traveling down a couple hallways, passing people leaving or going to their rooms.

"These people are probably wondering why I don't have any shoes on."

"Are you kidding? A hotel is the only place you can get away with not wearing shoes without having to worry about what people are going to say. People walk the halls in bathing suits and swim trunks. Nobody cares."

I grunt, but we keep going until we reach the room that holds the pool.

"It closes soon, so people likely won't be coming in," he says as he walks inside, the door propped open with a wooden wedge underneath.

Once we're both inside, he closes the door, then immediately rips his shirt over his head.

"If you're expecting me to skinny dip..."

"I wasn't, but that sounds like fun," he says with a flirtatious smile. He steps out of his tennis shoes, removes the socks, then pushes his jeans down. He's left standing in a pair of gray boxer-briefs. "Your turn."

I glance around, wondering if there's a way for people to look in here.

"No windows," he says. "The only other door is that one over there and they can't come in from outside. And we're not doing anything wrong, anyway."

When he walks down the steps that lead to the water, I remove everything but my underwear, tossing them to a plastic chaise lounge chair.

Jayden spins around, water up to his stomach as he walks backward toward the deep end. His eyes never leave me as I descend the steps.

"I've been wanting to see you naked and wet all day. None of my friends do it for me."

My lips pull up on one end. "I'm glad to hear it, but I'm not naked."

"Not yet."

I make my way to the side, dipping below the water before coming to a stop and standing near the five foot marker. I shake the water from my hair, and find Jayden swimming over.

He stands less than a foot away, his eyes hooded as he inspects me. With an arm outstretched, his fingers brush a few locks out of my face.

"I love your eyes," he confesses, looking slightly embarrassed before giving me a lopsided smile and shrug. "I can't quite figure out the color."

"I can't blame you. They're a mix of blue and green. Not just one color."

"Like mine. So dark you can't really tell the difference between my pupils and irises."

"Yours are rich, soulful, and deep."

The words come out unplanned, just what came to mind as I stared into them. His teeth sink into his lip briefly before grinning.

His hands find my torso under the water and they roam the ridges of my abdomen before dipping into the waistband and traveling to my ass. His legs brush against mine as he leans in and licks water from my neck.

"I want you so bad," he whispers. "I couldn't stop thinking about you."

"Then why are we here?" I question, my fingers dipping into the waistband of his boxer-briefs and tugging him forward.

"Because you need to learn to play and have fun."

"I know how to have fun," I grumble.

"Sure you do."

He pulls back, splashes water at me and swims away, leaving me to chase after him. For the next several minutes, we enjoy having the pool to ourselves like children left unattended. I dive under the water, swimming toward him as he attempts to get away. He swims through my legs as my eyes scan the moving water, trying to find him. He kicks water at me when he emerges, and I slip under and wrap my arms around his waist and tug him below the surface. We play and laugh, and I can't remember the last time I allowed myself time to have fun like this.

When he's in the corner of the pool, I approach, leaving him with little space to flee. "I think I win this game," I say with a smile.

He braces his elbows on the sides and then his legs wrap around my waist, yanking me into him. "I think I do."

Our faces are inches apart and my lips ache to feel the softness of his. Deep, dark eyes assess me, and my hands reach out to hold onto the edge, trapping him between my arms. Our chests heave with deep breaths, and I can tell he's waiting for me to make a move. He won't kiss me because he knows it's one of my rules, but I can break that rule right now. All it'll take is me leaning in.

The loud sound of the door opening has us breaking apart. A hotel employee stands at the door. "Pool's about to close, fellas. Gotta lock it up."

"Oh, all right," Jayden says, glancing at me longingly before swimming toward the stairs.

The man walks off, allowing us to get out of the pool without an audience. Jay tosses me a towel when I emerge, and we both dry off as well as we can before donning our clothes again.

"Fucking wet underwear and jeans is not comfortable," Jay complains, tugging at the material.

"This was your idea."

He smiles. "And I don't regret it."

"It was fun," I say with a grin.

"Did you say you had fun?" he teases, holding onto my arm. "My God, I never thought I'd hear it."

I shake my head, smiling. "Hungry?"

He looks me up and down, pure lust in his eyes. "Starving."

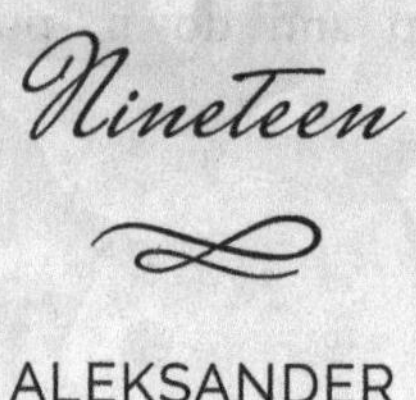

Nineteen

ALEKSANDER

ONCE INSIDE THE ROOM, Jayden quickly removes his jeans. "I think I need to shower again. I don't want you to taste chlorine when you worship my body with your mouth," he says with a wink.

"That's a good idea."

"Together?" he asks with a hopeful tone.

I inhale, knowing what I should say but warring with what I want. "Yeah. Let's use mine. It's bigger."

Marching through the living room, I bypass the bed and go straight for the bathroom, opening the glass door of the shower and turning the water on.

Before I can fully spin back around, Jayden's there, his body pressing against mine. His hips pin me to the glass wall of the shower, his lips planting kisses from my neck to my collarbone, and across my shoulder. His hands shove my pants and underwear down, and I quickly step out of them, my cock quickly coming to life.

I pull his shirt over his head and he pushes his boxer-briefs down before walking us into the shower, closing the door behind him.

Hot water from the raindrop showerhead pours down both of us, and while Jay runs his hands through my hair, keeping it out of my eyes, I reach down and grab his cock in my right hand.

He hisses with pleasure.

"I guess we should actually clean ourselves first, huh?" he pants.

"I'm just gonna dirty you up, anyway."

Jay reaches for a washcloth and squirts some body wash on it. "Yeah? With your cum?"

"If that's what you want."

He quickly runs the soapy material over his chest, stomach, and arms. "Maybe."

With another squirt of soap, he starts massaging the cloth into the same spots on my body. "Why maybe?" I ask, hoping my voice isn't as breathy as it sounds to me.

"Depends on what you'll do for me."

He rinses the cloth and puts more soap on it, washing the rest of his body before drizzling more of the liquid in his hand and stroking my cock.

"What do you want?"

"You know."

I allow my hands to gently caress his body, feeling every powerful muscle. I wish he could understand why. I don't do certain things because as soon as I think about it, the verbal assault I got for many years hammers its way back into my brain, calling me every slur you can think of, and probably even some you can't.

My dad's voice rings in my ears. *You bend over for another man like some sort of bitch? My son is a fucking fruitcake? If you like the taste of cock then you might as well be a woman. Only women suck dick, son. How dare you want to do such vile things? Aren't you ashamed of yourself?*

I spin Jay around, my fingers dancing down his back until

I reach the crack of his ass. I lean over his shoulder and whisper, "I want to bury myself deep inside you. No condom. You sure you're clean?"

He sucks in a breath. "Yeah. You?"

"Yes."

I grab the bottle of conditioner and squeeze a generous amount in my hand as well as above his ass, watching it drip down the middle.

My fingers slide in, pushing past the tight ring of muscle until I can move two in and out with ease. With a slight pivot, I get us to the bench at the back of the shower.

I spin him around, making him give me his back. "Ride me."

He angles his head over his shoulder, looking at me before lowering himself on my lap. He takes hold of my cock, gently guiding me inside him as the steam fills the enclosed space. With one hand clutching a bar on the side, he moves himself up and down, and I hold onto his hips, moaning as he takes me deep.

Jay fully seats himself, leaning back into me with a moan, and my arms snake around his middle, one hand on his cock.

"You're so hard for me," I whisper into his ear.

"You feel amazing," he breathes, rocking back and forth. "Fuck, I could do this all night."

My free hand runs up his stomach and chest, finding his throat where I give a gentle squeeze. "I could do it even longer."

He gasps lightly, moving faster. "Alek."

"What do you need?"

"I want to turn around."

"So turn around."

Jay gets up, spins, then lowers himself into my lap once again, this time, face to face. As soon as I'm buried all the way inside him, I realize the intimacy of this position. We're so close.

He rocks, moaning as he drops his head back. My hand skates up his throat, fingers gripping his jaw. When he locks eyes with me, I see a yearning in them. He's hoping I'll kiss him, and I'd be lying if I said I didn't want to.

My thumb brushes across his pillowy soft lips, my fingers pressed against the base of his skull. I could pull him in easily. Give in to the desire.

Jayden moves faster, his face transforming into one of euphoria. "Alek," he breathes. "I'm so close."

I reach between us and stroke him as he rides me, my other hand going to his lower back. "Yeah, you gonna come for me?" I breathe, watching his face change as the pleasure builds up.

"Yes," he cries. "Fuck yes, I'm gonna come all over you."

A low growl rumbles in my chest as my eyes drop to his cock. His hands land on my shoulders, fingers digging into my flesh as he quickens his pace. His dick is thick in my hand with a small amount of arousal at the tip. The desire to lick it off shocks and excites me.

My thumb brushes across the wetness, and I bring it to my mouth and taste the saltiness of his pre-cum.

"Oh fuck," he exclaims. "Alek. I—"

I wrap my fingers around his cock again, stroking him. "Come for me."

"Oh God," he cries, his body tightening and tensing up. "Yes. Yes. Yes."

Jayden's cum shoots from his crown, landing on my stomach and hand. "That's it," I coax. "Yeah, give it to me," I murmur, transfixed.

Jay moans, a shiver taking over his body. His head drops against mine, and our foreheads and noses touch—lips closer than they've ever been.

His forehead comes off mine, dark eyes meeting light ones. He moves a fraction of an inch, daring to come closer.

"Jay," I whisper softly, unsure what I'd even say next.

"Let me. You don't have to respond. Just let me."

He takes my silence as permission, and his hand cradles my face as he ever so lightly lets his lips touch the corner of mine. His mouth ghosts over my parted lips as he travels to the other corner, giving me another gentle kiss. The feather light pecks have my stomach tightening and my cock twitching in his ass. I close my mouth, my lips barely pressing into his. His exhale is soft, and his forehead dips to mine one last time.

Then he gets up, pulls me to my feet and turns around. His eyes meet mine. "Dirty me up."

Bending him at the waist, I thrust into his ass, my entire body on fire, pinpricks of pleasure dancing across my skin. I fuck him hard, needing my release but also feeling the need to erase the intimate moment we just shared. I enjoyed it and I shouldn't have, for more reasons than one.

This is about sex. Not feelings.

With each thrust, I attempt to block the terrible things that echo in my brain. The disgusting words and threats that I know are wrong—that I know shouldn't have a hold of me anymore.

I bury myself deep in him, hoping some of his goodness transfers to me. I envy his confidence. I hate that he can do what we do without a care in the world.

"Shit," I grunt, gripping him tightly. "I'm gonna come."

"Yeah," he pants. "Come in me. On me. Give me all of it."

My orgasm hits, exploding inside him before I pull out and stroke myself, emptying the rest of my release on his ass and lower back—painting him with my cum.

Twenty

ALEKSANDER

IF HE FEELS any sort of awkwardness, he doesn't show it, then again, why would he? It's not like he's the one with intimacy issues. He's probably not dwelling on the strange kiss we shared. Did we share a kiss if I technically didn't reciprocate? Is he angry about that?

Regardless of how he feels, I can't stop thinking about it. His lips were soft and gentle as his hand cradled my face. It felt...nice. However, my body was tense the entire time. Now I can't stop contemplating how that should've gone. I should've kissed him back. What's my dad gonna call me now? Nothing. He can't.

Is it smart, though, to break down those walls when you know it's not going anywhere? He's young and deserves to enjoy dating and fucking around. He can't tie himself to me. And how would I look? A man near his father's age dating him? Plus, I'm leaving. It wouldn't behoove me to give into any indulgences.

As I war with myself, fighting between shoulds and should nots, rights and wrongs, decisions of the heart versus decisions of the mind, Jay clears his throat.

"You okay over there?"

I glance at him flipping through the room service menu. "What's that? Oh. Yeah, I'm fine."

He gives me a look that lets me know he doesn't believe me. "Mmhmm."

Moving from the kitchen where I down a glass of water, I sit at the table that's become my workstation, my legs bouncing before I'm up and walking toward the TV. I feel agitated and restless. My body moves as fast as my mind is racing, and I can't sit still.

After a few minutes, Jay closes the menu, and the loud noise of his hand landing on top of it pulls me from my thoughts.

"What the hell's going on with you?"

"Nothing, what are you talking about?" I reply in a defensive tone.

"After we finished fucking, you've hardly spoken two words to me. You ignored me as we washed up, threw some clothes at me without so much as a glance in my direction, and now you won't stop pacing."

His words hit me in the gut. I hadn't realized I had come off so dismissive, but it's not surprising. My fear and underlying issues rear up, taking over any logical or reasonable thought process. Where I should assure him it's nothing to do with him, I lash out.

"I thought you said you didn't need rose petals and candles. I thought you said you didn't catch feelings, and now here you are wanting me to, what? Cuddle you? Whisper sweet words in your ear?"

His anger flares as he stands up, his jaw clenching as his fists do the same at his side. "I don't need those things, but I'm also a fucking person."

"You're here for me to fuck. The dinners and swimming were never supposed to be part of the deal."

He takes a few steps, bringing him closer. "You're the one who asked me to look at menus and order food. You're the one who offered to have lunch in the office. I made you swim, but it was you who said it was fun. So, what the fuck are you talking about?"

I shake my head, running a hand through my hair as I walk around him. "It doesn't fucking matter. It's done. We cannot have this weird psuedo fucking relationship. Sex. It was only supposed to be sex. No feelings. No emotions, No attachments."

Jay follows me. "Well, you're being really emotional about it right now. Must have some sort of feelings that are making you act that way."

I spin around and face him. "You're a fucking kid."

His nostrils flare and I know I'm poking the bear. His fury is boiling beneath the surface.

"You seem to enjoy fucking this kid." I grimace, hating the words as soon as they leave his mouth. "You know, Alek, you're so caught up on this age thing you seem to forget I'm bigger than you." He prowls forward. "Do I look like a kid to you?"

I swallow, trying to keep my anger in place, refusing to allow lust in the picture. "You may weigh more, but you're still the one bending over for me."

That's it. That's the comment that makes him snap. His eyes flare, his chest heaves, and every muscle in his body tenses. He storms toward me.

"Are you trying to say because I let you fuck me that that means something? What are you insinuating here, Alek? Huh? I'm soft? I'm less masculine than you because your dick has been in my ass? There's a problem with that way of thinking, but I'm not here to educate you. But if you think fucking me makes you less gay, let me tell you..." He chuckles, but it's laced with anger and lacks any sort of happiness.

"You're being ridiculous," I say with a scoff.

"Am I? You won't kiss, let me fuck you, or suck my cock. Is it because you're afraid you'll like it? Do you think that by having these *rules* you're not fully succumbing to your gayness?"

"Fuck off."

Another venomous laugh leaves his lips, and this time he inches closer, coming behind me and forcing me between him and my desk.

"You want me, Alek, but you're scared. Admit it."

"I'm not fucking scared," I bite, trying to spin around.

He forces me back in place, pinning his body to mine. His mouth finds my ear. "Let me tell you a secret." His hands land on my hips. "Bending over for a man doesn't make you soft." He pushes his hands into my loose, lounge pants, his fingers pressing into my thighs. "Sucking a dick doesn't make you any less of a man." One hand wraps around my cock and I moan at his touch. "By suppressing who you are, you're suppressing your pleasure."

He licks and then bites my neck, squeezing my dick in his hand before giving it a languid stroke. "Jay." I struggle to say his name with any sort of control. It comes out in an airy whisper.

With lightning speed, his hands come out of my pants and go to my back, forcing me to bend over the desk. His hips piston forward, letting me feel his cock on my ass. In a panic, I push up off the wood, trying to stand up straight, but he uses his strength and pushes me back down.

"Jayden," I growl.

He tugs my pants down, and because I didn't put on underwear after my shower, I'm left exposed to him. His fingers dance over the curve of my ass cheeks, causing me to suck in deep breaths. I want him to stop, and I want more.

I can't see what he's doing, but a shift behind me has me angling to look. Before I can get a glimpse, I feel his cock against my skin. He rests his heavy erection on top of my ass, guiding down between my cheeks. He doesn't ever try to penetrate, he's just teasing.

A groan escapes my throat as I grip onto the edge of the table. My breaths come faster and louder.

"Feels good, doesn't it?"

A gentleness I don't deserve is granted via a soft hand rubbing up my back, all while his cock slides between my cheeks. His weight covers me when he leans over, bringing a hand to my mouth.

"Spit."

Desire, fear, and annoyance at using my own actions against me swirl amongst each other, but I spit in his hand and he must use it to coat his cock, because I feel the wetness of the erection between my cheeks again. He moves, fucking me without actually fucking me, squeezing my cheeks together for friction against his dick. It's a tease and my cock throbs.

Jayden grunts and pants behind me, using my body for his own pleasure. I moan and squirm, wanting more. Needing more. I'm not altogether sure I'm ready for him to fuck me, but right now, I need something. I just refuse to ask for it.

"I knew you'd like it," he moans. "You have no idea how good I'd give it to you."

A fucking whimper slips between my lips. I almost say, *do it. Give it to me*. But I clamp my mouth shut.

"You want to feel me deep inside you, don't you?" he asks, still moving. Still tormenting me with his dick. "I know you're curious. You want to know how good it could be." He moans. "You want my cock filling your mouth, don't you?"

He steps back, his fingers replacing his cock, sliding

through the crevice of my ass, barely pressing against my hole. Using his other hand, he yanks me back, allowing himself room to grab my erection.

The smear of my pre-cum over my crown has my face flushing. I'm so turned on, and there's no way to deny it.

He groans low in his throat as he strokes. "Tell me you like it. Tell me you want all those things."

An orgasm is building, and he's doing just enough to keep it on the edge, but not enough to push me over. I'm desperate, pushing against the finger near my asshole, fucking the hand around my cock.

"Yes!" The word is ripped from me. "Yes, I fucking want it, are you happy now?"

He stops touching me altogether, moving away. I get up and spin around, my eyes wild as I look at him. He's pulling his pants back up, so I do the same.

"And that doesn't make you less of a man. Being a selfish asshole does." He reaches for his keys and wallet, gaze flying to mine once again. "You forced me to be like you. How does it feel to be used?"

"I wasn't using you!"

"You said I was only here for you to fuck. Just because I came each time doesn't mean you weren't using me. You wanted what you wanted and didn't care about my desires."

"Then why did you keep coming here?"

He levels me with a look, then shakes his head. "Guess it doesn't matter."

"I told you the first night that we were gonna do things my way and my way only. This is my way, Jayden. I was honest with you."

"Okay, then it's my fault," he says. "I guess I was confused by the invitations to share a meal with you, by the bits of yourself you offered at work earlier."

"I can't give you what you want. I'm not capable of it."

He sighs. "It's fine. I don't want it. I'll see you at work on Monday, boss. I'm assuming you'll be able to keep this and that separate, considering you don't have any feelings to get in the way."

He slams the door as he leaves.

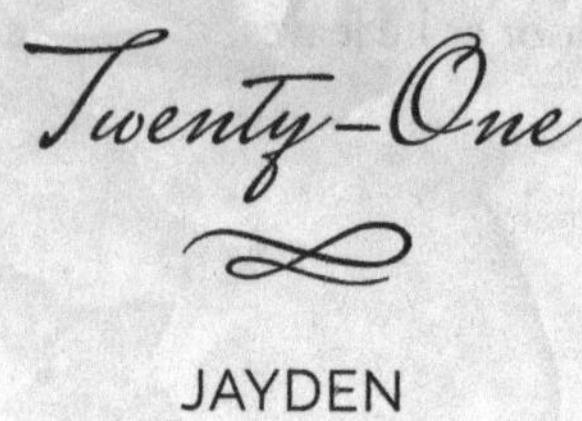

JAYDEN

AFTER LEAVING Alek's hotel wearing the clothes he gave me once I was out of the shower, I rush home to change into my own shit, not wanting any reminders of him.

I'm not a guy who gets easily angered, but tonight, he really pissed me off and turned me into something I'm not. I'm not spiteful and vindictive, but I wanted to use him in the way I felt he was using me.

I'm aware of his *rules*, but like I told him, it became confusing when he was asking me to eat with him, when he shared pieces of his life with me, when he let me kiss him. I thought he was opening up and tearing down a wall. Instead, tonight he basically said I was a hole for his dick and nothing else. I know I was fucked up toward people in the past, but I was never like this. I didn't tell them they were only good enough to fuck.

I get it. I know why there are rules in place. Don't fuck your boss because when shit goes south, you're left in this uncomfortable situation. He has the power. He can remove me from the program and make sure I don't get hired. I contemplate even showing up on Monday.

My anger fuels me, so once I'm changed, I go downstairs where there's a party raging, and I drink. I drink until I can forget about Alek, and how I actually started liking him even though I have every reason not to. I drink until I don't want to call him or send him a message, cursing him out for making me feel like shit.

"Hey, Jay." A brunette plops down next to me, but it takes me several seconds to see clearly enough to recognize her.

"Oh, hey, Tee."

I call her Tee, but she goes by Tia, which is just a shortened version of her actual name—Tatiana.

She laughs. "Wow, you're pretty drunk."

My grin is slow as she blurs into two people. "Ding ding."

"You okay?"

I shrug, or I think I do. "Yeah, fine." I try to scoot up from the bench that's pushed against the wall. "Was I ever an asshole to you?"

"What?" she questions with a giggle.

"You know, did I treat you like shit when we were hooking up?"

She pushes a curly lock of hair behind her ear. "Uh, no. Why are you asking me this?"

"I just wanna know," I say, the words stringing together. "I know I wasn't always the most romantic, but—"

"Jay, you were fine," she says, confusion marring her face. "You were always nice. Just because we weren't in a relationship doesn't mean you were a dick. I was aware of the situation we were in."

"Yeah, but did you feel used?"

"Did you?" she says with a laugh. "We used each other for sex."

I sigh. "I know, but it was different."

She touches my knee, her fingers giving me a little tap. "What's going on?"

I wave a hand through the air. "Doesn't matter. Never mind."

We end up chatting for a few minutes before she disappears and another one of my fuck buddies shows up.

"What is this? Ghosts of hookups past?"

Aiden, someone from at least a year ago, furrows his brows before letting out a chuckle. "What?"

"Nothing. What's going on, man?"

"Not much. Just checkin' on ya. You look like you're pretty wasted, and you're not out there having fun like usual."

I groan. "I'm fine. Let me ask you a question. Was I an asshole to you? Make you feel like shit? Used?"

He laughs nervously. "Uhh."

"Just be honest. I wanna know."

"You were never mean. We had some good times."

"I feel like there's a *but* coming."

He snorts. "I mean, I think I liked you more than you liked me, but that wasn't on you."

"Sorry, man."

"Don't be. I'm fine. It was a long time ago, but why are you asking this?"

"I don't want to be the guy who made people feel used and dismissed their feelings."

"Well, I never told you my feelings, so you didn't have the chance to dismiss them," he says with a laugh. "And I never felt used. I mean, I guess I wanted more than what I was getting, but that was probably because I liked you a lot. It was just unrequited."

"Hmm," I murmur, scratching my head.

Am I only upset because I actually do have some sort of feelings for him? If I had none, I wouldn't

care as much, right?

"Are you in my position now or what? You like someone who doesn't like you back?"

I scoff. "I hate him."

Aiden laughs. "You sure? Whoever he is has caused you to get drunk and be sad in a corner while reminiscing about past relationships. Doesn't seem like hate."

"Well, it's definitely not love, and I'm not sure if it's *like*. Maybe lust. But mostly, he's a selfish prick and I hate him."

Aiden humors me with a laugh, even though I'm sure what I said makes no sense.

"You're a good guy, Jay. Don't let someone make you doubt that. We all make mistakes and bad decisions, and I think everyone goes through a selfish stage, but we're all capable of change, and we're not the sum of every bad thing we've done."

I spend the next hour and a half or so, stuck to the wall, drinking myself closer and closer to a blackout. It's unlike me, and I hate that I've allowed Alek to affect me so much. I'm not this guy. I don't mope. Sulking isn't something I usually do.

After a few other concerned friends come over to check on me, I take my miserable ass upstairs. I thought I'd be able to drink Alek out of my mind, instead, it's having the opposite effect.

Drunk, with my brain as foggy as my vision, I pull my phone out and scroll through social media until I realize I can hardly focus on words or pictures. As stupid and cliché as it may be, and definitely something you should never do while drunk, I bring up Alek's name in my phone. My thumbs hover over the letters, ready to send a scathing text.

I'd only be repeating what I already told him, but the need to reach out, if only for him to respond, is strong. After writing and deleting several different messages, I eventually make the smart decision to not send anything. He's my boss, after all.

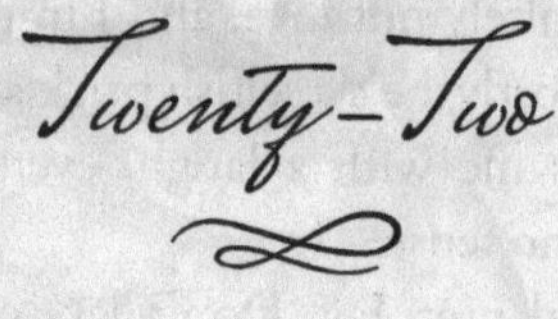

JAYDEN

AFTER I LEAVE CAMPUS, I have enough time to stop by a bakery on my way to work, so I pick up a few coffees and show up to Linda's desk five minutes before I'm due.

"Good afternoon," I greet with a smile, handing her a coffee. "Had them put an extra shot of espresso and an extra pump of hazelnut, just for you."

Linda grins, tucking her blond hair behind an ear. "You are the best. I definitely need this today. Somebody is on a warpath." Her eyes bounce over her shoulder, toward Alek's office, informing me he's in a bad mood. Good.

"Making everyone miserable?"

She tilts her head from side to side, like she doesn't want to talk shit about her boss, but the statement must hold a little truth. After taking a sip, she closes her eyes and holds the cup to her chest. Lowering her voice and leaning forward, she whispers, "I really hope you get one of the permanent positions."

I bark out a laugh. "From your lips to God's ears."

"I'm God in this office, so if you're expecting a position

128

here permanently, Mr. Brooks, I'd stop flirting with my secretary and get to work."

Linda's eyes go wide, and I glance over my shoulder to find Alek had approached us from behind. My body probably blocked him from being seen by Linda.

My eyes travel the length of his body before coming to a stop on his face. "Yes, sir," I say through gritted teeth.

Once he closes himself into his office, Linda exhales. "I had no idea he was out of his office. He must've left when I went to the bathroom. I'm so sorry."

"Don't worry about it," I tell her before heading down the hall and toward Luther's office.

After presenting him with his coffee and taking my own out of the carrier, we get to work.

Two hours in, and the interns are released for a break, so most of us gather in the break room on this floor. We snack on whatever we get from vending machines or what we manage to bring in with us. Typically it's nothing healthy. We survive on caffeine and junk food here.

With a few minutes to spare, I head to the bathroom. Mid-stream, Alek walks in. He stops short before moving forward, going to a urinal a few spaces away. The tension is thick and heavy, but neither one of us says anything.

At the sink, I watch him in the mirror as he turns around and walks toward me. It's really not fair how good he looks. He could've at least had the decency to look sleep-deprived or tortured in some way.

His eyes assess me as he washes his hands, and I find myself taking my time lathering my hands with soap like I'm about to perform surgery, because I don't want to leave the room yet. I want to give him time to say something. Anything.

I finally turn the water off and make my way to the paper towel dispenser, deciding he's not going to say anything. He'll continue to be a stubborn asshole, and that's fine. We shouldn't keep this going anyway. I'm clearly becoming too invested in someone who doesn't deserve it, and who checks all the boxes on who I shouldn't be with anyway.

"Jayden."

My back stiffens. I finish drying my hands and drop the used towel in the trash before I turn around.

"Mr. Drakos."

"About before."

I sigh. "I wasn't flirting with her. I brought her a coffee, because I'm a nice person. I brought one for Luther, and I'm definitely not flirting with him. I didn't bring one for you, because, well, you know." I take in a deep breath. "The only person I'm having an inappropriate relationship with in this office is you. Well, was. So, don't worry. I've learned my lesson."

He sighs. "That's not—"

He's cut off when the door swings open and Joel strolls in, his smile bright when he sees me.

"Hey, Jay. How was your weekend?" When my eyes bounce to Alek, Joel turns and notices who it is for the first time. "Oh. Hi, Mr. Drakos."

"Mr. Grenald," he greets stiffly.

"My weekend was okay," I answer. "Could've been better."

His eyes shift toward Alek, like he isn't sure how to talk in front of him, but Alek remains unmoved.

"That sucks. You should've called me. I went out with a few people and had a good time."

"You're right. I should've called you," I answer, using this moment to piss Alek off. "I'm sure I would've had a much better time."

Joel grins and I start to feel bad for leading him on. Fuck. I blame Alek for this.

"Yeah, well, maybe next weekend? Let me know."

He eyes Alek one last time before heading to a urinal.

"Will do. Thanks," I reply, moving to leave.

Alek's behind me soon after I start walking down the hall toward Luther's office.

"I think we need to talk," he says.

"We don't. I'm over it. It's fine."

"Dammit, Jayden."

I glance around, one person walking past us gives us a weird look. "Better be careful, Mr. Drakos. You're bringing attention to us. I'd hate for people in this office to think you're bending over for me. That wouldn't be good for your image, would it? Can't be the powerful, alpha male boss if you like dick."

His face reddens slightly as he clenches his jaw. He yanks me by the arm into an open conference room, locking the door.

"Will you fucking stop?" he seethes, keeping his voice low.

"What? That's what it is, right? You'll never be in a normal relationship if you don't understand that intimacy is a two way street. You're not supposed to only get what you want. You have to please the other person too."

"Are you saying you weren't pleased?" he asks, anger in his tone.

I stare back at him. "That's not what I meant, and you know it."

"This wasn't supposed to be about intimacy. I informed you of that. I didn't want it."

"Lots of people kiss, and it means nothing. Not everyone is in love when they makeout with someone. Getting on your knees to suck my dick doesn't mean you have to get on your knees to propose marriage. Just admit you're a selfish prick when it comes to sex and let's move on."

He slams his hand on the door. "Goddammit, Jayden. I'm fucked up." He gestures toward his head. "You have no idea what's going on in here. I...just can't."

My shoulders drop with an exhale. "I'm gonna say something I hope you don't fire me for, but it's something I believe is the truth, and maybe you'll take it for what it is—advice from someone who cares, rather than an insult. I think you need to talk to someone. A therapist. I think you might have internalised homophobia."

He steps back, his eyes widening before his eyebrows pull together. "I'm not homophobic."

"Just look into it. I've studied it a little myself, and I'm not insinuating you have every textbook example, but separating sex and love is one, because you fear intimacy. Shame and anger. Fear of people finding out. Look, you said your parents didn't take it well, and I don't want to speak badly about them, but it seems they might be classified as homophobic, and what they said to you may have stuck." I shrug. "It's up to you. I'm gonna get back to work. No hard feelings, okay?"

He nods absently, like he's not really hearing me, and I slip out of the room without another word from him.

I don't know why I hadn't put it together earlier, but I dealt with this once before. A guy I was hooking up with was the same way. His family was very homophobic, but he was gay. However, he was deep in the closet and was constantly afraid I was going to out him. We had to sneak to see each other, and he was afraid of getting too close, kissing too much, and never wanted to cuddle or lay in bed together afterwards. Around other people, he'd put on a front and act straight, almost to the point of hating on the LGBTQ community for no reason. It was fucking crazy, and I couldn't put up with it for longer than a few weeks.

Based on the little information Alek gave me about his

parents, I wouldn't be surprised if they instilled that same hate and disgust, and now it lives within him.

I feel bad for him and anybody who has to struggle to be who they are, but I think he needs time to figure that out, and he was right, we were never supposed to be anything more than fuck buddies.

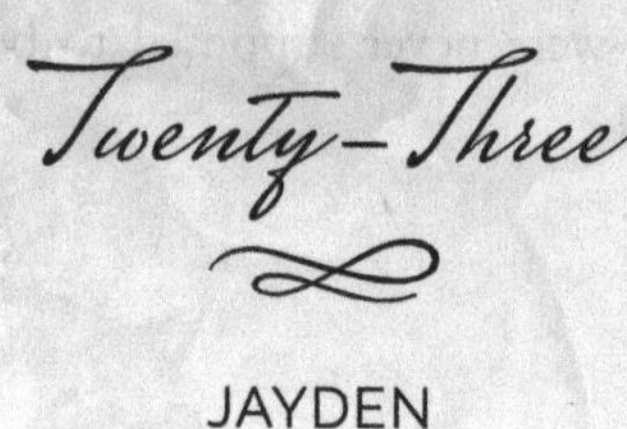

Twenty-Three

JAYDEN

THE REST of the week keeps me busy. I'm getting closer to the end of the school year, so studying for exams has taken up almost all my free time. I've partied less, focusing on both my schoolwork and work for MGD.

I won't lie and say I haven't thought twice about Alek, because I have. I've seen him a handful of times at the office, in the meetings, and occasionally when I walk past his office, but he never spares me a second look or more than a cursory nod. I'm not sure if he took offense to what I said, or if it'll be something he looks into. I guess it's not my concern.

On Friday, I stay a little late with Luther, Phillip, and two other interns, so by the time I have to cross in front of Alek's office, Linda is already gone, and his voice filters through the closed door. After a laugh, I hear him decline some sort of invitation, saying he already has plans.

Something akin to jealousy coils in my stomach before I shake my head at myself. He can have plans. Maybe I should make plans for myself. I haven't been out with my friends in a while. Maybe the guys will be up to head to a club, and perhaps I'll find someone to spend time with afterwards.

As I head to the parking lot, I pull my phone from my pocket, wanting to send a message to Trev, Renzo, and Dex to see if they have plans. Instead, my phone rings before I can even type two letters.

"Hello?"

"Hey, son."

"Hey, Dad. What's goin' on?"

"Oh, not much. Just checking in on ya. You doing okay?"

"I'm fine. Busy."

"Busy is good."

I laugh. "I suppose."

"You don't have any parties to go to tonight, do you?"

With a sigh, I ask, "Why?"

He chuckles. "Wondering if you want to have dinner with your old man," he says in a genial tone.

"What?" I exclaim. "Are you here?"

Dad laughs again. "Yep. Just got settled into my hotel about an hour ago."

"Holy shit," I say with a laugh. "Yeah, of course. Is Mom here?"

"No, she couldn't make it. Stuck with me, I'm afraid."

"No, that's fine. When do you want to meet up? I can go there now."

"Meet me in an hour. I'll send you the address."

"Okay, sounds good."

"See you soon."

"Bye. Love you."

"Love you, too, son."

I drive home to be able to shower and change, excited to see my dad again. I went home over Christmas, so it's not like it's been that long, but my dad has never been here before.

Excited that I may have time to show him around campus, maybe introduce him to a few of my friends, I don't even think about the fact that I've slept with his friend—our boss.

Not until I show up to the address I popped in the GPS and it brings me to the same exact hotel Alek is living in.

"Are you fucking kidding me," I say when I park in the lot.

Alek isn't one to roam the hotel anyway, so I hope I don't see him as I make my way to the lobby. However, I wonder if this is just a strange coincidence, or does my dad know he's staying here and picked this place on purpose? Does he plan on seeing him too?

I don't have much time to dwell on it because as soon as I step inside, I spot my dad sitting in an armchair, reading a newspaper. He notices me and stands up, a wide smile on his face.

We're nearly the same height, but he's far leaner than me, and where I'm almost bald, Dad is all the way there with the shiny head and everything. In a gray suit, he saunters over with a chuckle.

"Lookin' good, kid."

"Must get it from you. Lookin' pretty sharp yourself."

We embrace and laugh before he walks me back over to the sitting area he was in.

"Doesn't look like you're missing any meals," he says with a chuckle. "When I went to college, I swear I lost twenty pounds."

"Broke college kid eating noodles every day?" I ask.

"Something like that."

"I've been eating like crap lately because I'm not in any sports, so I feel less disciplined, but during a season, I'm pretty strict with my diet."

"Well, you look good. Your mom's complained you don't FaceTime her enough, so we'll have to be sure to do that while I'm here."

"I know. I get caught up in life and...yeah, I should be better."

He grins. "Don't worry about it."

"I see you're getting a few more gray hairs in that beard, Dad. Gettin' old, huh?"

He rubs a hand over the hair covering his jaw. "Getting better, son."

I laugh. "Oh, that's what we call it."

"You better believe it."

"So, what's with the sudden visit? How long are you here for?"

"I just wanted to see you, and decided to use the weekend to come out. Of course we'll be back for graduation, so you'll see your mom and sister then, but I figured we could have a nice father/son weekend."

"Dope. I can think of a few things we can do."

"Good, but first, dinner. I'm starving."

"Where do you wanna go?"

"I made reservations in the restaurant here." He glances at his watch. "Let's head over."

Opposite from the front desk, we walk to a restaurant in the corner called Tito's. Any concern I had about Alek showing up quickly dissipates the longer we're seated. We get through appetizers and the main course, talking about everything from my schooling, dad's job, my sister and what she's been up to, and Mom's plans to open her own restaurant in the future. We laugh and have a good time, and finish our meal without a hiccup.

My dad is known to bring up my plans for the future and harp on me not taking life seriously enough, but he doesn't preach to me about any of that now. Maybe he's satisfied with the internship I have, with the hope that I'll have a permanent position at the end of it.

"There's a bar in here somewhere," he says at the end of the meal. "Want a drink?"

"You want to drink with me?" I ask, surprise likely etched over my features.

"I know you drink, so don't act brand new. Didn't I tell you your sister shows me the pictures?"

I roll my eyes. "It's college. We're supposed to drink. I think it's an unspoken rule."

"Right," he says with a snort. "We'll have one drink. One."

"All right, all right."

"And then you'll come to my room for at least an hour to make sure you're sober enough to drive home."

I bark out a laugh. "Okay."

When we get to the bar, Dad orders an Irish whiskey, and I decide on sticking with a beer from the tap.

After he disappears to the bathroom, I respond to a few texts from friends, telling Bryant I may be able to meet up with him later. He's wanting me as a wingman as he attempts to shoot his shot with a guy who works at a diner.

When I put my phone down on the bar and glance around, my lips part when I find Alek walking in.

Frozen, I stay locked in on him until his eyes meet mine. The atmosphere changes with his presence, it's like he sucks all the air from the room while stealing everybody's attention. My body stiffens, my heart thumps against my ribcage, and the noise disappears as our gazes stay connected.

Shit.

Before I can even think about what I should do, my dad is back, and he notices Alek right away.

"Hey!" he greets excitedly. "You made it."

The room comes back to life as I snap out of my daze. My eyes bulge as my head swivels between the two. When my dad gives me a strange look before going to greet his friend, I fix my face.

When Alek disengages from the handshake with my dad, he glances at me before clearing his throat. "Uh, Calvin, I wasn't aware your son would be joining us. I'm not sure it's right that we have drinks together, considering he works for me."

My father laughs. "Oh, Alek. Who's gonna fire you? You're the boss. You're not getting in trouble, and don't forget, I work for you, too."

Dad takes his seat next to me, all smiles. Alek runs a palm over the center of his suit jacket in what appears to be a nervous gesture.

"I don't want anybody to think I'm giving any intern special treatment. That's all."

I almost snort, but instead take a sip of my beer.

"Just stay for one drink," my dad says. "Come on, nobody from work is coming to some small corner bar in a hotel."

Alek looks like he wants to bolt, but he gives in with a nod. "Okay."

Dad grabs his drink and nods toward an open table. "Let's head over here."

Swiping the beer from the counter, I study Alek for a few seconds while he waits to order a drink, then I follow my dad to the table.

With Dad to my left and Alek to my right, I find myself trapped in the middle while they talk about what's going on in the Chicago office, what's been happening here, and only minor things about people I don't know.

What was only supposed to be one beer turns into two. After a while, Dad seems to remember I'm here.

"Sorry, son. Just doing a little catching up. Alek's a good man, right? I told you you'd learn a lot from him. You enjoying your internship?"

My eyes cut to Alek before I answer. "Yeah, learning a whole lot."

"He's a good kid," my dad tells Alek. "A bit more social than I ever was, but he's got a great work ethic, too."

I want to curl up and die hearing my dad describe me as a good kid to the man who railed me on his balcony, bed, and in the shower.

Alek presses his lips together in a forced smile and nods. "Yeah, he's doing well."

"Can we not talk about work?" I ask. "Probably not the best idea, considering."

"Sure, sure," Dad says. "How's school?"

"I'm passing."

Dad laughs. "You're not usually so tight-lipped. You got a girlfriend?" He pauses. "Boyfriend?"

I let loose a sigh that I didn't mean to sound so fed up, but being next to Alek and talking about this is the last thing I want to do.

"Neither," I answer. "But I have options." I add the last part, wanting to see how Alek responds.

His eyes flicker to me, his jaw tense before he reaches for his glass.

"Well, you're still young," Dad says. "You have time."

"I suppose. I've had enough play time, though. My oats are sowed."

Me and Dad laugh, but Alek remains stoic.

"Don't rush into anything," Dad preaches. "When you find someone you really like, you'll know. It'll come when you least expect it."

I nod, taking another sip of beer. My phone rings, and after a quick glance at the screen, I say, "Excuse me. It's Bryant. I have to take this."

I walk out of the bar and stand near the window. "Hello?"

"Hey, man. What're you doing right now?"

I look through the glass and find Alek watching me before focusing on what my dad is saying.

"I'm out with my dad and boss."

"Yikes."

I laugh. "Exactly. They're friends. It's weird."

"Yeah, sounds fun," he says with a chuckle. "Well, shit. I was hoping I'd have you as my hype man when I go see Jackson."

I glance at my watch before looking through the window again. Dad gives me the don't be rude face, gesturing toward Alek with his head.

"My dad is giving me the parent look. Apparently, I have to act like I want to hang out with my boss."

"Damn. Well, I'll let you know how it goes. Wish me luck."

I chuckle. "You got this man. I'll call you later."

"Have fun."

I roll my eyes. "Right."

He laughs before ending the call, and I make my way back to the small table. "Sorry about that."

"Who's Bryant?" Dad asks in a teasing tone. "He one of the options?"

I open my mouth to tell him the truth, but pissing Alek off and making him jealous seems like the better option.

"Maybe," I reply with a coy smile.

Dad shakes his head with a good-hearted laugh, looking at Alek. "This kid." Dad aims his gaze at me again. "Well, you've always had your fair share to choose from. Everybody's always been drawn to you. Just remember to stay considerate of people's feelings."

I nod, chancing a look at Alek.

"You thinking of having kids, Alek, or is that not in the cards for you?" Dad asks.

"Oh." Alek shifts, clearing his throat. "I'm not sure about that. For a long time I didn't think it would be possible." When Dad cocks his head, Alek continues. "Long hours. Always working. You know?"

That's not what he meant at all, but he's not about to come out to my dad.

"It'll never be the right time. Me and my wife had Jay when we were pretty young, then we thought when we had his sister that we'd be more prepared, but we weren't. It's hard no matter when you have them," he says with a laugh. "But worth it."

"I'm probably too old now," Alek admits.

"Nah," Dad answers with a chuckle. "Oh. Lanie came by looking for you a couple times. Didn't you two used to date?"

My head snaps up and my eyes lock onto Alek. He doesn't look in my direction, but I know he's aware of my gaze.

"Oh, we went out a few times. Nothing serious."

"She seems pretty serious about you. Said to let her know when you were back in town."

Alek quickly changes the subject, and I finish my beer.

I can't help but dwell on the fact that Alek dated women. He said he was into men. Strictly men. He didn't say he was bi, so if he's dating women, he's farther in the closet than I thought. He's acting like he's straight. I'm torn between feeling bad for him and being annoyed.

Does he plan to fuck men on the low but date and eventually marry a woman, just for appearances? Because his parents led him to believe he had no other choice? That's fucked up.

By the time I snap out of my own thoughts and listen in to the conversation, it takes a few seconds to catch up.

"So, if you were dating Lanie, how did Piper fit in? She hung around for quite a bit."

"Cal, I'm not sure we should talk about this here," Alek says, eyes bouncing to me.

"Oh, Jay's not gonna judge you. It seems like you two may be cut from the same cloth." Dad laughs, and it's then that I notice his eyes. He's drinking more than he planned, too. Dad doesn't drink often, so he's probably gonna regret getting so comfortable with his boss later.

"Well, I think I'm gonna head out," I announce, not wanting to hear about Alek's dating past, and thinking they might be more comfortable talking about things without me here.

"You sure?" Dad asks.

"Yeah, I can hang out with Bryant."

"I'm not so sure it's safe for you to drive right now," Alek chimes in. His faux concern about driving while barely intoxicated is actually jealousy. He doesn't want me hanging out with a guy he thinks I could be into.

"Oh, that's right," Dad says. "And you had one more beer than you planned. You should stick around a while."

"Dad, I'm fine. I don't feel drunk or even tipsy. I'm okay."

Alek gives my dad a look, and I swear to God if my dad wasn't here, I'd have plenty to say to him right now.

"Just go up to my room and hang out for a little bit. I'll be up soon."

I grit my teeth. "Fine. I can text Bryant from there, I guess." Dad turns to talk to the waitress, so I whisper to Alek. "Maybe he'll come visit me here. Give me a goodnight kiss."

I wink at Alek as his nostrils flare, then turn to get my Dad's attention. "Okay, see you soon, Dad. You don't care if I invite someone over, do you? We'll just be watching TV."

He waves a hand at me. "Yeah, that's fine. Just no funny stuff. I don't want to walk in at a bad time."

I laugh before looking at Alek. "We'll probably be on the balcony." Then I leave, a grin on my face.

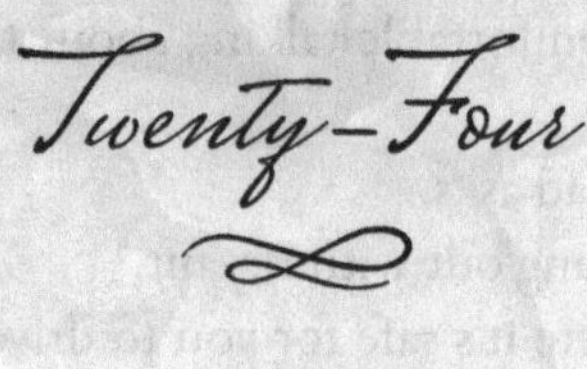

Twenty-Four

JAYDEN

THIRTY MINUTES into being in my dad's room with absolutely nothing to do but text or call friends—most of which go unanswered, because they're all probably having fun, I get up and search for the remote to the TV.

Dad's room is smaller than Alek's but bigger than a typical single-bed room. There's a mini-bar, small balcony, and a separate bedroom from the living area and kitchenette.

Just as I'm thinking I can probably leave without my Dad knowing, my phone starts ringing. When I look at the screen, I see my dad's face.

"Really? FaceTiming me to make sure I'm where I'm supposed to be?"

Dad laughs. "Told you he'd be pissed."

"Who are you talking to? Al—Mr. Drakos?"

"Calm down. We're just making sure you're not drinking and driving."

"Oh? Mr. Drakos cares?" I murmur.

Whether he heard me or not, I don't know. Dad laughs at something else, and I roll my eyes. "You getting drunk, Dad?"

"Of course not."

I shake my head. "Uh-huh. I'm tellin' Mom."

"Oh please. Just stay put a little longer so I know you're safe."

"I think I need to make sure you're being safe."

"What's that?" he asks, his face disappearing from the screen for a few seconds. "Oh. Jay, is your friend over?"

My curiosity is piqued. Is Alek actually asking my dad if I have someone over?

"Well, I gotta go. See you later, Dad. Have fun!"

I wait another fifteen minutes before I grab my keys and head to the door. There's no point sticking around. My dad's enjoying his vacation and getting drunk with his friend. He likely won't be up for a while, and I'm far from feeling intoxicated, so I'll just leave and deal with my dad tomorrow.

When I pull open the door, I'm met with both my Dad and Alek on the other end.

I step back and sigh. "Oh great."

"Hey," Dad laughs. "What does that mean? We're not that bad."

Alek chuckles, and it's the first time I'm noticing he's probably a little tipsy, too. Less drunk than my dad, but not sober.

"Well, y'all can have the room. I was about to leave."

I don't miss Alek's eyes scouring the area, searching for another person. When he realizes it's just me, he seems to relax, giving me a sort of smug smile.

I purse my lips. "I have someone to meet. So, you're good?" I ask Dad.

"Come on. Stay. Let's have a guys night in. We got drinks in the mini-bar."

"I don't really want to have a sleepover with my dad and his friend, and if I have even one more sip, you're gonna make me stick around even longer. No thanks."

"I thought you liked staying in hotels," Dad says. "You did when you were younger."

I glance at Alek. "I've had my fill."

He arches a brow at me, and I stare back at him.

"Well, I'm gonna use the bathroom. I'll be right back," Dad announces.

As soon as he's out of the room, Alek approaches me, backing me into the wall. "I don't find your little games amusing. Didn't I tell you I don't play them?"

"No, you only play games according to your rules, but they're games, nonetheless."

"I don't appreciate you trying to make me jealous. The thought of you in here with anyone else..." He lets it trail off as he inhales deeply through his nose.

"What? Makes you jealous? You know what that means, right?" I say with a smirk.

"It means nothing."

"We're not fucking anymore, Alek," I say, stressing his first name. "You made it clear you're not capable of pleasing me."

He clenches his jaw. "You made it clear you're not capable of sex without forming attachments."

"I'm hardly attached to you. I wasn't lying about having options. I could call up three different people tonight."

"Then why didn't you?"

"The night's not over," I say with a shrug.

"I think it's because you're hung up on me."

I choke out a laugh. "Funny, coming from the guy asking my dad if I had anybody in the room. Just admit you care more than you want to." I step forward until my chest touches his. "Admit you're still thinking about how much you want to kiss me."

His eyes travel to my lips briefly, but before anything can happen, the bathroom door opening has us stepping away from each other.

"Okay, so who's ready for another drink?" Dad asks, entering the room.

"I'll take one," Alek answers.

"I'm gonna leave."

"All right, fine. I get it. You don't want to hang out with two old folks," Dad says with a laugh. "I'll call you tomorrow. We'll get together and do whatever you want, okay?"

"Try not to have a hangover," I say with a smirk. I give him a hug before pausing in front of Alek. I have to be polite, otherwise my dad will get into my ass about it later, so I extend a hand to him. "Mr. Drakos. See you Monday afternoon."

He slips his hand into mine, squeezing it firmly while his beautiful eyes penetrate mine. "Yes, I'll see you soon."

Taking my hand from his, I spin around and walk out. By the time I get into my car, I realize my mood has shifted and I no longer want to hang out with anybody. I could join my friends wherever they are, but I feel too agitated. I wouldn't be any fun.

I regret the way I've been acting, but he's brought out this side of me I'm not used to. What is that? Why am I so bothered?

Yeah, I probably like Alek more than I should, but that doesn't mean I can't be without him. I just want him to be honest with himself and with me. We could easily still have a friends-with-benefits situation that doesn't require emotions, but can include kissing and blowjobs.

Nearly thirty minutes later, I'm still in my car, just driving around and listening to music. At a red light, my phone vibrates with a text so I check it before the light turns green.

Come to my room.

. . .

My heart leaps, and as excited as I am to read that message, part of me is still holding onto frustration and I don't want him to know how eager I am to be alone with him again.

I wait until I can pull off the road and into a nearby parking lot before I respond.

Why?

Just come.

You're not my boss outside of work, you know?

Why are you acting like you don't want to see me?

I just did see you.

Your age is showing.

Fuck you.

Do you want to?

My stomach clenches as my heart stutters in my chest before warmth floods my veins.

Don't play with me.

Please come over.

His use of the word *please* has any resolve I had crumbling. I doubt he uses that word much. I don't respond to him, I just drive.

Fifteen minutes later, I'm in the elevator, on the way up to his room. After I knock, he doesn't take long to answer, and though he's still showing signs of being a little drunk, his shoulders appear to sag in relief when he sees me.

With a half empty glass already in his hand, he walks to his bar. "Drink?"

"I'd have to sleep over."

He snorts but starts pouring. His bare feet pad toward me, arm outstretched, offering me a glass.

"I think we need to talk."

I put my drink down. "Oh Lord. If this is the, *it's not you, it's me* talk, it could've been done over the phone."

He struts to the couch and plops down. He's still in his slacks and button up shirt. The top two buttons are undone, the sleeves are rolled up, and though he looks a little tortured, he still looks damn good.

I follow his lead and sit across from him. He takes two drinks before he speaks.

"I'm sorry I was a dick. I didn't mean to make you feel like you were being used. I thought we were both on the same page, and I didn't stop to think that maybe I was hurting your feelings."

"When you say it like that you make it sound like I was at home crying. I'm not sad about anything. Just frustrated. I'm not saying I haven't been with someone who hasn't wanted to suck dick, but usually it's been a woman, and that was because it was a one and only hookup situation. Gay men can have a lot of differences, but one of the similarities is liking cock. And I've never been with anyone who was opposed to kissing." I shrug. "Saying it out loud now, I get that it sounds trivial."

"It's not. Look, I know that I'm the abnormal one, but I have reasons. They may not make sense to anybody else, but to me they do."

"Okay," I say with a nod.

"I told you a little about how my parents reacted, but that was just scratching the surface. Growing up, I didn't have it easy. I knew I was attracted to the same sex when I was about twelve. I fought that attraction for a while, because I was confused, but then I met a kid a little older than me. We became close, and I guess I saw things differently than he did, so when I tried to kiss him, he became enraged. It wasn't until later, after he told his older cousins, that I knew just how upset he was.

"They caught me in an alleyway as I was walking home and made sure I knew to never come near that boy again. That was the first time I heard the slurs and felt the hate, but it wasn't the last time."

"Alek."

He holds a hand up, stopping me from saying more.

"I lied to my parents about why that happened, feigning ignorance. I said it was just a random attack and that maybe they were just wanting money. I was afraid for a couple years to even try to get close to another guy again. I thought everyone knew and would only be attempting to catch me trying something just to have an excuse to attack.

"I was angry, too, and in my fear of being found out, and anger for being a victim, I became friends with people who I thought would protect me. They were angry kids just like me, but because of their own reasons. We were constantly getting in trouble for doing stupid shit. They hated people who were like me, and I had to pretend I hated them, too.

"They beat up a kid for being gay. It was for fun. They had no reason to hate him, but they heard he was a homosexual and wanted to punish him for it. I wasn't there that day, but they told me about it later. That only instilled more fear into me." He takes a breath and runs a hand through his hair. "Fast forward a couple more years, and I'm working at a restaurant, where I meet this guy. We both worked until close, having to clean the kitchen, and we became good friends. One day he said something about an ex-boyfriend, and I was so surprised at his honesty. Besides the shock, my first feeling was fear. What if he was laying a trap? Trying to get me to admit to being gay?

"A long while went by before I realized he was a genuinely good person. He was two years older than me and not even in school anymore. One night after we had closed up, we ended up messing around a little. That went on for a few weeks, and I was finally accepting that I was gay and it wasn't a big deal. I liked what we were doing, and he was a good guy."

Alek stops talking and takes another drink. His eyes find mine, and I can tell whatever comes next is important. I'm almost afraid to hear it. He already admitted to being attacked. Maybe that's where the scars on his torso came from. I can't imagine it getting worse.

"My dad decided to come pick me up one night. Usually, it was my mom, and typically she waited out front. My dad was impatient, though, and he drove around to the back. We always kept the back door cracked for fresh air, and when he came in looking for me, he found us in a compromising position."

I take in a sharp breath as my eyes bulge, imagining the scene. "Oh."

Alek nods. "He walked in on us as Phillippe was...well, entering me."

My eyebrows shoot up. "Oh shit."

"To keep a long story short, he lost his shit. He shoved Phillippe away, knocking him into a table. He tried fighting him, and I jumped on him in an attempt to protect Phillippe. It turned into a messy brawl that ended with me being forced to quit my job. I never saw or heard from Phillippe again. My dad beat me even more when we got home that day, and after that, it was non-stop verbal attacks mixed with a few physical fights.

"Mom found out and cried for weeks. For a long while, I rebelled. I stayed out, got in trouble with friends, drank, did drugs. I did a lot of shit I regret. Dad had enough right before I turned eighteen and refused to have me do anything that would stay on my record once I was legally an adult. He moved us to a new town and forced me to work for him.

"The slurs never ended. He wanted to make it known that he was disgusted by homosexuality. He said only women sucked cock. He told me I was a bitch for bending over for another man. He hated me and wanted me to hate myself. He told me I should be ashamed and embarrassed. Both of my parents eventually got to the point where they pretended like they didn't know, but that was only when I stopped fighting. They broke me over time, and I was done trying to defend myself. They'd never understand. They introduced me to women, they talked about grandkids, and made it known I was to have a son take over the company. They said they hoped to have a real man in the family again, hoping I wouldn't ruin a child with my sickness."

I stand up. "Alek, I can't even listen to this anymore. This is awful. Fuck. I'm so sorry."

He finishes his drink and drops the glass to the table noisily. "That's the gist of it. It was hell for a long time. Their deaths brought a minute sense of relief, but the damage had already been done. Mental abuse lingers. People are always concerned with physical abuse, but my wounds have healed. The ones in here," he says, pointing to his head, "are very much still raw and open."

I sit next to him, unsure if he wants any sort of affection or not, but being close seems better. "I know there's nothing I can say that'll make you feel better, but I wish I could take that away from you. Nobody deserves that."

He holds my gaze. "I think you're right. I probably should talk to a therapist."

I barely nod, my lips pinched together. "I'm sorry for making you feel like shit when this is what you were living with."

"I shouldn't expect people to know, and you'd think I'd be more aware of people's feelings considering that's all I wanted from my parents—some sort of consideration and under-standing."

I sigh. "I like you, Alek. More than I should, probably, since you're my boss, my dad's friend, and leaving soon. I know nothing will come of this, and continuing will only make it harder when you do leave."

"Feels like there's more to that."

"But I don't want to stop."

His lips quirk up slightly. "I don't either, but I can't promise you anything will change."

"I get it."

"Okay."

"Okay."

He laughs. "You want to stay over?"

"Of course," I say, rolling my eyes.

"Good."

I drop to my knees between his legs and start undoing his pants.

Twenty-Five

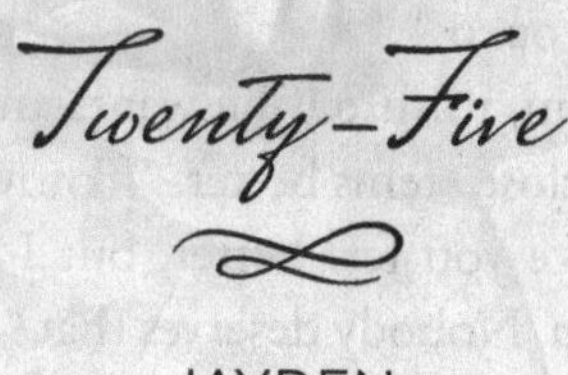

JAYDEN

I TAKE MY TIME, wanting to slowly unravel him. He's still holding a lot of tension in his body from the conversation about his past. My heart aches for him, and I know I can't do anything to make it better and I can't take his pain away, but right now, I can make him feel good.

Flattening my tongue, I run it up the underside of his shaft, flickering when I get to his swollen tip. He holds my gaze as I tease him, licking every side of his cock but never taking him into my mouth.

I suck one of his balls into my mouth, gently caressing it with my tongue as I moan around him. He hisses, his head dropping back as I work him over, bringing my hand to his shaft to stroke.

After a few minutes, I remove my hand and plant soft kisses on his shaft, moving up to his stomach. I unbutton his shirt and kiss all the way up his chest until I reach his neck, swiping my tongue across his Adam's apple.

"No kissing. No blowjobs from you. Those are your rules, right?" I ask.

He watches me with lust burning in his eyes. "Yeah."

"Okay. Trust that I'm not breaking those, but let me do something else."

His dark brows furrow briefly. "Okay."

I lean back in, rubbing the scruff of my face against his, nibbling on his neck while he raises his hips, letting me feel his cock against my torso.

"You're killing me," he breathes, a hand coming to squeeze my hip.

I back away, grinning at him. His other hand comes to my face, holding me right in front of him, his thumb grazing my chin. My breath hitches as he studies me. I don't know why I never saw it before, but I do now. The pain in his eyes is evident. It's not that he doesn't want to kiss me, because I can see that he does. But he's allowing the pain and abuse from his past to lasso his desires and yank them back. I watch the war happening as I get lost in his eyes, and I no longer feel frustrated for myself. I'm angry alongside him.

I smile again, letting him know it's okay. "Let me make you feel good."

Traveling down the length of his body, I make sure to pay attention to every square inch, kissing, touching, and licking. I kiss over a couple thick scars, wondering if those came from the kids who jumped him, or from his own father.

Once I finish removing his pants and underwear, I push his legs further apart, giving me room between them as I take his cock into my mouth. He holds onto my head and fucks my mouth, touching the back of my throat with the head of his dick.

"You're so good," he pants. "Being in your mouth...fuck."

I pull off, dropping lower, licking his balls. When he moans with pleasure, I let the tip of my tongue dance further down, barely grazing over his perineum.

"Shit," he gasps, sitting up.

I place my hands on his inner thighs. "It's okay." He sucks

in a breath and nods. "Okay," I repeat, grabbing a hold of his legs and tugging him down, bringing his ass to hang over the edge of the couch.

I start by stroking him before my tongue travels down his perineum again, this time continuing to his ass.

"Oh," he moans, his voice nearly giving out. "J-Jay."

I groan, loving how my name sounds coming from his mouth, especially when he's not growling it with frustration.

It takes a couple minutes before he loosens up, letting me push his leg up a little, allowing me more access. My tongue slides over his hole making him gasp. I don't try to penetrate, but I do enough to give him pleasure. When he reaches for his cock, I feel a little victorious.

"That...that's, oh God," he says, stumbling through his sentence.

I get lost in the moment, relishing in the sounds he makes. Savoring the shaky breaths and whispered curse words. I never want to stop. I want to devour him.

"Get up here," he says through harsh pants. "I can't take it anymore."

I stop, worried I've pushed him too far. "Are you okay?"

His eyes are wild—passion and need burning brightly in their depths. "No. Far from it. I need to be inside you."

"Let's go to your room," I say, reaching for his hand. "I need to prepare for that cock of yours."

He lets me pull him up, and we walk to his room hand in hand. While he pulls the lube from his drawer, I remove every-thing except my boxer-briefs, the material tented with my erection.

I watch him as he moves, his thick cock stealing my atten-tion. "Fuck, I kind of want you in my mouth again."

He turns to look at me, his eyes perusing my body. "I'm afraid I'll come if you do what you were doing again."

I bite down on my bottom lip, grinning. "I'm glad you liked it."

Alek struts toward me, pushing my underwear down. "Mmhmm." His fingers brush against my pre-cum and he looks down. "Shit, you're leaking."

"That's what you do to me."

His eyes meet mine while he smears the wetness over my crown. "Just from..." He stops himself. "Fuck."

"Lube?"

He wraps his fingers around my shaft, giving me a long, slow stroke. "Huh?"

I chuckle. "The lube."

"Oh. Yeah."

I push the underwear down my legs and he brings me the bottle of liquid. I position myself on the bed and spread my legs, reaching between them to slide a finger inside.

"Fuck," I hiss.

Alek stands at the side of the bed, watching.

"Like what you see?" I tease, sliding another finger in.

"I do," he answers, eyes lifting to mine for a fraction of a second before moving back to my ass.

"Ah," I moan, grabbing my dick. "Just slather some of this on your cock and come fuck me," I say, throwing him the bottle while I continue to finger my ass.

I get on my hands and knees and slide to the edge of the mattress. Alek's hands curve over my hips and up my back before I feel his forehead drop to my back and his nose skate down my spine. I wait to feel the soft press of his lips, but it never comes.

"No. Turn over," he says.

I turn to my back and he squirts some lube in his hand before coating his dick, then his fingers push into my ass before he guides himself in.

"God," he breathes, slowly pushing inside.

"Fuck me, Alek. Hard. Give it to me."

A growl rumbles in his throat before he slams into me, making us both cry out.

"You like that?"

I shake my head. "I love it."

He groans, pulling out and diving back in. "Good. Remember that when you threaten to go to someone else."

"Ah!" I exclaim as he thrusts deep. "I—I was kidding. I wouldn't..."

I can't get the words out.

"The thought of you with someone else on the balcony." Thrust. "In bed." Thrust. "I hated it."

"Fuck, Alek," I gasp. "I just wanted to piss you off."

"Mission accomplished. Don't do it again."

"I only want you anyway." He pauses, and I open my eyes to look at him. "Don't stop."

He slams into my ass, dropping down to hover above me as his hips piston back and forth. "Tell me it's mine."

I moan. "It's yours."

"I wish I could give you more," he whispers, his movements slowing to a teasing pace.

"Alek," I pant, reaching around to grab his ass. "Don't torture yourself, and don't torture me. Fuck me and I'll be happy."

His lips curl up into a smile and he fucks me into euphoria. We're a mass of tangled limbs, muttered words, heavy breaths, and something else. Something deeper and stronger. Something neither of us will delve into, because it's something we've never dealt with before.

Twenty-Six

JAYDEN

WE WAKE up in bed together Saturday morning, but after a quick smile, he slides out from under the covers and disappears into the bathroom. Once I hear the shower turn on, I stretch before deciding to get up. Knowing I could very well head to the bathroom in the other room, I choose to use the one Alek's in.

"It's me. I'm gonna use one of these hard ass toothbrushes they supply."

He laughs. "Okay."

My eyes keep flickering to the foggy glass shower, catching blurry glimpses of his body as he moves. My already semi-hard cock comes to life even more when I remember our previous time in the shower. Before everything sort of went to hell.

After I'm done brushing my teeth and washing my face, I lean against the wall that faces the shower. "Are you as hard as I am right now?"

Once again, he grants me a soft chuckle. "Can't say. I don't know how hard you are."

"Would you like to know?"

The water shuts off and he struts out like he just walked

out of one of my wet dreams. His body is toned and fit, rivulets of water cascading down his skin like tiny waterfalls, droplets clinging to his sculpted face. His cock isn't exactly hard, but not fully flaccid either, but it makes my mouth water nonetheless.

He grabs a towel and starts rubbing it through his hair as he steps up to me, his hand molesting my cock through my underwear. "Feels pretty hard."

"Mm. Gonna help me with that, or should I rub one out while I shower?"

His hand dips inside my boxer-briefs, grabbing my erection and giving it a squeeze. "When you're with me, this is mine. When you come, it'll be because I make you."

Fingers graze my balls as he continues touching me. "Fuck. Make me come, then."

"Shower first. Meet me on the balcony."

"In the daytime? Mr. Drakos," I say in a teasing voice.

He withdraws his hand and smacks the side of my ass before taking his towel and wrapping it around his waist. "Hurry up."

I take the quickest shower I've probably ever taken, while still making sure to thoroughly wash all my intimate parts. I don't bother getting dressed when I'm done, only taking enough time to dry and moisturize with some of Alek's body lotion.

Taking a couple minutes to stroke my cock to life, I decide to walk out completely naked. When I don't spot him on the balcony, I make my way to the living room to find him with a phone balanced between his ear and shoulder, and halfway dressed.

"Yeah, I have it in my office. I'll head over right now."

He spins around to grab a tie off his desk and his eyes collide with my naked body. "Oh God." He clears his throat. "Oh, no. It's nothing."

I grin, feeling a little triumphant over his reaction. I keep moving, grabbing the tie for him and settling it around his neck, tying it for him. He watches me closely with curious eyes, doing a decent job focusing on his conversation while my cock prods against him.

Alek ends the call before I'm done with the tie, but stands still, letting me finish.

"Thank you," he says in a husky voice. "I have to run to the office. Want to come?"

"Should I come like this?" I ask, glancing down at my naked body.

His teeth drag across his bottom lip as he studies me. "I'd kill anybody who looked at you too long, so I'm thinking no."

I smile so wide I nearly start laughing before I turn on my heel and head to his room. "Let me get dressed, but you owe me. I was really looking forward to being back on the balcony with you."

~

What I thought was supposed to be a quick trip to take care of whatever Alek needed to do turns into forty-five minutes of him on the phone with multiple people, faxing paperwork, sending emails, and even jumping on a zoom call. It's nothing I know about or can help with, so I busy myself with cleaning up an already clean break room before heading back to his office and dropping to the chair on the opposite side of his desk.

He ends the call and blows out a breath as he relaxes into this seat. "Sorry. I didn't mean for it to take this long."

I shrug. "I don't have anything going on. It's fine."

Alek runs both hands through his hair before bringing his fingers to his temples and rubbing circles. "Fucking headache."

I get up from the chair and walk around, coming to a stop behind him. "Let me help."

"It's the start of a migraine. I get them fairly often, but I didn't bring my pills with me."

"My mom suffers from them, too," I reply, pressing my fingers to the base of his neck, seeking the pressure points there and pushing upward.

He moans as I massage around his hairline, then I use my thumbs and focus on the pressure points between his neck and shoulders.

"Feels good," he murmurs.

"I'm pretty skilled with my hands."

He makes a noise but doesn't say anything. I continue for several minutes before I tell him to drop his head back slightly.

His eyes open up and connect with my gaze as I use my thumbs to press between his eyebrows, massaging gently. We stay locked in on each other for a couple minutes before he closes his eyes again. After another sixty seconds or so, I stop, strolling around to stand in front of him.

"I hope it's a little better."

"It is. Thank you."

The air between us feels heavy—thick with an undercurrent of feelings neither of us is ready to talk about. Something shifted after he opened up. We both say we know nothing will come of this, and he says he can't change, but there's an understanding now. I get why he's the way he is, and though I wish it could be different, I'm not annoyed by it anymore. I want to make him happy. I want to show him that men can be together and how it doesn't mean you're lesser than.

"Can I admit something?" I ask, wanting to get back to what we're comfortable with.

"What's that?"

"I've thought more than once about doing something in here."

His brow arches perfectly. "Like what?"

I laugh. "A little of everything, if I'm being honest. But, let's start with this," I say, getting to my knees. "Maybe it'll help with your headache."

He spreads his legs, a smirk on his lips. "In the name of science, I think we should try."

I grin and undo his pants, reaching into his boxer-briefs to extract his cock without having to remove his clothes.

My own erection throbs in my pants as his hardens in my mouth. I take him deep, then stroke him expertly while my tongue swirls around his crown. I cup his balls in one hand, massaging them gently before lowering my mouth and sucking them in my mouth one at a time.

"Fuck," he hisses, his hand landing on my head. "Your mouth. I'll never tire of this mouth."

I moan, letting my tongue drag up his shaft before I envelope him between my lips, his cock sliding over my wet tongue and touching the back of my throat.

"I'm gonna come," he grunts.

My eyes find his as I bring him to the peak of his desire, and then his head falls back as he comes undone, exploding in my mouth with a guttural roar.

It takes him a minute to catch his breath, and as I'm swiping a thumb over my lips, he gazes down at me, and the vulnerability in his eyes is apparent. "I don't know how I'm going to be able to leave."

Twenty-Seven

ALEKSANDER

A MONTH after opening up to Jay about my past, and he's still willing to be with me in the only way we can be—secretly and without the promise of much more than sex and a quasi relationship that might look weird to anyone but us.

We keep things at work professional, and he's been doing exceptionally well. According to the marketing managers, he's in the top three of the group, which means he'd likely be offered a job here once it's all said and done.

Thinking about that makes my stomach knot up. The idea of him having a job here just really solidifies that his life is here and mine is in Chicago. I'm actually heading back in four weeks and this will officially come to an end.

Our relationship, if you will, has developed into a little more than just sex. We hang out in my room, watching TV and laughing. We've shared numerous meals together, but only in my suite, and he's gotten me back down to the pool a couple more times.

He hasn't brought up the fact that I still haven't kissed him or taken him in my mouth, and it honestly makes me like him even more. It's not normal. I'm aware of that. So the fact that he's been able to move past that says a lot, probably more than he realizes.

When we sleep, we touch each other now. He'll either end up under my arm and on my chest, or I'll have an arm draped over his torso as we lay side by side.

Tonight, he'll be spending time with his friends, because usually we're holed up in my hotel, and his friends have been asking questions.

"You sure you don't want to come?" he asks, resting his chin on my shoulder as I stand in front of the sink.

I laugh. "I don't think that's the best idea."

"My friends are cool, though."

"Your friends are going to be confused if we show up together. Plus, you're supposed to be hanging out with them, not me."

His arm snakes around my waist before his hand reaches for my crotch. "But I don't get to do this with them."

I finish washing the vegetables I'm about to cook and shut the water off, spinning to face him. "And let's make sure it stays that way, hm? But you know I'll be here when you're done."

"But you actually have groceries in here and you're about to cook. I should help you eat."

I smile as I study his face. "I'll save you some."

He groans. "Fine. I'll go have fun without you."

I grab his wrist as he moves to step away. "Hey. You know I'd go if the situation was different."

He slips his hand in mine and smiles. "I know. I'm just giving you a hard time." He winks and struts toward our bedroom.

My bedroom.

Before he leaves, he stops back in the kitchen, smelling like citrus, mint, and cedarwood. My favorite cologne of his. I give him a onceover, hating how good he looks before going out to a club where every person with eyes will be staring and trying to get with him.

"Maybe I've changed my mind. I think I should tie you to the bed and never let you leave."

He grins. "I'll tell you now, I will develop Stockholm syndrome."

"Have fun."

Jay leans in and kisses my neck. "I'll talk to you later."

I watch him leave and hate the empty feeling I have once he's gone. When he's here, his personality and presence fills the space with joy and light. Now it just feels quiet and dark, and I've started to realize I feel his absence more and more each time he leaves. I've gotten too used to him, but I'm selfish enough to keep him around even though I know how it'll end.

After I finish making and eating dinner, I wash the dishes and then put on the news while I do some work. It feels like several hours have gone by before I check the time, but it's only been two.

By ten o'clock, I'm bored out of my mind, now used to always having someone to talk to, whether he's here or texting me. We've spent so much time on the phone before that he may as well have been here with me.

I take a hot shower then get in bed, knowing Jay would make fun of me for going to sleep before midnight. I told him eventually you get to the point where staying up late for no reason just doesn't make sense. Then he usually gave me a reason to stay up late, because he'd strip naked and make it impossible to even think of sleep.

My phone trills from the nightstand next to me, startling me out of unconsciousness. I squint at the clock, trying to figure out how long I've been out. It's almost two in the morning.

"Hello?"

"Hey!" Jay exclaims loudly, dragging the word out. "I've been trying to text you."

"Are you okay?" I ask, sitting up.

"M'fine," he says, mashing the words together.

"Sounds like you had fun."

"I miss you."

I chuckle. "It's been very quiet and boring here without you."

"So, you miss me too."

I shake my head, a grin on my lips. "Where are you? Did you make it home?"

"No. I'm still out."

Multiple voices in the background blare through the phone.

"What are you doing?"

"Who are you talking to?"

"Leave me alone," Jay tells them. "I was trying to have privacy."

"In a bathroom? Are you having phone sex?"

"Everyone is starting to leave. Do you want me to call you an Uber? Or is your boyfriend gonna come get you?"

I hear Jayden laugh. "Boyfriend," he says drunkenly, addressing me. "Do you want to come get me from the bar orrrrr should I get a ride from someone else? Not that I want to ride anyone but you."

"Hey, hey," a voice in the background says. "TMI, but excuse me? Are you committed?"

"What the fuck is this? Trev, do you know this boyfriend of Jay's?"

"I'll get you," I tell him. "Where are you?"

"Um. Lily Pad."

"Okay. Keep your phone on you. I'll call when I'm there."

"Kay. Thanks. You're the best."

Loud conversations start up and I end the call, throwing

on some clothes and grabbing my keys. After putting the name of the bar in my GPS, it takes me fifteen minutes to get there.

When I pull up alongside the curb, I spot the logo on the sign on the building—a rainbow colored frog sitting on a lily pad. Based on some of the patrons exiting the building, a few of which are coupled up, it would be safe to assume it's a gay bar.

I call Jay's phone and wait for him to answer, but he doesn't pick up. I try another time but it goes to voicemail. Before I'm about to step out, my phone rings.

"Hello?"

"Hey, this is one of Jay's friends. Are you his ride?"

"Yeah. I'm outside."

"Okay. He's pretty drunk and back at the bar. We'll get him out there in a minute."

"Okay."

The call ends abruptly and a couple minutes later, Jay emerges with his usual wide smile. Another guy who matches Jay's size has an arm around him as he walks him out.

I roll the window down slightly and Jay's voice floats in. "Yeah, that's the car." He runs up to the window and peeks in. His eyes are low and red, but he's cheerful. "Hey, you made it."

The muscular guy with bronze skin and dark hair approaches Jay. "You good?"

"Yep. Thanks. I had fun."

The guy snorts and opens the door for Jay. A blonde man walks over to join them. "This the boyfriend?"

"No," Jay replies. "A friend."

He gives each of them a fist bump, but the blonde says, "You said boyfriend on the phone."

"Nice car," the bigger one says.

Then like I thought would happen, they both bend down

enough to peek inside. It's dark inside the car, but the bigger of the two seems to be sober and something flashes in his eyes as Jay climbs into the passenger seat.

"Oh shit. Mr. Missionary," he whispers, glancing back to Jay. "Are you fucking kidding me?"

A trilling sound from Jay's lips turns into a full blown laugh. "No! We gotta go."

His friend points at him. "We're gonna talk about this later."

The blonde grabs his hand. "Come on, babe. Let's go home."

Once Jay closes the door, he sinks into the seat. "I'm sorry."

"Seatbelt. Who is Mr. Missionary?"

He struggles to fasten the belt as he laughs. "You."

"Me?" I ask, helping him buckle it.

"It's a long story."

I start driving and he shifts, resting his hand on my thigh. "I want to fuck you so bad right now."

"I think you're too drunk to do anything."

"Never," he says with a laugh. "I'm still young enough to be able to drink and get hard."

"I want to know about this missionary thing."

"That was Dom. He works at the bar we met at. He saw me walk over to you. He said you looked old and boring."

"Old and boring?"

"Maybe I'm paraphrasing, but he said you probably only fuck in the missionary position. Then you went and fucked me on the balcony. If only he knew."

I shake my head as his hand keeps inching toward my cock. "I really did miss you though."

"I doubt it," I say with a laugh. "But I'm glad you had fun."

"I was just trying to forget you're leaving soon. Hey, are you coming to my graduation?"

The shift in topics has my head spinning. "I don't know. I didn't plan on it. How would we explain that?"

"Yeah, I guess."

He keeps touching me, and every time I glance at him, he's watching me with a drunken grin.

"What?" I ask.

"You're really fucking hot," he states. "Like, so beautiful it makes no sense."

"I think you're really drunk."

"Yes, but it's true. I really like you, you know?" He sighs, turning to look out the window.

I hesitantly put my hand on top of his as it rests on my thigh. His head swivels to look at me, but I keep my eyes on the road.

"You like me too."

My only response is to give his hand a small squeeze.

Twenty-Eight

ALEKSANDER

ON THE WAY UP to the room, he continues to be handsy. In the elevator, he hooks his arm through mine and rests his head on my shoulder.

"I think I'm drunk."

With a snort, I say, "I know you are."

"But I still wanna fuck."

"I think you're gonna pass out as soon as you get in the bed."

"No, I won't. Promise we'll go to the balcony again," he says with a mischievous grin.

"We will. At some point."

He rolls his eyes, leaning back against the wall of the elevator. "I'd love to have you at graduation. It's in two weeks."

"Your family will be there."

The doors open up and I reach for his arm and pull him out.

"I know, but you're their friend. Maybe you can come as a friend of the family." He snorts, finding that amusing.

I reach for my key and unlock my door. "Let's get you in bed."

"Naked. With you naked."

I ignore him, aware he's probably way too drunk to do anything. As soon as he hits the bed, the room will start spinning.

"So, the friends you were with...they're together?"

"Who? Oh. Dom and Trev? Yeah. They fell in love and moved in with each other. We're all on the same football team. Or were."

He drops to the edge of the mattress and tries kicking off his shoes, but doesn't get very far. Instead, he chooses to take off his watch, but he can't get his fingers to work correctly.

"Let me help," I say, unlatching the watch band and putting it on the nightstand. "So, just you and them tonight?"

He shakes his head. "Nah. Ronan and Renzo were there. They're gay, too. Dex was there. He's straight but he doesn't care about going to gay clubs with us. Uhh, Bryant and Ivy were there, too."

I help him take off his shirt, but still at the name Bryant.

"Bryant? The one you said was one of your options?"

He smirks at me. "Jealous?"

"Jayden," I warn. "Don't mess with me."

He bites his lip flirtatiously. "I'm sorry. I like when you get all growly and possessive. Bryant was never an option. He's a friend. That's it."

I squat down, helping him remove his shoes and socks, leaving him only in a pair of jeans. He stands up, unsnapping the button and dragging the zipper down, pushing them past his hips until they fall to his knees. He reaches down and tries taking something out of his pocket, but his phone drops to the floor along with a clattering of coins and balled up dollar bills.

"Shit."

"Let me get it," I say, squatting back down to pick up

whatever he dropped, knowing he'd probably fall over if he attempted it himself.

Once I've gathered everything in my hand, he's taken his pants off and stands in front of me in his snug boxer-briefs. I glance up, not used to being down in this position while he towers over me. Something about it makes my stomach flip and my heartrate pick up speed, then he runs his fingers through my hair.

"How do you see me right now?" he asks.

"What do you mean?"

"Have you ever thought of me negatively?"

My brows furrow as I stand up. "No, never. Why would I?"

"Well, I've been on my knees for you countless times. I've been bent over for you. I've done all the things you haven't because you're afraid that'll make you 'soft' or 'less of a man' or whatever bullshit your parents made you believe, and yet you've never thought that of me, have you?"

"Jay," I say softly.

He sits down and gazes up at me. "Just know I'd never think differently of you. Don't feel self-conscious around me." He lays back and closes his eyes. "Oh shit. The room is spinning."

I pull the covers back on his side. "Come on. Get under the comforter."

He scoots all the way over, nuzzling his face into the pillow. "Lay with me?"

"Of course."

I climb onto my side and he makes his way to me, pushing his face into the crook of my neck. "You smell so good."

I wrap an arm around his shoulders and hold him close to me. He kisses my neck a couple times before going still. It doesn't take long before his breathing evens out, succumbing to sleep.

Angling my head, I press my lips to his forehead and give him a kiss. My chest expands, filled with warmth and contentment. The small act of affection didn't make me feel miserable or disgusting. It didn't make me feel inadequate. In fact, I'm only regretting doing it because he's asleep, and he should be aware that I did it.

I know it may not make sense to many people. How can I not want to kiss or do certain things with men when I'm still actively attracted to and fucking them? Believe me, I struggle with the same thoughts. My dad beat it into me that being submissive was for the weak. Bending over and kneeling for men was not what another man should do. In my fucked up head, I somehow twisted it and thought that as long as I wasn't doing those things, it wasn't as bad. After all, a hole's a hole, right? The difference between a woman's mouth and a man's can't be that different. If I fucked a woman in the ass, what makes it different if I fuck a man's? Things were only different if I was being fucked, if I was sucking dick, if I was kissing men.

I shake my head, furious with my parents. Enraged with myself. All these years I never allowed myself to be with a man more than a couple times, and there haven't been many men in my life. Jay's the first guy I've been with this long, and as weird and fucked up as our relationship might be, it's the closest I've had to a real one. We hang out, talk, laugh, eat, and fuck. We don't kiss, and the fucking so far, has been one-sided, but it's still a very real relationship, even if I've been trying to convince myself it's not.

I wish he wasn't so drunk, because I'd wake him up and kiss him right now. I'd tell him I'm sorry for being so stupid. I'd offer him anything he wanted, because this means something to me, and I'm just now realizing it.

As my excitement looms, reality sets in. I'm still leaving Michigan. He's still going to live here. His Dad will want to kill me if he ever finds out. There isn't a future for us. This is all we have. Three weeks at most. I leave shortly after his graduation.

Now anger burns in my veins. I wasted so much time. I know in the beginning it wasn't supposed to be anything serious. It was sex, but somewhere over the past few weeks, something changed. I know it and he does, too, and yet I still chose to play dumb. I still pretended this wasn't anything, because I needed to keep that separation. I couldn't develop feelings. I couldn't make it harder for us, but now it feels like I stunted something that could've been better.

Not every story needs a happily ever after, right? Ours could've been greater, even if we knew it was going to end. Sometimes, it's about the journey and the lessons learned and memories made.

Twenty-one days. That's all we have.

"Jay. Jay." I shake him slightly, trying to rouse him, wanting to talk.

"Mm," he mumbles.

"I have to say something."

"Mm." His brows lift but his eyes remain closed.

"Wake up."

"Babe," he groans, turning over. "Let's talk tomorrow."

He wiggles his ass into my crotch, seeking my hand with his and pulling my arm over his waist. The term of endearment mixed with his need to cuddle has me grinning like the Cheshire cat.

"Okay."

Twenty-Nine

ALEKSANDER

JAYDEN DOESN'T USUALLY sleep in very late, but the alcohol has him still unconscious around eleven o'clock. I've already had breakfast and am planning for lunch while taking care of some work. Close to eleven-thirty, he strolls through the doorway, scratching the back of his head and squinting at the sunlight flooding the room.

"Hey."

I grin, putting my paper down. "Hi. Feeling okay?"

He makes a face. "Headache mainly. Sorry for being such a drunk ass."

"You weren't as bad as you think."

"Well, thanks for coming to get me."

I nod. "Of course."

He smiles. "I'm gonna go brush my teeth and put on some clothes. I'll be back."

"Okay."

Nearly fifteen minutes later, he rushes in, phone in hand. "I have to leave. Apparently there's something happening at the frat house. I need to be there."

I get up. "Oh okay."

"Maybe we can meet up before I see you at work tomorrow," he offers.

"Yeah. Just let me know."

He walks over and gently clasps his fingers around my wrist before wrapping his arms around me in a hug. "Thanks for last night."

My arms snake around him. "Anytime."

As he eases away, his eyes linger on mine and I can tell he has something he wants to say, but he holds it in. "Bye."

"Bye."

Once he's gone, that empty feeling settles in. I had gotten used to being alone, but now I'm finding that I hate it. The silence has never been so loud.

After my realization last night while curled around Jay, all I've been thinking about is trying to make these last three weeks be the best they can. However, I still war between what I want to do versus what's smart to do.

I know I have a lot to work on, and the past trauma will likely affect me for a good while, but once Jayden told me about internalised homophobia, it really triggered something inside me. My first instinct was to be angry. How could I be homophobic if I know I'm gay? But I did look into it, and some of it does register with me. Self-hate is a very real thing lots of people go through for different reasons, and I can't deny that I hated myself for a long time. If I wasn't gay, then my parents wouldn't have treated me the way they did, and our relationship would've been better. If I wasn't gay, those kids wouldn't have attacked me.

I allowed myself to think I was only accepting those dates with women because my parents wanted me to, but it went a little further than that. I didn't have to sleep with them, and I did. I wanted to test myself. I wanted to know if I could. I led women on, continuing to date and sleep with them, because I believed in the whole fake it till you make it thing.

However, I was still finding other men to have sex with, because that's what I wanted, but it was always very discreet and usually with men who were also in the closet, because I knew nothing would ever come of it.

All of that to say, I've scheduled some therapy appointments for when I'm back in Chicago, so I can start to work on myself. I never understood the phrase, *you have to love yourself before you can love someone else.* I think I get it now, though.

I spend the rest of the afternoon waiting to see if I'll hear back from Jay, hoping he'll be able to come back over, because I really do have a lot I want to tell him. However, the hours pass, and by the time nine o'clock rolls around, I know he won't be coming back. He has school, and I have work to get to in the morning. Usually, during the week, I keep our interactions short and minimal. He's too tempting to have around in my office, especially alone.

At ten-forty, when I'm getting ready for bed, I get a text from Jay.

Sorry, it was a crazy day. We have several events to finish planning plus a community service project. Blah blah, boring college kid stuff to you, probably. I can't believe I'm almost done with this, though.

I don't think it's boring. I don't know much about what you do when you're not with me.

We party a lot. The stereotypical stuff, you know? Mixers and socials and other events. We've done a lot of work for the community, though. Raising money for charity and volunteer work.

> Sounds like you stay pretty busy.

Typically, but I enjoy it all. I don't like down time. Gives me too much time to think. Haha

> I guess we're similar in that way. However, I have been thinking about a lot more lately.

Oh yeah? Like what?

I hesitate to answer, because the truth is it has a lot to do with me, him, and us. Probably not a conversation for late night texting, and definitely one I'd prefer to have in person.

> Self-reflection, I suppose.

I see.

A couple minutes goes by without either one of us saying anything else. When my phone lights up, I snatch it up.

I have a lot of work to do this week. I won't be able to be back over there with you until the weekend, probably.

> I understand.

Which sucks because I know you leave soon.

Yeah, I know.

Guess I'll see you at work tomorrow.

Can't wait.

He sends me an emoji of a huge smiley face followed by a black heart, and those stupid little emoticons have me feeling like a love-struck teenager. The smile on my face doesn't disappear until I'm asleep.

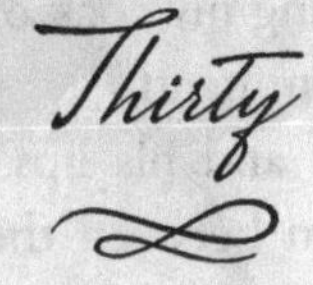

Thirty

ALEKSANDER

"HAPPY TO SEE ME, BOSS?" he asks when he enters my office at the end of the day.

"I'd be happier if this wasn't the first time I had you alone."

His perfect teeth sink into his bottom lip as he grins at me. "I can't slack off. I hear the boss is a huge dick."

I approach him, walking him backwards until his back hits the door he just closed. I grab his hand and put it on my crotch. "Huge dick sounds about right."

"Don't tease me," he moans, squeezing me in his hand.

"I'd apologize, but..."

"You're not sorry. I know," he says, quickly undoing my button and zipper, slipping his hand into my boxer-briefs.

He strokes my cock, and I'm instantly as hard as a rock. "You know how much I love this dick."

"Do I?" I ask, my voice airy.

"Wasn't a question. You should know by now."

"Mm."

"I want you to fuck my mouth," he says huskily.

"We shouldn't. Not here."

"You started this, Mr. Drakos. And you weren't sorry."

He drops to his knees, and seeing him down there as he licks his lips, eyes full of sexual longing, I want nothing more than to give him what he wants.

I step forward, pulling my cock out and guiding it to his lips. "Your wish is my command."

His eyebrow arches and his lips begin to form a smile before I push my crown between them. He holds onto my thighs while my hips piston back and forth.

"Oh fuck," I grunt, trying to keep my voice low.

The murmured voices of people walking through the hallway can be heard through the door, and Linda's voice trickles in as she talks on the phone.

"Your mouth is fucking magical," I whisper, holding myself up with a hand against the door. "So good."

He moans around me, hollowing his cheeks as he sucks, using his tongue to swirl around my shaft, and using his hand to stroke while he teases my crown. He does everything he knows I love, and then pulls off my cock to let his tongue dance over my balls.

"Fuck, baby," I murmur, not even planning on using the word. It just slipped.

His eyes snap up and meet mine as he moans, then he takes me in both hands, stroking me hard and fast while holding my crown on the flat of his tongue, waiting for my load.

I squeeze my eyes closed, my muscles flexing. I'm thrown into paradise, surrounded by bliss and infused with passion as I come, gasping and cursing as quietly as I can.

He groans as he tastes me, like he loves the flavor.

Barely easing away, I grab a hold of my shaft, squeezing the tip as a few more drops of cum drip out and land on his lip.

When I step back, he stands up, moving to wipe his

mouth with his hand, but I stop him. My cum glistens, capturing my attention, and after I meet his dark gaze for a few seconds, I lean forward slowly and lick the remnants from his lip.

It's the first time my tongue has touched any part of his mouth, and a shiver runs up my spine as a thrill of excitement shoots through my veins. Warmth swirls in my stomach, and he gasps lightly, watching me with wide, curious eyes.

"Just cleaning up my mess," I whisper.

He licks his lips, and is about to say something when Linda's voice blares over the intercom on my desk.

"Mr. Drakos, Mrs. Nelson wants to know if you're available to meet tomorrow at five. I don't have anything on your calendar."

"Shit." I shove my cock back into my pants, fastening them up as I walk to the desk. "Yes, that's fine. Thank you."

"You're welcome, sir. I'm about to leave soon. Do you need anything?"

"No. Thank you, Linda. See you tomorrow."

"Oh, sir. I'm sorry. Mr. Pemberton is here now. Can I send him in?"

Jay quickly adjusts himself in his pants and does another swipe of his mouth with his hand. "I can leave," he whispers.

I nod. "Okay, give me a minute."

After rounding the desk, I make my way back over to the door where Jay lingers. "Talk to you later?"

"Yeah. I'll text you."

"Okay."

I pull open the door and let him out so I can let Luther in. The two of them nod and smile at each other, saying goodbye, and then I'm enclosed in the office with Luther—the only person who knows almost everything about me.

Maybe it's time to open up to him about my current situation.

"That's a good kid there. Hard worker. Likeable. I think he'll have a good career here."

I sit down at my desk. "Hm. Oh, Ja—Mr. Brooks? Yes, I agree." Luther eyes me carefully, but I ignore him. "So, what can I help you with?"

"You're leaving soon, so I'm wondering if you have plans on who will be taking your spot here."

I smirk at him. "Luther, I think you know you're gonna be the boss when I leave."

"Because I'm the oldest?"

"The most experienced. Why do you think I brought you out here?"

"Because I'm the only one who didn't have a family to uproot?" He grins.

"No. You know what to do and you'll do a good job. The branch is doing well, and we'll keep growing. The interns who get chosen will fill this place up, and from what I can see, we'd be good to get any of them."

"There's a young lady—Patricia Patterson. She's actually wanting to move to Chicago when she's done with college. Think there's space for her up there? Or would you rather someone else take that spot?"

He tacks the last part on there several seconds later, and when I look up at him, he's watching me again with scrutiny.

"What are you talking about?"

He shrugs. "Nothing."

I sigh, rubbing my fingers at my temple. "Luther, what do you have to say? I can nearly see the words trying to crawl out of your throat."

He chuckles. "I know you better than most, and I think you'd agree to that. I knew your parents, and your dad didn't mince words, so I'm aware of a lot more than you may think."

"So you know he was an asshole. Most people did."

"Alek," he says, dropping formalities. "Do you like Mr. Brooks?"

My brows furrow, instantly and easily choosing annoyed confusion. "What do you mean?"

"I know you're gay, and I'm probably the only one here who does. I also know Mr. Brooks is bi, and considering I've been working with him fairly closely these past several weeks, I'd like to say I know him pretty well. I see things. Notice things. He talks about you in a way that's not unprofessional, but it's clear he has a crush at minimum."

My heart flutters in my chest. "Okay, and?"

"And you like him. He's in here quite a bit. Definitely more than the other interns. I've seen you two when you've thought nobody is around. You've never done anything blatantly obvious, but sometimes all it takes is a look and a smile. There's something there. Your eyes always find each other when you're in the same room, while everyone else seems to avoid your gaze."

I sigh. "Luther."

He holds up his hand. "I know it's not my business and I know you're my boss, but I'm old, Alek. I've been around the block and back. You confided in me way back when, and I know the things your dad had to say about you. I can only imagine he was worse when actually speaking to you, but I want you to know that he was wrong. Everything he said was wrong. His entire thought process was wrong."

"I don't know why you're telling me this."

"Because I want you to have someone in your life tell you that it's okay to be who you are. There's nothing wrong with you." He stands up and knocks on the desk. "You're a good man, Alek. You're a thousand times better than your father. If there's something brewing with you and Mr. Brooks, then go with it. He's an adult and you run this company. Nobody's getting in trouble."

"I'm leaving, Luther. I don't live here." It's as close as I get to an admission to something happening between us.

He shrugs. "You could, or he could move there. That's his hometown."

He walks out before I can wrap my head around everything he just dropped on me.

Thirty-One

ALEKSANDER

TUESDAY GOES by and besides a couple glimpses of Jay through the halls, I don't see much of him, and I never get to talk to him prior to leaving for a meeting before the end of the day. He reaches out to me while he's studying, and we text back and forth for a little while before he disappears into his studies.

Wednesday is nothing but stress when it comes to my job, keeping me occupied while I put out fires with numerous calls. Jay has a community service job with his frat that evening, so we hardly talk.

I find myself just waiting for Friday to roll around, because that's when we get most of our time together, but that means a week will have been lost before I've even been able to talk to him about everything I've thought about regarding us. I wanted to be better. I wanted to attempt more. And now we're almost down to two weeks.

"Is it weird that I just want to lay with you?" Jay asks when he calls me Friday evening. "I'm finally done with my work, but now I just feel stressed and tired and I think only you can make me feel better."

I smile. "It's not weird. Come over and I *will* make you feel better."

"Mm. Sounds like a little more than laying down, but I think I'm up for it."

"I don't mind just laying together. I've been wanting to talk to you, anyway."

"Uh-oh."

I laugh. "It's not bad. Come on. I've missed you."

Silence sits heavy between us. It's the first time I've said that, though not the first time I've felt it.

"Okay. I'm coming."

Half an hour later, Jay's at my door, and when I let him in he steps forward, wrapping an arm around my waist as he kisses my neck. I put a hand on his lower back, keeping him close before encasing him in my arms completely.

"Oh, you missed me, missed me."

I snort. "Shut up."

"Let's cuddle," he says, taking my wrist and tugging me to the couch on the balcony.

Outside, I sit in the corner of the small sectional, one leg outstretched on the cushions as Jay settles between my thighs, his back to my chest as his long legs stretch to the end of the couch. He wiggles and then rests his head on my chest.

"This is nice."

I rest a hand on his hip before moving it down to caress his upper thigh. "I agree."

We sit in comfortable silence for a few minutes before he speaks up. "What did you want to talk about?"

I clear my throat. "Well, I'm not too sure how to begin, but you know how I told you I've been doing some self-reflecting?"

"Yeah."

"I want you to know that what you said about internalized homophobia really hit home and whether that's what it is, or just self-hate, something is definitely affecting me, and I've made appointments with a therapist back home. I want to be better."

He grabs my hand and squeezes. "I'm happy for you."

"I also have a confession."

"Should I be scared?"

"No," I answer with a chuckle. "Remember when you came over while you were drunk?"

He groans. "Mostly."

"Do you remember when you said you'd never look at me differently?"

"Yeah."

"It made me think. You've done so much. Everything I've told myself I'd never do for whatever dumbass reason I thought made sense, and not once, ever, did I think of you like I've assumed I'd think of myself. My dad called me a bitch, a sissy, and many other awful things I don't want to repeat. I've been doing or not doing whatever I thought would keep me from being those things. I realize the ignorance, but those thoughts are threaded in my brain."

Jay shifts, turning to face me. "It is ignorant. Bottoms in male/male relationships shouldn't be demeaned and called names. I'm aware of the stereotypes. I know people assume one person has to be the 'woman' in the relationship, and therefore they're supposed to be effeminate and whatever," he slices his hand through the air, annoyed. "But there's no one way to be in a queer relationship."

I take his hand. "I know. I'm sorry. I've not been the best version of myself, and to be honest, I don't know what that is yet. I just hope to get there. But you were right, I've never had any negative or bad feelings about you. In fact, I've felt jealous. I've wished numerous times to be more like you."

"I'm glad you're like you, though."

I grin. "I'm glad you like me despite my flaws."

"What was the confession?"

"Oh." I feel my cheeks heat slightly. "I kissed you."

His eyes bulge. "What? When?"

"That night. When you were drunk."

"Are you kidding me?"

"It sounds a little creepy now that I say it."

He shakes his head. "Help me understand."

"You were asleep, laying on my chest. I turned my head and kissed your forehead. Nothing too crazy."

"I missed a forehead kiss?"

I grin. "After I did it, everything felt right. There wasn't any sort of negative reaction. I felt happy. I wanted to do it again, but I wanted you to be conscious. And it made me regret not having done it sooner, but the reason was two-fold. On top of my own issues, I assumed a lack of intimacy would make it easier to end things."

"It's not gonna be easy, Alek."

I shake my head. "No, it's not."

My heart thumps in my chest as I stare at his lips, ready to kiss him properly. Time freezes around us, the cars below go quiet, and it's only us. He doesn't move, probably waiting for me, hoping I don't get cold feet.

When I lean forward, he does the same. I watch him closely as the distance between us disappears, and when our lips are a hair's breadth away, I shut my eyes and press my mouth against his.

His lips are soft against mine, and our moans blend together, creating a bliss-filled symphony as we come together for the first time.

My heart pounds in my chest, wanting to leave my body and join his, like it knows it belongs with him.

We shift, our bodies moving while our mouths don't steer far from each other. He's down on his back as I hover over him, kissing him softly at first, before I slide my tongue between the seam of his lips and into his mouth.

Jay makes a noise as he exhales, his hands around the back of my neck. Our tongues twist and twirl, dancing to the music we make with each moan, hum, and gasp we expel.

My cock hardens against his and I thrust my hips as I taste the mint from his tongue. He cradles the side of my face, sucking on my tongue briefly before mashing his lips against mine.

Everything is perfect until the loud knock on the door snaps us apart.

"That was amazing," I tell him, leaning down to kiss his lips again.

"You've always enjoyed my mouth."

"Now I can enjoy it in another way."

The knock comes again, so I stand up and adjust myself.

"Looks like you might need help with that."

"We can do plenty as soon as I get rid of whoever's at the door."

"Good, because we have a lot of time to catch up on, and I'm nowhere near being done with that mouth of yours."

I wink at him as I step away and into the open sliding glass door. It doesn't take long to walk across the living room and kitchen, and soon, my hand's on the knob.

Two things happen simultaneously: I open the door, and Jay steps inside and says, "No, wait!"

But it's too late, the door is open. I turn to face him and see panic written all over his face as he holds his phone, the screen lit up like he was reading a message.

"Alek," Cal's voice says before he sees past me and spots his son. "Jay? What the hell is going on?"

Thirty-Two

ALEKSANDER

WE'RE all frozen in place, shock stealing the words from each of us. I take a step back, opening the door wider, allowing Cal the opportunity to come in. Jay steps through the sliding doors, entering the suite and slipping the phone in his pocket.

The only silver lining here is that neither of us is in any state of undress, but just the fact that he's here at all is suspicious and highly inappropriate from a business standpoint. There's no way we're talking our way out of this, and I'm not sure if I should be the person to speak first.

Calvin strides in, eyes focused solely on Jay. "What is going on here?" he questions, his body tense.

"Dad," Jay starts, glancing at me for help. "I...uh. I came here for..."

I can tell he's gonna try to lie. That's everybody's first instinct when getting caught doing something they know they shouldn't be doing. Lie. Deny. Lie some more. I can't blame him.

"This seems highly inappropriate," Cal says, turning his attention to me briefly. "To be in your boss's hotel. At night."

The insinuation is there. Cal knows his son is into men, but he doesn't know about me. That might be the only thing keeping him from instantly jumping to that conclusion.

"You're here," Jay says defensively.

Cal pins him with an intense look. "I'm his friend. You are an intern. There should be no reason for you to be here." He turns to face me, and I try to remain relaxed, sliding my hands in my pockets. "Unless you called him here for a specific, work-related reason. Is that it, Alek?"

He's giving me an out, and I could take it. I should take it. It would be easy to say I needed him to pick up some papers for some project, but I think we'd all know that was bullshit. I inhale deeply, my eyes finding Jay. He gives me a shrug and a look that lets me know I can tell him if I want.

"It wasn't work-related, Cal. I won't lie to you."

Calvin inhales deeply through his nose, his jaw clenched tight as his fists ball up at his sides. His chest heaves with each breath as he stares at me, but he quickly turns to his son.

"You...you're sleeping with..." He can't get the words out, and he takes in another breath as he tries to steady himself. "What the fuck is happening here? Is this how you try to secure a job?"

Jay's face contorts. "That's not what I'm doing."

"Well, what is this?" Calvin faces me. "Alek, what are you doing? This is my son. My son!" he yells.

"Dad, I'm an adult. It's not a big deal."

"It's not a big deal?" he questions, spinning back toward Jay. "He's damn near my age, and he's your boss. He's *my* boss! This isn't right."

"Cal, it's not a serious relationship. We're just..." I trail off, not wanting to say what we've been doing.

Jay looks at me, his brows drawing in slightly. "Fucking. We're just fucking. Did you think I was a virgin? I've slept with plenty of people. Do you want to know who they all are?"

He's angry, and he's pushing his dad's buttons. Calvin explodes. "You need to watch it," he spits, pointing a finger at him. "I'm talking about this situation specifically. You should know better. You both should," he says, throwing a furious look in my direction.

"We met before he started working for me," I offer. "I didn't know he was your son when we first...in the beginning."

"I don't give a shit. You should've ended it the minute you saw him in that office. That's the responsible thing to do. And you should've told me." He turns back to Jay. "Or you should've." Something dawns on him and his eyes widen and his lips part. "We all had dinner together. You both sat with me, eating and drinking, and neither of you thought to tell me you were sleeping together."

I run a hand over my forehead. "We weren't really...it's complicated."

"We had a fight. We weren't talking then."

"A fight? Couples fight. People who are just having sex don't fight. Are you trying to tell me this is serious?"

"No," I answer. Maybe too quickly based on the way Jay looks at me. "Fuck. I don't know what to say here. You're not gonna like it no matter what."

"You're damn right, I won't."

"I understand this is shocking, but you were never supposed to know. What we've been doing has been under wraps. Nobody knows. It always had a termination date. Alek goes back to Chicago soon."

"Alek," Cal says through a humorless laugh. "You call him Alek. He's your boss!"

"He's a lot more than that!" Jay fires back before taking a breath. "You don't have to understand."

Cal's brows shoot up, surprised by his son's words. He ignores them for now, focusing on me. "I didn't even know you were into men."

I shrug. "Not many do."

"Jesus Christ," he says, running a hand over his bald head. "Your mother and sister are here. They're in our hotel room. What the hell am I supposed to tell them?"

Jay's back straightens. "Whatever you want. Look, I'm not ashamed. I don't know if you think I should be, but I'm not. I like Alek. We've had fun together and we haven't allowed that to interfere with work. You know how he is, so you should know he's kept everything professional. I'm not glued to him all day. He's not giving me special treatment. I mainly work with other people, anyway. If you think I should care about the age difference, I don't. So, I don't see the problem. It doesn't affect you or anyone else. You've preached to me about growing up and being an adult, and yet, you still act as if I'm a kid. Trust that you've raised me to make the best decisions for myself."

Cal's quiet for several seconds before shaking his head. "I can't believe this. I really can't."

"I'm sorry, Cal," I say. "I understand you feel betrayed in some way, but Jay's right. We're both adults and capable of making our own decisions. I know our friendship adds another fucked up layer to this, and I tried to cut it off but...well, it didn't work."

Jay smirks at me from behind his dad's back.

"This ends now. Termination date is to-fucking-night. This is wrong on many levels. Jayden, come on."

"You're my dad, but you don't control who I fuck, regardless of whether you know them or not."

"Watch your mouth," Cal snaps. "We're here for the week leading up to graduation. You will spend most of your time with us anyway. When is this internship over?"

"Next week," I answer.

"I know you're the head of the company, but I can still report this. You sleeping with an intern is wrong."

"Dad, stop," Jay pleads.

"It's fine," I say. "He's right and is entitled to his feelings. Cal, I'll head back to Chicago early."

"What?" Jay exclaims. "No. Fuck that."

"It's fine."

"No, it's not. That wasn't the plan. What about my graduation? What about…" he trails off as his dad's expression changes.

"Graduation? You want him at your graduation?"

Jay ignores him. "Alek, please. We had two weeks."

"I'm sorry."

"Then stay!" he says, storming toward me, clasping my wrist with his fingers.

I run my thumb over the back of his hand. "It was always leading to this. You're about to graduate and start your life here. Maybe at MGD. My life is in Chicago."

He presses his lips together as he stares into my eyes. His dad clears his throat, reminding us of his presence.

"Jayden, let's go. Alek needs to start packing." He levels me with a look. "I know you could fire me, but I hope considering the circumstances, you'll allow me to keep working, but I think we can agree our friendship is effectively over."

I nod once at him before looking back at Jay. With his father here, it really messes up the moment. I probably shouldn't kiss him, but I want to. We only got the one in, and regret settles deep in my core. There's so much I want to say, but Cal's fuming and staring holes into both of us.

"Bye, Jayden."

He shakes his head slightly, like he doesn't want to say bye. "I wouldn't change a thing," he says before storming out of the room ahead of his father.

Thirty-Three

JAYDEN

AFTER I LEFT Alek's room, I rushed ahead of my dad, finding my family's hotel room before he could catch up with me in the elevator. I was only able to find it because my sister texted me. She's the reason I knew my dad was here before Alek opened the door.

Just as he was about to see who had been knocking, I checked my phone and saw a few messages from Janae. She told me they were in town and staying at a hotel, and mentioned Dad leaving to see a friend who stayed in the same one. I read them all a second too late.

Once I made it to the room, Dad showed up a minute later, and Mom and Janae could tell something had happened. Mom pushed it aside, instead focusing on seeing me for the first time in several months. We talked about graduation, work, their new puppy, and how she's happy to be on vacation. Dad fumed silently, grunting responses, and I avoided looking at him. He didn't mention Alek, so I didn't either. I only stayed an hour before needing to flee, promising Mom and Janae that I'd be back tomorrow morning so we could go have breakfast.

I wanted to go straight back to his room and plead with him to stay, but I guess it wouldn't do any good. He's made up his mind, and he's right, it was always going to end. I just hate that it's ending right after our first kiss. We could've had two weeks of kissing. We could've had more.

After leaving the hotel, I drove around for hours before finally making it home and dropping to my bed. The desire to text Alek was high, but I didn't, and I never heard from him either.

Now, as I'm getting ready to go meet my family for breakfast, dread knots up in my stomach. I'm not ready to face my dad again. I don't know if he told them anything and if I'm about to be met with three people telling me how wrong and stupid I was to sleep with Alek.

I pull up outside the IHOP my mom told me to meet them at, and as soon as I step inside, I spot my mom waving me over to a table near the window.

"Hey, baby."

"Hey, Mom."

"Hi, ugly," my sister greets, barely looking up from her phone.

"What's up, snitch?"

She looks up, tucking a long braid behind her ear. "What?"

"I know you're keeping Mom and Dad up to date on my social media posts."

She snickers. "Oh. I was mad at you."

"For what? I'm all the way over here."

"I think it was when you said you wouldn't buy me those shoes I wanted."

I shake my head and Mom laughs. "We told her no, too. She needs to learn to save up some of her allowance, plus who pays over two hundred dollars for shoes?"

Dad's quiet in the corner, not chiming in like he usually would.

"So, what's been going on, baby?" Mom asks, looking over the menu. "How's life? Are you excited to be done with college?"

"Yeah, I am excited, but I also can't believe it either. Now that it's almost over, it feels like it went by really fast."

"That's how it goes," she says with a nod. "And your internship? How's that been?"

Both me and Dad stiffen. Clearly he hasn't mentioned anything to her. "It's been really good. I've learned a lot. It's definitely been more hands-on learning than in class." Dad scoffs but hides it by clearing his throat before drinking his coffee.

"That's good. When do they choose who gets the job?"

"The end of next week."

"You're working with Mr. Drakos, right? I really like him. Kind of stiff, but friendly."

Dad pins me with a glare. I look away and notice Janae watching us. I give her a forced smile before responding to my mom.

"Yeah. He's nice."

I keep it simple, hoping to keep my dad from popping a blood vessel.

Once we start eating, Dad begins to join in on the conversation. We're able to act like we're not avoiding each other by responding to the same questions, giving our responses one after the other, however, we're still not actually communicating. If Mom notices, she doesn't bring it up, but Janae seems to be more aware.

After we're done eating, we all go to the zoo. My mom likes to visit the zoo no matter where we visit, so we walk around looking at animals and feeding the ones we're allowed to. At one point, me and Janae are left alone while Mom and Dad wander around a gift shop.

"What's up with you and Dad?" she asks.

"Nothing. Why?"

She scoffs. "Stop lying. It's so obvious."

"He's mad at me. Well, I'm mad at him, too. It's not a big deal. Don't worry. We'll get over it."

"I'm just confused, because we hadn't been here that long and as soon as we saw you for the first time yesterday, you're already pissed, and then Dad comes in pissed, but he was supposed to be seeing his friend, and you know, shit doesn't add up."

I peer down at her. "Are you supposed to be cussing?"

"Don't change the subject. But also, don't tell Mom and Dad," she says, looking over her shoulder.

"Don't worry about it. Me and Dad are fine. But we do need to talk about you snitchin' on me. What's that about?"

She allows me to change the subject, and eventually our parents catch up to us, so I never have to answer her question. We finish our day with a trip to the mall and then dinner before they retire to their room and I go back to the frat house.

Sunday is full of stuff my mom wants to do—breakfast, taking family pictures at a park, then going back to the hotel to swim. Unfortunately, all that does is remind me of the times I got Alek in the pool. I wonder if he's still here.

As I lounge in one of the chaise chairs, Mom gets out of the pool and sits next to me.

"What's goin' on, baby? You seem down."

I force a smile. "I'm fine."

"Mmhmm. You know your momma knows what that means. I've said it many times in my life, and I almost never mean it when I do. Especially when you plaster on that fake smile."

I laugh, shaking my head while I watch Dad and Janae in the pool. "It's nothing."

"You and your dad seem to be on shaky ground. He won't tell me what happened, but it's obvious something did."

"I suppose I disappointed him."

"I doubt that," she says instantly. "We're so proud of you."

"It's a long story, and one that I guess doesn't need to be told. We'll be fine, though."

She studies me for a while. "You can talk to me if you need to."

"I know, Mom. Thanks."

When Monday rolls around, I almost hope to see Alek at the office, but as soon as I step inside the building, I know he isn't there. Not only was his car not out front, but his presence isn't felt.

At Linda's desk, she informs me that Luther is now occupying Alek's office and tells me Mr. Drakos had to hurry back to Chicago for an important business matter. Only I know the truth.

I didn't anticipate feeling the way I do with him gone. It started off as meaningless sex but along the way, it turned into more and I didn't seem to realize it until it was over.

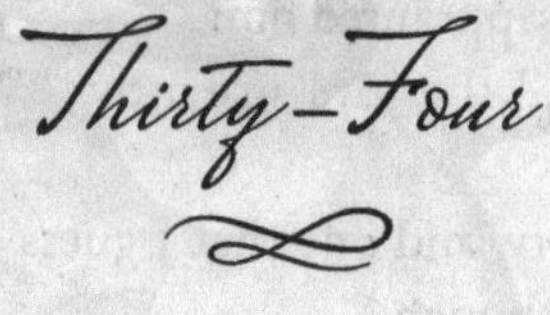

Thirty-Four

JAYDEN

ON THURSDAY, it's announced that I was one of three interns chosen to work at MGD. On Friday, I graduate from college.

My parents and sister cheer for me when I walk across the stage, but I still can't help scanning the crowd, hoping to see a familiar face with blue-green eyes staring back at me.

The morning stretches into the afternoon with tons of pictures being taken after the ceremony is done. After chatting with my friends for a while afterwards and going over the plans for celebrating tonight, I depart campus for the last time.

My parents take me out to eat, and once we're done, we head back to their hotel.

"I'm so proud of you, baby. You've done so well. I can't wait to see how you shape your life," Mom says, squeezing me into the fiftieth hug today.

"Thanks, Mom," I reply, hugging her back. "I'm extremely grateful for your and Dad's help getting me here."

Dad gives me a hug once Mom releases me, our fight behind us for the most part. "Congratulations, son. Like your mom said, we're beyond proud of you. You're going to do great things."

"Thanks, Dad."

"We're going to be heading back early in the morning," Mom says from her bed. "So it'll be an early night for us tonight, but I'm sure you have plans," she says with a grin.

"Yes, be safe tonight," Dad adds.

"I will."

"You don't have a special person in your life?" Mom finally asks. She's always questioning who I'm dating, and I'm surprised she's gone this long without bringing it up.

"Honey," Dad says, probably wanting to stop this before it starts. "Leave him alone. He's young. He has a lot of time."

"What? I'm just curious. I figured if you had someone we'd probably meet them today."

"There's nobody," I tell her. "It's either the wrong person, wrong time, or wrong circumstance."

"Wrong circumstance?" she questions.

"Honey," Dad says again.

She ignores him. "What does that mean, Jay?"

I don't look in my dad's direction when I reply. "He doesn't live here."

"Does he live nearby? How'd you meet?"

Dad fidgets next to me as he sits in the chair near the window.

"Not that close. He was only here for a short time."

"I'm sorry to hear that," Mom offers. "If it's meant to be, you'll work it out."

I force a grin and nod.

"It's not going to work," Dad says, unable to hold his tongue any longer.

I sigh, my shoulders dropping as I anticipate whatever the hell is about to happen now. Janae looks up from her phone as she lounges on the bed, aware the mood has shifted.

Mom's brows furrow as her head snaps to her husband. "What are you talking about?"

Dad gestures to me, his arm outstretched as he looks at my mom. "Caroline, your son was fu—doing whatever with Alek!"

I don't miss when Janae sits all the way up, her eyes as round as saucers as her mouth forms an O. Mom flinches back before bringing her gaze back to me.

"Aleksander Drakos?"

"Yes. I caught them our first night here. Our son was up in his hotel room. Apparently, it wasn't anything serious," he says, his voice dripping with disbelief.

"Is that true?" Mom asks, her tone calm but her face giving away her shock.

"Yes, it's true, but I don't know why we're talking about this. Dad said enough that night, even threatening to report Alek. He left already. Went back to Chicago early to make Dad happy."

"Well, I'm still not happy," he says.

"And you don't have to be," I snip. "What should matter is whether I am, and I'm not. Not at all." I stand up, ready to say what I have to say and leave. Looking only at my mom, I say, "I met Alek before I started work. We did what adults do and then I showed up to work on Monday and found out it was him. He said he wouldn't have done anything if he had known who I was and was ready to end it then. It was me who pursued him. When we decided, as adults, to continue what he had started, we made sure work was never compromised. Everything remained professional. Our time was spent alone and we knew it was a short-term thing. He left. He's gone, so it's over. What is there to talk about?"

Mom remains silent for several seconds, processing, as Dad begins to pace in front of the window.

"I had no idea he was...but okay, umm." She stands up,

hands in the air. "I can understand how your father might feel, and the age difference is there. However, my parents have quite a gap in their age. Fifteen years. But they've never had issues, and they've always been happy."

"Caroline, please don't condone this," Dad says.

"There's nothing wrong with it," she offers in a gentle tone. "I know you look at it a little differently because he's your friend and boss, but I know him, too. I like him and you know he's a decent man."

"He's the boss. It was inappropriate and he should've known better. How can I invite this man into my house again? He took advantage of my son."

Having heard enough, I speak up. "I wasn't taken advantage of. I told you I pursued him, but I'm not going to sit here and talk about this anymore. It doesn't matter. I don't know how many different ways I can say that. He doesn't live here. I'll never see him again. Dad, you get your way, and I'll eventually move on."

"Sweetie," Mom says, stepping closer and grabbing my hands. "I think it does matter. To you. And you're right, we don't get a say in our children's partners. If that was the case, I wouldn't have married your father."

Dad scoffs and I look between them, but Mom gives me a grin. "Dad didn't like him. Thought he was a troublemaker." She winks. "But he's been the best husband anybody could ask for, and he's a great father. He's just trying to look out for you."

"I get it," I say with a sigh. "But I'm not planning on bringing people to you to get your approval, I just have to hope that you both like whoever it is I happen to want to be with."

"If they make you happy, that's all I care about," Mom says.

Dad exhales loudly. "Son, you know I want you to be

happy, but you have to understand how this makes me feel. I'm sure you'll find someone else."

"I'm gonna go," I say, attempting to force a smile. "I'm glad you all came to visit. Thanks for everything. Really. Let me know when you make it home. I'll plan a visit for Thanksgiving."

Mom wraps her arms around me, her head coming to my chest. "I love you. So proud. Don't forget that. Be happy, baby."

I squeeze her back and kiss her cheek. "Yes, ma'am. Thank you." I walk around to the bed, and wrap an arm around my sister. "Love you, kid. Stop being a snitch, yeah?"

"Shut up. I love you, too."

After a quick glance at my dad, and the years of being taught to respect them no matter what, I march toward him and extend my hand. It's not the best form of good-bye, but at least I'm not ignoring him and walking out.

"Have a safe trip."

He keeps my hand in his. "I mean it. I want you to be happy."

I nod before spinning around and leaving the room.

Thirty-Five

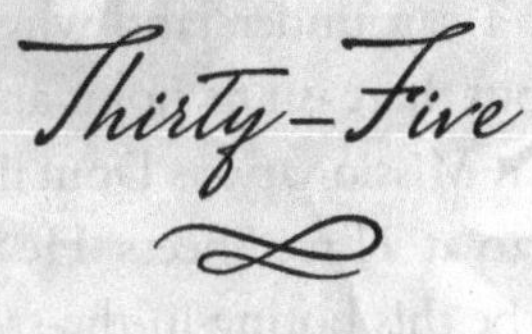

JAYDEN

"WHAT IS WRONG WITH YOU?" Renzo asks as I sit on Trev and Dom's couch while everyone around me is either drinking or dancing.

"Nothing."

He drops down next to me, nudging my side. "I know you're full of shit. We just graduated, dude! Everyone's having a good time except you."

"I was drinking. I *am* drinking," I amend, holding up my beer.

Renzo takes it from me. "First of all, this is full and warm."

"I don't know, man. Just got some shit goin' on. I'm fine."

"Talk to me," he says with another nudge. "I may have overheard something about a secret boyfriend. Is it that?"

I snort. "Who was it? Dom or Trevor?"

He pretends to lock his lips shut, but it doesn't matter because soon Dom marches over and plops down on the other side of me.

"Why are you all depressed over here? Mr. Missionary?"

I shoot him a look before Renzo pipes in. "Who?"

With a drawn out, dramatic sigh, I figure I may as well open up. I gave Renzo a little shit for not letting me know what was going on with him and Ronan, and then Trev kept the fact that he was gay *and* sleeping with the new running back a secret. Now I can understand why you want to keep things to yourself, but there isn't a point anymore.

"I met a guy. Mr. Missionary, as Dom likes to call him, at a party I was invited to at Three Sheets. He was a bit older and Dom thought he'd be this boring-in-the-sack type of guy, but I'll have you both know, he's far from boring."

They exchange a look and laugh, but I keep going.

"Anyway, surprise surprise, he turns out to be my boss."

"At the marketing company?" Renzo asks, eyes wide.

"Yep. Runs the company, in fact."

"Holy shit," Dom says.

"Anyway, long story short, we kept sleeping together, deciding it was a sex only type thing. I found out later he was due to leave shortly after graduation, but over time, I guess we got close. There's a lot of other details you don't know, as far as issues he has due to past trauma, but right at the end, he was opening up and our sex only situation was turning into something else." I wave my hand through the air. "Anyway, oh, I forgot to mention—he's friends with my dad, and my dad showed up to his room while I was there last weekend and everything went to hell."

"No!" Renzo gasps.

"It was a whole mess and Alek left early. I haven't talked to him since then. He's in Chicago now and my Dad's still pissed, and I don't know. I'm just feeling annoyed and stressed."

"I feel like I'm in a soap opera," Dom says, making Renzo snort. "Oh, shut up. My mom watched them a lot."

"So, you ended up really liking this guy," Renzo says.

"I guess," I answer with a shrug.

"How old is he?" Dom asks.

"Forty-one."

Renzo lets out a low whistle. "Forty-one?"

Dom peeks around me and looks at Zo. "He's hot though. Not gonna lie."

"I don't know what to say, man," Renzo says. "I mean, he doesn't live here. Have you thought about moving back home? Maybe it'll work then."

I shake my head. "So we can have double date dinner nights with my parents?" I joke. "Nah, I don't want to live in Chicago. I like it here. I have a job here now. The beginnings of a career. Plus, I don't know how he feels about us. He hasn't reached out. He said goodbye, so it felt pretty final."

"Have you texted him?" Dom asks.

"No, but only because I'm afraid he won't reply or he'll tell me not to text him again."

"You won't know till you know," Renzo says with a shrug.

"Come on, man. Get up, get drunk, let's celebrate, and you can figure out your shit with Mr. Missionary another time. Right now, it's your time."

I playfully punch Dom in the arm. "Okay, okay. No more sulking. Who wants to play shot roulette?" I yell loud enough for everyone to hear.

A few groans mixed with a few cheers echo back to me, and our group of friends celebrate the ending of our college lives.

After having a couple more conversations with my friends about my love life situation, I start to feel a little better. Nobody's judging me for Alek being older or my boss. Surprised, maybe, but nobody has anything negative to say. Which I feel should be the case for everybody's relationships. As long as it's a legal, consenting relationship, it shouldn't matter the gender, race, or age of the people involved as long as they're happy. I don't know why everyone gets so caught up in what or who other people are doing, loving, or fucking.

However, I am at the beginning of my adult life. I'm turning twenty-three next month and I have a job lined up and ready to start in two weeks. I'm going to live with Trev and Dom until I can find an apartment. There's nothing close to my job, and I'm not wanting to commute over forty minutes back and forth to work every day. Plus, they're building some new complexes a couple miles from MGD and should be ready to move into in the next month or so. Everything is looking good for my future. Maybe it just wasn't my time to settle down. Perhaps I need to settle into my life a little more first.

"Hey, you good?" Dex asks me from across the dining room table we're playing beer pong on.

I snap myself out of my thoughts and smile. "I am. Let's go. I'm whoopin' everybody's ass."

The group laughs and we get absolutely wasted and end up having a sleepover with nearly a dozen people sprawled between two beds, a couch, and a makeshift fort in the living room.

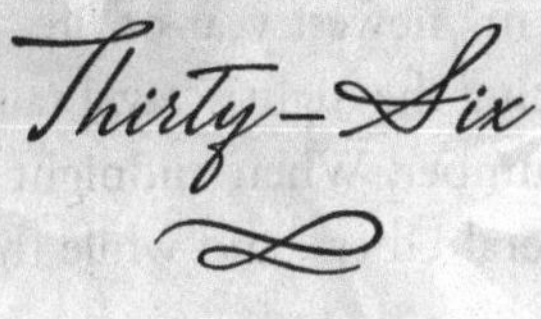

Thirty-Six

JAYDEN

"HAPPY BIRTHDAY!" Linda shouts from her desk when I walk past.

"Thank you," I reply with a grin. "You comin' to the festival?"

"Are you kidding? Of course, I am!"

"Dope. I'll see you there."

"Got any plans for your birthday?"

"Me and some friends are going to a couple clubs."

"Well, have fun."

"I will. Thanks."

I leave the office building, done for the day. Luther, or Mr. Pemberton as I now refer to him, has been a good boss. I've worked here almost a month now, and I'll move into my apartment in two weeks. As much as I love Trev and Dom, you can only live with a couple for so long before shit gets a little awkward. There's not much space between the rooms, and I'm sure they'll enjoy their privacy again once I'm gone.

Tomorrow is the music festival I spent so much time working on, and it'll be nice to be there, but it reminds me of

Alek. I still haven't texted him, though I've been tempted many times.

When I get home, I shower, eat, change, and wait for everybody else to be ready to leave. By ten o'clock, we're at Toast, drinking to my newest year of life, falling off mechanical bulls, and dancing the night away. I talk to a girl there and she gives me her number. When midnight hits, we're heading to Lily Pad via several Ubers, and while there, I dance with a couple cute guys.

I don't feel any sort of excitement or searing attraction, but they're nice enough. One lingers around, offering to buy me a shot, and is more flirtatious than anybody has been in a while. I consider jumping head first and hoping that if I just give someone a chance, I'll wash Alek out of my system. Who's to say who or what he's been doing back in Chicago. Maybe he called that woman back and took her out. Maybe he found another closeted gay man to hook up with. The thought of either of those things makes my stomach roll.

At one-ten, I spot Ronan standing between Renzo's legs as Zo sits on a barstool, their arms wrapped around each other, lost in their own little lovers bubble. Trevor and Dominic are further down the bar, taking a shot together before collapsing into laughter and falling into each other. Dex left to go be with Violet around twelve-thirty, and Bryant and Ivy are on the dance floor together, making new friends.

"Hey, I think I'm gonna call it a night," I tell Zo and Ronan.

"You sure?" Renzo asks. "You okay?"

"I'm good. Feeling a headache coming on," I lie. "I think I'm just gonna go home and lay down, but I had a good time. Thanks for coming out."

"Yeah, man. Happy birthday. We'll see you tomorrow at the festival."

"Definitely."

I say bye to Bryant and Ivy before heading toward Trevor and Dom. "Hey guys. I'm gonna head back."

"Why? You okay?" Trevor asks.

"Yeah, just a headache."

"Okay, well, we'll be home later," Dom says.

"I'll probably be asleep. Don't worry, I have my earplugs."

"Fuck off," Dom says with a laugh.

"Thanks for tonight," I tell them before leaving, waiting outside the club until my Uber arrives.

As soon as I'm in the backseat of the black sedan, I drop my head back and close my eyes. Two minutes later my phone buzzes in my hand and I open my eyes to read the screen.

> Happy Birthday. Sorry I'm a little late.

I jolt up, my heart attempting to leave my body through my throat. I read the message three more times to make sure I'm not just drunk. Alek's texting me. After a month and a half.

> Thank you. I'll let it slide this once.

I deleted four variations of that text, unsure what to say. Should I have left it at *thank you*? Should I have asked him how he was, how he's been, and if he misses me like I miss him? Okay, that last one is a definite no.

> It won't happen again.

Good. So, how are you?

I'm okay. You?

Same. Okay.

A few minutes go by before he replies, and I stare at my screen the entire time.

No birthday plans?

I'm leaving a club now. Going home.

Well, I didn't mean to take up a lot of your time. I wanted to wish you a happy birthday and say congratulations on graduating. Luther tells me you're doing great at work.

You're asking Luther about me?

Of course. Keeping tabs on my employees.

All of them?

Just my favorites.

I smile at my phone, feeling an insane amount of happiness at just a few words.

How many favorites do you have?

One

A laugh escapes through my lips as my euphoria builds.

Nice to know.

Goodnight, Jay.

My smile drops at his abrupt goodbye and I don't reply until I'm inside the house.

Goodnight.

~

The music festival is pretty long, so I show up around three-thirty, shortly after it starts, and talk to a few people I know as well as make new friends with other festival goers. It's the extrovert in me.

Around five, I stand under the shade of a tree, talking to the other people who worked on marketing this festival before heading to a food stand and chatting with the girl working it.

Bryant finds me a little later, and we sit on the grass watching the bands for about an hour before I get up to find a bathroom. On the way there, I run into Linda and end up talking to her and her friend for half an hour as we browse the tables of local small businesses.

Once I'm done with the bathroom, I check my phone and read messages from Trevor and Renzo, telling me they're on their way. I go back to Alek's message thread and debate whether I should text him. I chew on my lip, my fingers hovering over the keys.

What are you doing?

On instinct, my head snaps up and my eyes roam the surrounding area, wondering if he's here. Was it just a coincidence?

I'm at the festival. You?

Ah. The festival. You enjoying yourself?

I guess.

He doesn't reply, so I slip the phone back in my pocket and find Trevor, Renzo, and Ronan shortly after. Trev tells me Dom had to work, and Dex and Violet are supposed to be heading over in a little bit.

The four of us grab some beers and squeeze into a spot near the main stage, staying there until we need more beers. At ten-thirty, Joel shows up with a friend of his, and I end up talking to him near some henna station where two teen girls are getting their hands done.

He's flirting with me, sticking close to my side and making sure to touch my arm or shoulder every so often. Renzo watches from several feet away as they scarf down some wings and raises his brows at me.

I shake my head and grin, focusing on Joel. He's a good guy. Attractive, and somebody I'd definitely give a chance to.

My phone vibrates in my pocket, and I expect some smart ass text from Zo when I pull it out and look at it.

I have a question.

Alek.

My pulse spikes for an unknown reason. Maybe it's because this means he's still thinking about me. He wants to talk and that has to mean something.

What's that?

Is it still mine?

A surge of excitement shoots through me and desire thrums in my veins when I read and reread his text. I hold my phone in both hands, fighting a smile as I stare at the screen, deciding how to respond.

Do you want it to be?

Just answer the question.

I laugh at the screen, glancing up to see Joel standing in front of me, talking to his friend. His eyes flicker to me, curiosity burning in his eyes.

"Sorry," I tell him. "Old friend."

He grins, giving me a slight nod.

Yes.

Then why are you talking to the man who wants to get into your pants?

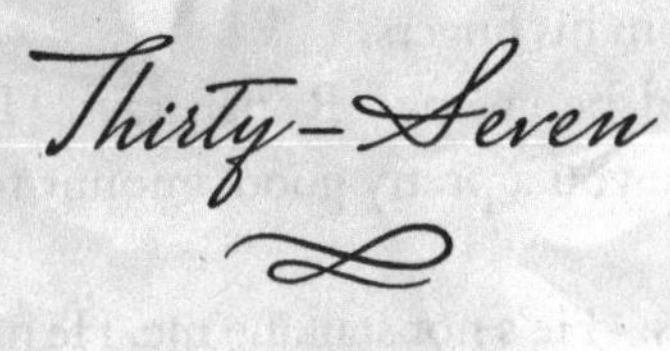

Thirty-Seven

JAYDEN

MY HEAD SNAPS UP, eyes scanning the area around me. He's here.

"I'll be back," I tell Joel before jogging toward my friends. "I think he's here."

"Who?" Trevor asks.

"Alek. He texted me and knew who I was talking to."

"What?" Trevor looks around even though I'm not sure he knows what he looks like. The only time he saw him, he was fairly drunk.

I keep spinning around, searching for his face in the crowd. It's packed, especially now that the headliners are about to start performing. He was close enough to see that I was talking to Joel, though.

Where are you?

He doesn't reply, and I'm left wondering where the hell he is. There's no way he'd know who I was talking to unless he was nearby.

"Maybe he has someone spying on you," Renzo offers as he licks sauce from his fingers.

"That would be creepy," Ronan says. "But also telling. He'd have to like you a pretty good amount to have someone stalk you."

I roll my eyes. "He's not stalking me. He must've come for the festival, but where the hell is he?"

As I study the faces in this little food court area, I notice Trevor and Ronan glance past me as Renzo stays focused on his food.

Before I can turn around completely, I hear his voice. "I'm right here."

My eyes widen, looking down at my friends who stare at him. I spin slowly, coming face to face with the man whose eyes have haunted my dreams, and whose touch I still crave.

"Looking for me?" he asks with a grin.

I smile back at him, my lips stretching wide across my face until my cheeks hurt. "Hi."

His head dips, a lopsided smile on display as those hypnotising eyes land on me. "Can we talk?"

"Yeah," I say with an eager nod. "Yeah, of course." I turn to my friends, who are unabashedly watching our interaction. "I'll be back."

Alek's hand lands on my back as we make our way through the tables until we reach the outskirts of the festival, hanging out behind all the tents and food carts.

Nerves twist in my stomach, and my first instinct is to be thrilled he's here, but I worry he's only in town for the festival and this conversation is only going to lead to another goodbye.

"You look good," I say, my eyes traveling up and down his frame.

Not in his usual suit, he's still not completely casual, wearing a pair of khaki-colored chinos and a light blue button-up shirt.

"Thanks," he replies, drinking me in with his eyes. "You too."

"What're you doing here?" I ask, cutting to the chase.

"A man can't come to a music festival?"

"Not one that lives eight hours away."

"I've missed you, Jay," he admits, stealing the air from my lungs.

"I've missed you, too," I reply immediately.

He releases a breath like he was afraid I wouldn't feel the same. "I've been going to therapy. She's really earning her money with my twice a week sessions."

I smirk. "I'm glad you're going."

"Me too." He inhales deeply, shoving his hands in his pockets. "I hate the way things ended. I'm not a man with many regrets, but I regret all the things I didn't do or say when it comes to you."

"I hate that that night was ruined by my dad. Have you talked to him at all?"

He shakes his head. "He's doing his best to ignore me."

"Figures."

"We have a lot to talk about. Are you willing to go out with me? Dinner maybe? Drinks?"

My eyebrows rise. "Dinner? Not to your hotel?"

Alek shakes his head, an amused smile on his lips. "I'm not trying to hide anymore."

"Wow. Well, of course I'll go out with you."

"Tomorrow? I know you're busy tonight."

My stomach drops. I don't want him to leave. I want to

spend the rest of the night with him. I want to sleep over and go back to the way it was before he went back to Chicago.

"Tomorrow works."

Alek smiles, stepping toward me. His knuckles graze my cheek as he stares into my eyes. "See you then. Please kindly tell Joel to fuck off."

I bark out a laugh as he strolls away.

When I get back to my friends, they look around, wondering where Alek is.

"Well? What's going on?" Renzo asks.

"He asked me to go out with him tomorrow since I was busy tonight."

"Busy? With us?" Trevor questions.

"Dude, go get him," Ronan says. "You're with us all the time. He came back here for you."

"Well, I don't know if that's true," I say.

"Go find out then," Renzo says.

"You sure?"

Zo rolls his eyes while Trevor scoffs. "Go."

"Y'all are the best. I'll be in touch," I say before running off, hoping I can catch up with him.

I pull my phone out, ready to call if I don't see him, but it's quite a walk before you get to the parking area and I spot him still making his way through the empty field.

"How about we have dinner tonight?" I ask as I walk up alongside him.

Surprise transforms into delight when he sees me. "Sure. Want a ride?"

"On the first date?"

He smirks. "I'll be a gentleman."

"Mm. Too bad."

Thirty-Eight

ALEKSANDER

WE SIT across from each other in a small booth at a local place called Nicola's Pizza. There's a handful of patrons, but Jay asks the guy to seat us in a corner away from most of them, allowing us some privacy.

"Connections?" I ask, quirking a brow.

"Oh, baby. I have connections all over this town," Jay teases. "But really, I just know a lot of people, plus I come here pretty often."

I nod and glance at the menu. When my eyes flicker up, Jay's watching me.

"Don't need to look at the menu?"

"Nope. I always get the same thing."

"You don't want to try anything new?"

"Why stray from something I know I already enjoy?" He cocks a brow, seemingly talking about more than pizza.

"Hmm. Well, just get a large of whatever you usually get, and I'll share."

We don't say much until the waiter's already taken our order and dropped off our drinks. When we know he'll be gone a little while, Jay speaks up first.

"So, you in town for the festival?"

"Partially," I admit.

"And the other part?"

My lips twitch, pulling into a grin. "I think you know."

"I don't know anything, if I'm being honest," he says. "I know what I hope, but considering I haven't heard from you in almost two months..." he trails off, shrugging his shoulders.

"I wanted to call you. I brought your name up on my phone more times than I can count, but I knew that if we talked, I had nothing to offer you. What could I say?"

"Anything. I would've taken anything over nothing."

"I'm sorry. I wanted to be better. You made me want to be a better person. I had to work on myself, and I still have a ways to go, but I couldn't let even more time go by. I kept thinking you'd find somebody else soon."

His eyes widen slightly upon hearing my truth. "You haven't been dating?"

I shake my head. "No. You?"

"No."

The sense of relief I feel is immediate and the smile on my face portrays that. "It's really good to see you."

His lips draw into a bright smile. "Why didn't you tell me yesterday that you were gonna be here?"

"I felt like wishing you a happy birthday was a good excuse to reach out, and thought if you didn't want to hear from me, you would've either ignored me or told me to fuck off. When you replied, I decided I'd make contact with you today."

"You were afraid I was going to be mad at you? Did you forget the last thing I said?"

I shake my head. "It plays over and over in my head constantly."

"I meant it. I wouldn't change anything."

Stretching my arm across the table, I take his hand in mine. "Jay, I'd change almost everything."

His brows dip in the middle. "What do you mean?"

"When we started, I said everything we'd do would be whatever I'd allow. I never gave you a chance. I was selfish in my refusal of certain things. I should've treated you better, even if you were just supposed to be a fuck buddy. You were right. I didn't treat you like a person with feelings. I was only concerned about myself."

"Alek," he cuts in. "I wasn't aware of why you were the way you were. I wouldn't have said those things had I known."

"It doesn't matter. I was wrong, and every day since I left, I've regretted not being better for you. You went above and beyond and I remained stuck in my ways. You're one of the nicest people I've met and you deserved better."

"You're acting like I wasn't happy. I was. I loved being with you. It was the first time," he pauses, swallowing while staring into my eyes, "I had met someone who didn't bore me. Being with you was always exciting, even if we were just eating while watching TV. It was the first time I didn't have the urge to get up and run away, needing to find my friends or something else to do."

The waiter appears, so we pull our hands back and let him put the pizza on the table between us. "Let me know if you need anything," he says before leaving.

"Anyway, that's what I mean when I say I'd change things. I'd want us to be equal and not just me controlling how we do everything. I'd be less afraid. I'd try more. I'd be better."

Jay rubs a finger over his bottom lip. "Are you saying you want to try again? You want something more this time around?"

I dip my head. "If you want to."

"How would that work? My dad. Our location."

"If you want it to work, I'll find a way to make it."

His lips quirk up slightly. "Let's do it."

My heart nearly leaps into my throat. "Okay."

We finish our dinner, and I drive him back to the music festival where his car is parked. It's cleared out quite a bit, but there's still plenty of people lingering.

"How long are you in town for?" he asks.

"I don't need to be back until Tuesday."

"Okay. Do you want to get together tomorrow?"

"Of course I do," I reply with a smile. "You're why I'm here."

His face lights up. "Okay. Well, I guess I'll text you tomorrow?"

I nod. "Okay."

He leans forward slightly before stopping himself. "Um."

Leaning over, I place my hand on the side of his neck and gently press my lips to his. When I ease back, I stare into his eyes for several seconds while my thumb caresses his skin. "Goodnight."

"G'night," he says huskily.

It takes everything in me to not demand he come back to the hotel with me. I'm desperate to feel him, kiss him, and merge our bodies into one as we succumb to our sexual desires. But I don't want our second chance to be the way it was before. Last time it was only about sex. I want him to know I want and care about more than that.

He looks back at me twice before he gets into his car and drives away.

Thirty-Nine

ALEKSANDER

JAY CALLS me around noon on Saturday and gives me the address to where he's staying, so I pick him up, and together we drive to a sandwich and salad shop, properly titled S & S. There, we pick up a couple to-go salads, club sandwiches, and fruit cups. We take our food along with a couple bottled drinks with us back to the car, and I drive out to Lake Renap upon his insistence.

"It's the nicest park here," he says. "They have picnic tables and a walking trail that circles the entire lake."

We take our food to one of the empty tables and enjoy our park lunch date under the hot summer sun.

"How's work?" I ask him.

He grins. "I'm enjoying it. It was a smooth transition from intern to employee. My new boss is not nearly as attractive as my last one."

With a smile, I say, "Technically, I'm still your boss."

"Should I call you sir?"

I arch a brow. "If you want to."

He snickers, digging into his salad. "How's the other branch?"

227

"It's doing fine. I'm thinking of appointing someone to take my place."

"What?" he exclaims.

"It'll still be my company, but I can get someone to act as CEO in my absence."

"Absence?"

I smirk at him. "Right. If I were to leave Chicago."

"You'd leave…" He trails off while his thoughts spin in his brain. "You're thinking of leaving Chicago and stepping down as CEO to be here? With me?"

"It's an hour and a half flight. I can go between here and there pretty easily, and the company is still my main focus, but there are tons of qualified CEOs."

"Does that mean you'd take your job back here?"

I shake my head. "No. Luther will remain where he is. Of course, I'll be aware of everything, but I can work from home. I've spent a long time working myself to the bone, needing to be involved in every single aspect, but I can focus on the bigger things while the CEO works on everything else. I'm not losing money."

He chuckles. "Right. I bet not. So, you're moving here?"

I nod, watching him carefully. "We can't have a proper chance if I don't, and I wouldn't ask you to move to Chicago when you're just starting out."

"Wow. Alek, that's incredibly selfless."

"It's about time, right?"

He makes a face. "So, I guess that will solve one problem, but we still have another."

I pin my lips together and nod. "How do you feel about that? Possibly ruining your relationship with your father?"

"If he can't love me because of who I choose to be with, then that's on him, right? He can't think I'd pick my partner based on how he feels about it." He takes a drink of his lemonade before capping the bottle and putting it down. "Plus, we've been fine. There've been many phone calls and FaceTime conversations with him and my mom, and everything seems to be normal. He isn't acting pissed at me anymore. Maybe he's calmed down."

"We'll need to talk to him."

He nods. "Yeah."

"Until then, let's talk about other things," he says with a smile. "I move into my own apartment in a couple weeks."

"That's good. Your first time living alone, right?"

"Yeah, I'm probably gonna hate it. I enjoyed the noise in the frat house. I like knowing someone is always around. There's always someone to talk to. The silence bothers me, but I gotta grow up, right?" he says with a chuckle.

Once we finish our meal and throw our trash away, I grab his hand in mine and we walk along the trail, enjoying the shade from the large trees that surround us.

Jay looks at our joined hands and smiles, glancing up at me. "You out?"

I shrug. "I guess so. I don't know many people here, so it's not like I've had to tell anyone. Luther already knows."

"He does?"

"Yeah. I didn't get the chance to tell you, but he seemed to be onto us. He confronted me about it."

Jay hisses. "Was he pissed?"

"No," I reply, shaking my head. "He was quite supportive."

"Wow, that's crazy."

"I never felt the need to have a coming out moment because I was never with anyone for a long time, or in public. I didn't think I'd ever be able to be in an actual relationship with a man, so it wasn't necessary. But I want you to know that I really like you and I'm not trying to keep what we do behind closed doors anymore."

He smiles, blissfully happy, and leans over and kisses my neck like he used to. "Therapy for the win."

I laugh. "Yeah, I'll have to find a new one here, or maybe mine in Chicago will allow me to have sessions with her over Zoom. She already knows all my baggage and history."

"I'm really proud of you, you know? A lot of people are afraid to go to therapy, but you seem to be getting a lot out of it."

"I don't think mental health should be a taboo topic. We all deal with our own issues, and though some might be more serious than others, I think it's nice to be able to have a non-judgmental person listen to you and offer you advice and help."

"I agree."

"I don't know when it happened, but I think it was within our last month together that I realized I was starting to form attachments to you. I wanted more, but I held back for several reasons, and I hate myself for that. However, the phrase, *absence makes the heart grow fonder* seems to be true. Our separation really helped me realize just how much I enjoyed our time together. Sometimes you don't know until you don't have it anymore."

"God," he says with glee, a huge smile in place, "I didn't know you had this whole other side to you." He stops walking, standing in front of me and placing his hands on my hips. "And as much as I'm enjoying it, I still hope my bossy, demanding Alek is still in there, because I think I really liked that side, too." He bites his lip as he watches me.

I circle his wrist with my fingers and tug him off the trail and up against a nearby tree with a thick trunk that'll hide us from prying eyes. I pin my hips against his as my thumb brushes against his soft lips before I push it between them.

"Suck it."

He does, twirling his tongue around my digit. "Mm."

"Just because I can admit my feelings for you doesn't mean I don't want to force you to your knees and shove my cock between your lips. You've always looked so good with my dick in your mouth," I say with a smirk.

He moans, dragging his teeth against my thumb as he pulls off. "You still owe me a balcony fuck."

"I owe you a lot," I admit. With my hand moving to his growing erection, I lean in and kiss the spot below his earlobe before I whisper, "I can't wait to find out what you taste like."

"Oh fuck," he groans.

After we leave the lake, I take Jay to a movie and then we eat dinner before I drop him back off at his friends' house. I see the disappointment in his face when I don't invite him to my hotel.

"I want you as much as you want me," I tell him while we're parked outside the house. "I just don't want to do things the way we did last time. Let me woo you. Date you. I've never done it before and you deserve it more than anyone."

He can't help but smile. "Well, when you say it that way."

I lean across the console and grab his face, kissing him. I let my lips linger and barely touch my tongue to the seam of his lips before giving him another peck. "FaceTime me later."

"Is that a demand?"

"Yes. Be in your bed when you do."

He bites his lip. "Okay."

"Good. Now go."

"Yes, sir," he teases before stepping out of the car and strutting to the front door.

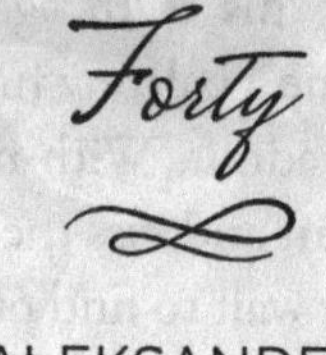

Forty

ALEKSANDER

ON SUNDAY, I don't see Jay until almost five o'clock, as
he had plans with his friends that were set before I decided to
come into town. He offered to ditch them, but I told him it
wasn't necessary. I was able to get a session in with my therapist over Zoom, so everything worked out well.

At four-fifty, my phone buzzes with a text from Jay.

Same hotel?

Yeah.

Same room?

No. Same floor. Are you planning on
coming over?

Yes, because you won't invite me over, so
I'm inviting myself.

My excitement grows knowing he's on the way. We'll be alone, in a private space, with beds, couches, and balconies at our disposal. I'm not sure how much self-control I'll have.

Five minutes later, Jay lets me know he's getting on the elevator. Forty seconds after that, the doors are opening as I lean against the wall and wait. Three seconds and three strides later, Jay cradles my face in his hands as he devours my mouth in a passionate kiss.

When he finally pulls away almost a full minute later, we're both breathing heavily, our cocks hardening against each other.

"Wow," I say on a breath.

"I missed you."

"Eager to see what you'll do when you see me when I come back."

We walk to my room, shoulders brushing. "How long will you be gone for?"

"Not sure. I have interviews set up when I get back. I'm seeing a few CEOs and taking care of some other business. I was thinking maybe I'd talk to your dad then, too."

He makes a face. "Maybe I should ease him into this."

"Whatever you think will work best." I unlock and open the door. "I can fly you out next weekend. Then you can do it in person, and maybe we can all discuss it."

"You'd do that?"

"Of course."

As soon as the door closes behind us, he pounces, kissing me again. We fight for control, my tongue plunging into his mouth and then him sucking on it like it's a candy.

"I'm trying to take things slow," I say through heavy breaths.

He unbuttons my shirt, kissing my neck and chest. "Alek, I'm wooed, okay? I like you." He rips my shirt off, moving to my pants. "I *really* like you, and it's been nearly two months since I've had sex, and I need you."

Any sort of control I was clinging to is ripped away when he says he needs me. I pull his shirt up over his head, throwing it to the side, and then both of us shove our pants to our ankles, kicking out of our shoes and remaining clothes in a frenzied rush.

While we touch and grope, our mouths come together in a rough kiss all while we walk through the room, heading to the bedroom. I bite on his bottom lip, eliciting a hiss from his throat, then he plunges his tongue into my mouth.

In the room, I back him into the mattress until he falls back, sprawling across the covers, his hand going to his dick, stroking it as he watches me.

I get on my knees, straddling him as I lean over, giving him a soft kiss. "I want to taste you."

His lips quirk up. "I've been waiting to hear those words for a long time."

Chewing on my bottom lip, I study him, trepidation creeping up. "I may not be the best."

Jay reaches up and cradles my cheek. "You already are. Don't worry."

I lower myself, making my way down his muscled body, leaving small kisses across his chest and stomach until his cock is in view.

Taking it in my hand first, I give him a few strokes before dropping my head and opening my mouth. I lick around his crown first before encircling it with my lips.

"Ah, yeah," he moans.

I move lower, taking him deeper in my mouth, reveling in

the hard cock wrapped in velvety soft skin sliding across my tongue.

He's so big. I stretch my lips around his wide shaft as I attempt to get as much of him into my mouth as I can.

"Yes, baby," he whispers, his fingers combing through my hair. "Fuck, that feels good."

Spurred on by his words, I keep going. I suck, bobbing up and down as my hand stays wrapped around his base, pumping it at the same time.

"God," he murmurs, his hips lifting off the mattress, pushing his dick deeper into my mouth. "Alek."

His words and moans keep me motivated. I want nothing more than to make him feel good. To give him this pleasure.

I focus my tongue around his tip, stroking his dick with fervor until he's tensing up. "I'm gonna come if you don't stop," he breathes. "And I really want to come with you inside me."

Pulling off, I wipe my lips and move to grab the lube. When I'm back at the bed, I drop to my knees on the floor and pull him down by the legs until his ass is on the edge. Without any words, I lean in and swipe my tongue over his perineum before letting it travel lower.

He gasps. "Oh shit. You're gonna kill me."

I flick my tongue up and down a few more times before squeezing lube onto my fingers and gently massaging his hole. I take my time stretching him, loving his moans and grunts and the visual of him stroking his cock.

When I stand up, he scoots back enough to give me room, and then I hook a leg over my arm as I guide my dick into his entrance.

My crown disappears, and we both release grunts of pleasure. Once I slide all the way in, I rock back and forth slowly, giving him time to adapt to my size before I pick up speed and thrust harder.

"Yes," he cries. "Yes, give it to me."

I bury myself in him, giving into my carnal desires. I've thought about this moment almost every single day since I left. This, and having the roles reversed, but I suppose we'll get there.

"You like that?" I ask, pushing deeper.

"God, yes," he moans.

"Did you miss me? Miss my dick?"

"Fuck, I missed everything. Alek, oh my God," he bellows.

"Yeah, baby. I love when you scream my name."

He whimpers. "Fuck."

Jay wraps his hand around his dick, stroking vigorously as I plunge in and out, deep and steady.

"Make a mess for me," I whisper huskily. "I want to see it."

"Oh yeah." He closes his eyes briefly, his perfect, sculpted body flexing with his movements. With a gasp, his eyes pop open and his jaw drops. "I'm about to come."

I take my speed up a notch, already feeling the beginnings of my orgasm building, my balls drawing up. My nostrils flare as my gaze stays trained on his cock, and when his release shoots out, landing on his stomach, I envy the flesh. I want it in my mouth, on my skin.

"Fuck!" he roars, drawing the word out as his body convulses.

I watch him come apart, his face contorted with absolute bliss and his cum painting his skin, and then his dark eyes meet mine. His lips are parted as he sucks in air, and it's the sexiest fucking thing I've ever seen. He's perfect.

"Oh shit," I gasp, my climax coming in fast as I enjoy the vision below me. "Oh. Fuck. Jay. God," I cry, punctuating each word with a thrust before I release deep inside him.

"Yes," he mewls, his hands gripping my biceps.

When my body is spent, I collapse on top of him,

breathing heavily. He caresses my shoulders, back, and ass, his fingertips dragging up and down.

"God, that was good," he says on a breath.

I force myself up and look into his eyes. A million different thoughts bounce around in my head, but I just lower my mouth to his in a soft kiss before slowly pulling out of him.

"It's still early," I say as I walk toward the bathroom. "Maybe we can visit the balcony later."

He chuckles. "I won't say no to that."

Forty-One

ALEKSANDER

MY TIME in Michigan went by too quickly, but being in Chicago again means more steps closer to permanently being in the same town as him.

We've already chosen a new CEO, so the transition period starts now. I've taken care of almost everything I need to, even if that means delegating certain tasks to people I know can handle them. I'll be readily available for any problems that arise, but I've made it to where the company can run without me needing to be a constant presence.

However, it's already the weekend and Jay's here to help break the news to his parents about our relationship. I hope Cal will take it well, and I hate the idea that it could impact their relationship, but I have high hopes that he'll love his son enough to move past any issue he has. He has to have heard about there being a new CEO, so I'm sure he has questions, but he's done his best to avoid me since returning to work.

I leave the office for the day and make my way back to my place where I know Jay awaits. I wasn't able to get away to get him when he landed, but I gave him my address and instructed the doorman that he was to be let inside.

When I open the door, I don't see him right away, but after removing my jacket and dropping my briefcase on the couch, I spot him looking out the floor-to-ceiling window.

When he hears my steps, his head swivels, and a grin stretches across his face when he sees me.

"This view is incredible."

"It is," I reply, not talking about the city or Lake Michigan.

He spins, his back against the glass as I trap him between my arms, pushing my body into his as I kiss him like I haven't seen him in years rather than days.

Jay cups my ass through my pants, moaning into my mouth before pulling away. "Happy to see me, boss?"

I thrust my hips into him. "Can't you tell?"

He smirks before turning around, pushing his ass against me. "But really, this view." His head angles over his shoulder. "Too bad there's not a balcony. We could bless it."

"There's a terrace pool a little lower, but it doesn't offer as much privacy," I reply, resting my chin on his shoulder. "How was your flight?"

"It was good. Also, I don't think you should be able to call this an apartment. I wasn't expecting so much opulence."

I chuckle. "Have you talked to your parents yet?"

"Yeah. They know I'm here. They're expecting me in an hour."

"You ready?"

"I think they're already suspicious, but yeah, I'm ready. Do you want to come?"

I step back and then lean against the window as I watch him. "I'm not sure if that's the best idea. Maybe you can soften them up first."

He chuckles. "Just drop me off and linger around in case the coast is clear."

With another kiss, I say, "Okay. Whatever you say."

"Mm," he murmurs, an eyebrow perfectly arched as his fingers dip into my waistband and yank me forward. "I might like that game."

"Maybe we'll get to play later. I guess we should get ready to go."

He sighs. "Fine, let's get this over with."

After a quick shower, we travel down the sixteen floors of this building in the elevator and make our way to my car. Traffic makes the trip about forty minutes, but we still manage to arrive with five minutes to spare. I park around the corner from his parents place, choosing to sit inside a coffee shop while Jay goes ahead. Only a few minutes go by before he's back, stepping inside the small café, eyes landing on me.

"What's wrong?" I ask, standing up.

"Nothing. I want you with me. Let's do this together and face it together."

"You sure?"

He nods. "Yeah."

I take a deep breath. "Okay."

I won't lie, my heart pounds a little as we make our way up the street, passing multiple townhomes before we get to theirs.

"Ready?" he asks before knocking on the door.

"As I'll ever be."

The door opens, his mother's face coming into view, a large smile stretching her lips until she spots me. It drops briefly before she gets it back—this time, more tense. "Oh," she says simply, her eyes bouncing between us.

"Hey, Mom," Jay greets.

Her friendly smile is back as she opens her arms to bring

him in for a hug. "Hi, baby. I'm so happy to see you. This is quite the surprise."

"Yeah," he says, pulling back. "Is Dad here?"

Her eyes find mine again before she nods. "Yeah. Come on in, Aleksander," she says with a grin. "It's good to see you again."

"You too, Caroline. Thank you."

I don't think that she's too unhappy that I'm here. It seems to be mostly surprise and hesitancy because she isn't sure how Cal will react.

We follow her through the house, passing the dining room and bypassing the long, narrow kitchen before entering their cozy living room.

"Have a seat," she says, gesturing to the couch. "I'll go get him."

As she heads upstairs, Jay rubs his palms over his jeans, glancing at me. "Mom was never really the issue."

I nod, and then the clicking of footsteps descending the stairs gets my attention. Caroline gives us a smile, but Cal is emotionless when he spots us.

He puts whatever he might be feeling aside to hug and greet his son, and I stand up alongside him, but he doesn't extend his hand for a shake.

Jay's parents sit across from us in the loveseat, clearly awaiting some sort of announcement. When nobody says anything for what feels like an eternity, Caroline speaks up.

"So, what's going on? This is a surprise," she says, gesturing between us.

She doesn't look angry at all, just curious. Cal, on the other hand, remains fairly stoic, but something in his expression tells me he knows what this is about. After all, why would we be here together after all this time?

"Well," Jay starts, "I wanted to tell you guys about me and

Alek. We're going to be together, and I didn't want to have to hide that from you."

Caroline nods absently as she stares at her son. My eyes flicker to Cal.

"I have to tell you, I'm stepping down as CEO. The company remains mine, and all the work I do won't be done from either building."

Jay's mom's eyes widen. "So, you're moving to Michigan?"

I nod. "I am. It'll take a little time, but in order to give this a real chance, it's the only way. I wouldn't ask Jay to give up his job as he's just starting out."

She grants me a little smile before looking at her son. "This is serious then."

"You were right. It did matter to me," Jay tells her, referencing a conversation I wasn't a part of. "The separation really put that in perspective."

Cal remains silent, hands clasped as he watches the three of us talk.

"Dad, I know how you felt when you found out, but as I hope you can see, this is more than just a fling. Yes, it started out that way, and I didn't anticipate actually falling for him, but I did. Nothing we're doing now is inappropriate. He's giving up a role in his own company and moving his life to another state, and I think that shows a lot. I hope you can understand that this is something we both want and hope to grow into something more. I'm sorry I happened to fall for your friend, but since you did like him enough to consider him one, you should know he's a good guy."

"Cal," I say, jumping in. "Caroline, you too. I want you both to know that I really care about Jay, and I can admit he's probably too good for me, but I'll do everything I can to be better and to earn the right to be with him." Jay's hand lands on my knee, giving me a squeeze. I meet his gaze momentarily, smiling at him. "Our age difference has never been a huge concern or anything we felt we needed to devote a lot of time to. It's obvious I'm older, but he's such a brilliant and confident man, and I think I can speak for him when I say I don't believe he ever felt like I was taking advantage of him."

"I can put him in his place if I need to," he teases with a grin.

"Well," Caroline says, glancing back at her husband while she rests her hand on his leg. "I think it's very admirable to make such drastic changes for our son, Alek. I can appreciate the effort you're putting into this, and he must mean a lot to you to do so. Especially considering you aren't sure how this may turn out."

I nod.

"I figured something like this was coming," Cal finally says, breaking his silence. "I knew you were hiring a CEO, and as soon as we got the call that Jay was in town, I put two and two together." He sighs, running a hand over his beard. "I know I never allowed another moment for you to talk about Alek and what was going on between you, but I knew that night that it was more than a fling. I could see it in your reaction to him leaving. I could read it on your face for the rest of that week. You were affected heavily."

Everyone sits in silence for a while, unsure of what to say, or where to go from here. He isn't exactly excited, but he's far less upset than that night in my hotel room.

"I only care that you're happy," Caroline tells Jay. "You know that. I've never cared about who you chose to spend your time with, I just wanted you to be happy. If being with Aleksander is what brings you happiness, I'm fine with that." She turns to me. "My kids are my whole world, and I wish I could protect them forever, but he's a grown man capable of making his own decisions. If he chooses to be with you, I trust he knows what he's doing and I hope that you'll protect his heart to the best of your ability. Just as I hope he does the same for you."

"I appreciate that, Caroline. Thank you."

"You have to understand how taken aback I was," Cal says. "I never would've guessed, and yes, it's probably more so because you were my friend and less about age. The boss and employee dynamic bothered me because I know how it can be for young employees to feel like they have to do certain things if the boss that they're sleeping with says so. The power imbalance is why those types of relationships aren't allowed, but I guess I should've known my son better."

"I tried explaining that he wasn't taking advantage. He attempted to do the right thing but I was the one who kept after him. Yes, he gave in, but I'm pretty charming," Jay says with a smile.

His mom makes a face, but her lips quirk into a grin anyway.

"Well, this is your decision," Cal says. "I hope everything works out the way you want it. You're right, you're both adults and I don't have a say in your personal life, but like I said, I was just blindsided and didn't know how to react."

Caroline pats his knee, a small smile on her face.

"Thanks, Dad," Jay says, standing up to give both his parents another hug.

Caroline embraces me, and Cal shakes my hand. He doesn't look at me the same as he used to, but I supposed the knowledge of your friend fucking your kid probably changes things a bit. I can't blame him. I still feel a slight tinge of awkwardness around them both.

After a while, Cal offers me a drink, and Caroline whips up a quick meal. Jayden's sister comes home shortly after and gets caught up to speed fairly quickly, and is the only one who's the least bit concerned.

A couple hours later, we leave their house feeling a lot lighter, and make our way back to my home with smiles on our faces and lots to look forward to.

Forty-Two

ALEKSANDER

I miss you. When are you moving again?
Tomorrow?

I wish. I'll be there soon, baby.

IT'S BEEN three weeks since Jay was here in Chicago. There's been a lot of FaceTime calls and countless texts. I've been using this time to finish all business related work I need to, find a place to live in Michigan, and hire a company to pack and ship all of my belongings.

We decided we wouldn't attempt to live together right away. We want to give this the time and space a normal relationship would have. It's not like we've been together a long time, but I have a feeling living with Jay would be easy.

Question. Do you want to FaceTime
tonight?

Why would that ever be a question?

Okay. Another question. Do you want to give me a strip tease while we're on FaceTime? I miss a certain part of you.

We just had video phone sex two days ago.

I'm a fiend.

Call me, but you better already be naked.

Yessir!

Five weeks since I've seen Jay and I'm starting to go crazy. I've finally secured a place to live, thanks to a lot of phone calls and video chats with a realtor and the help of Jay. He's been my proxy, checking out the apartments in my stead. My furniture is set to ship out in a few days. We're getting closer.

While it's been hard to be away from him for such a long time, we've definitely learned a lot more about each other through all the late night phone calls.

My friends want to meet you. Are you ready for that?

You make it sound like I should be afraid.

You never know.

Of course I want to meet them. They're important to you.

So are you.

I drive into Michigan on an early Friday afternoon and get the keys to my apartment. My furniture is already in storage here, so I call the moving company I've previously been in contact with and meet them at the facility. A few hours later, everything that'll fit in this condo is unloaded and placed in my new home. There's still quite a bit that'll sit in storage until I move into a larger place, but a two bedroom condo is all I need. While that's what I had in Chicago, this one is a little smaller.

Jay's still at work and has no idea I'm in town, considering I told him I'd be in tomorrow. So after I unpack a few boxes, I take a shower and drive over to MGD.

I lean against the side of my car in the parking lot, hands in my pockets with one foot crossed over the other, and watch as he exits the building with two other people. Lost in conversation, he doesn't look in my direction right away. I can't help the smile that forms on my face as I watch him. He glances up briefly, then does a double-take. The sun is bright, and he brings his hand up over his brow, squinting in my direction.

"Oh shit," he exclaims before he jogs across the parking lot with a huge grin on his face.

As he gets closer, I stand up and brace for his large body to slam into me. He wraps his arms around my back, laughing as we embrace.

"You fucking sneaky ass. Why didn't you tell me?"

"I wanted to surprise you."

He pulls away just enough for us to be able to kiss, our lips coming together in a succession of quick pecks before I slide my tongue into his mouth, desperate to get a taste of him.

"God, I'm so glad you're here. I almost can't believe it."

"I'm here," I tell him, running a knuckle from his temple to his chin, capturing it between my fingers before I place another kiss on his lips. "Want to come to my place? We can order some dinner."

"Sounds perfect. I'll follow you."

He moves to walk away but I grasp his hand and yank him back into me. "I'm not ready to let go yet."

Later that night, after he's helped me unpack some more boxes, and we've had our dinner, we sit together on the loveseat without a TV to watch since the cable isn't connected yet.

"It started to feel like this was never gonna happen," he says. "I can't believe you live here now."

"Me either, but it already feels like home."

He gazes up at me, his head in my lap as his long legs drape over the side. "Tomorrow, my friends are coming over to my apartment for dinner and drinks. You have to come, meet them, woo them, make them love you."

"And if they hate me?"

"They won't. Not possible. But on the off chance that they do, it doesn't matter. I like you."

I run my hand over his head. "Then I'll turn on my charm. Make sure they do."

"Well, don't be too charming. Four of them are gay. They may try to steal you from me."

I chuckle. "Aren't they in relationships with each other?"

"Yeah, but you're definitely *leave my relationship* worthy."

I shake my head. "It's a good thing I only want you then."

His lips part. "Okay," he says, standing up and reaching

for my hand. "I can't restrain myself any longer. Let's go to your room. I have some things I need to do."

"Good thing I made sure to get the room as set up as possible," I say as we make our way down the hall.

We're not in the bedroom for more than fifteen seconds before we're both ripping clothes off each other, falling into the bed mostly naked.

Our bodies lie side by side, facing each other as we kiss and touch. Jay moves quickly, pushing me onto my back as he kisses across my torso, dragging his tongue across the scars I got when I was a teenager—attacked for being who I was. And now I have him and he gives me nothing but pleasure.

His lips travel lower, and after he's pulled my boxer-briefs down, his hand wraps around my erection and then I'm enveloped in his warm, wet mouth.

Jay moans as he tastes me, quickly bringing me to the precipice of bliss with his skilled hands and tongue.

"Wait," I manage to get out between heavy breaths.

He looks up, dragging his mouth from my cock but continuing to give me languid strokes. "Mm?"

"I..." I prop up on my elbows, staring down at him. "I want to try more."

His brows draw in. He's clearly aware we've already been down the kissing road, and I've sucked him off three times now. There's only one other thing we haven't done.

"Are you sure?"

I nod. "I've been preparing. I've had a lot of alone time."

His lips quirk up. "Okay."

He disappears to grab the lube from the dresser and he's back between my legs in no time. I've thought about us getting to this moment for a long time. I've been curious about it. I want to feel him inside me and give myself to him in a way that almost nobody's had. The only time I attempted this was when my Dad caught us, and it had barely started before everything went to hell.

I know Jay switches, but from some of our previous conversations, he was mostly a top, and I feel bad for being selfish.

"You ready?" he asks. "I'm about to blow your mind."

I barely get a response out before his tongue is dancing over my balls and traveling to my ass. His large hands hold my thighs up and apart as he tongues my hole, making fireworks explode behind my eyelids.

"Holy fuck," I gasp, grabbing onto the covers.

He moans, using that magical tongue to do deliciously dirty things to my body. Jay absolutely devours me, switching from poking and prodding to flattening his tongue and licking a long path up and down.

"Jesus," I cry, unable to process what I'm feeling. It's a unique sensation, but it feels so fucking good.

When he stops, I take a second to breathe, but then I hear the cap open on the bottle of lube. My gaze connects with his as he pours some onto his fingers.

"You trust me?"

I nod.

His fingers slide between my cheeks, but he uses his other hand to grab my cock and lowers his mouth over the crown, giving me something else to focus on while his slick fingers push against my hole.

"Oh shit," I gasp. "Jay. Oh God."

"I got you, baby. I'm gonna make you feel so good."

One finger tip pushes inside me, stealing my air. He pauses before he inserts it the rest of the way, using small movements to thrust in and out.

My eyes roll into the back of my head as I pull on my hair, gasping and moaning.

After a while, he drizzles some more lube on his finger and

my ass, and begins to push a second digit inside.

"Oh, God," I cry.

He continues his slow movements while he sucks my cock back into his mouth. Gradually, his fingers push in harder and faster, and he starts spreading them slightly, stretching me. After he's able to get three fingers in, my cock throbs with the need to release.

"Jay, please," I beg. I feel overwhelmed and desperate.

He removes his fingers and quickly coats his cock with the slippery liquid before spreading more around my entrance.

"I'm gonna go slow, but let me know when you want me to stop."

I bite my lip and nod. "Okay."

His wide crown prods at my entrance and I instantly clench up.

"Relax, baby," he says softly, rubbing a hand over my hip. "I've been dying for this. To know what you feel like on the inside." He moans as he pushes in a little more. "Fuck."

"Ah!" I exclaim as his tip pushes in, bringing with it a slight burning sensation.

"Oh God," he groans. "So fucking tight."

Another minute later, he's fully seated, his massive cock filling me up.

He rotates his hips, ripping a moan from my throat before he lowers his body, hovering over me.

"You feel incredible," he whispers, kissing me.

I wrap my hands around the back of his neck, forcing him to stay there, plunging my tongue into his mouth. I focus on the kiss as he rocks his hips back and forth, plunging in and out of me.

A few minutes later, he eases back, and probably for my benefit more than anything, he squirts more lube on his cock before he pushes back in.

"Watching my cock disappear into your ass is so fucking

hot. You're squeezing the hell out of me. I love it."

"God, Jay," I moan. "It's so good. So big. Fuck. I don't know what I'm saying."

His hand grips my cock, stroking it while continuing to fuck me. Both sensations are insane. My body is on fire, my brain misfiring, unable to come up with cohesive sentences to explain how it feels incredible, even with the bite of pain. I'm so full and ready to explode. His hand swirls around my crown before traveling down my shaft. His movements come faster, pushing harder, and I grunt through the pain, enjoying the pleasure that comes with it.

Jay's face contorts as his breaths come in hard pants. "Stroke it, baby," he directs me.

I take over, jerking my dick as he chases his orgasm, using my body to get there.

"Oh, yes, yes," I chant, my muscles tense as my climax gets closer and closer.

"I'm gonna come," he says. "Fuck, Alek. I'm gonna come deep inside you. Mark you. Make you mine."

I cry out, and when his back bows and his cock twitches inside me, I detonate.

His cum shoots inside me while I explode all over my hand and stomach. With quivering breaths, we endure the aftershocks of our orgasms, bodies quaking and sweat dripping.

Jay pulls out slowly, and I grimace when he comes free. He's gone briefly, searching my bathroom for the small items we unpacked earlier. He comes back with a cloth, but instead of handing it to me, he wipes the mess himself.

"That was..." he pauses, looking at me. "I have no words. Thank you for trusting me."

I prop myself up on my elbow and reach for his neck, bringing him back in for a kiss. "Thank you for opening my eyes to so much."

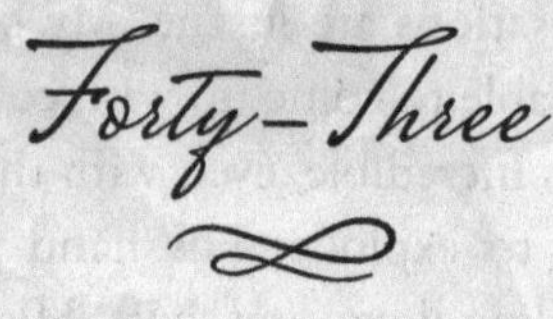

JAYDEN

"I THINK I LOVE HIM."

The room explodes. Renzo, Trevor, Dom, Dex, and even Ronan, who's generally pretty quiet, create a ruckus in my small apartment when the words leave my mouth.

"Are you kidding me?"

"For real?"

"Are you just in a sex daze?"

"It's about time!"

"Holy shit."

I make a face at all of them. "Okay, it's not that crazy."

"He just got into town," Renzo says.

"Right, but we've been talking on the phone for over five weeks. Every. Single. Day. Before that, we spent nearly two months together, either physically together, or again, on the phone. So it's not just sex. I know him. He's opened up so much to me. We developed this amazing friendship."

"The age difference doesn't bother you?" Ronan asks.

"No. I hardly think about it. I guess you can tell we're not the same age, if only because he mainly dresses in suits and I'm still a jeans type of guy, but it's not like he's got white hair and wrinkles. He's in his early forties, which is hardly old. Just older than us. And he's so fucking hot it makes me sick. People will trip all over themselves to get a piece."

They laugh at that.

"So, are you gonna tell him?" Dom asks.

"No!" I drag the word out as I arrange dishes on my kitchen counter. "No way. I'm not about to freak him out."

A knock on the door has me scrambling around the counter, heading through the living room. My friends laugh at my excitement but I ignore them. When I turn the knob and yank the door open, my lips pull into a wide smile.

He ditched the suit and came in a pair of dark blue chinos and a white Polo shirt. His eyes sparkle when he sees me, and I can almost read the lewd thoughts behind them as he looks me up and down.

"Hey."

My teeth sink into my lip before I respond. "Hey."

He leans in for a kiss, his hand gripping my hip.

"Ahem," an obnoxious Renzo says from behind.

I roll my eyes. "Brace yourself."

After closing the door, we walk the few steps to the kitchen area where my friends congregate around the food I have out.

"This is Renzo, Ronan, Dominic, Trevor, and Dex." I turn and glance back at my man, standing confident with an easy smile. "This is Aleksander."

He shakes each of their hands, offering a *nice to meet you* or *how are you* to each of them.

"So, you're the one," Renzo says with a sly grin.

Alek drapes an arm over my shoulder, his other hand dipping into his pocket. "Which one is that?"

"The one that got our Jayden to settle down," Zo says with a wink in my direction.

I throw him a look, but Alek chuckles, glancing at me.

"Maybe I made him want to settle down, but he made me want to live. I suppose we've both done something for the other." When everyone, including me, is stunned silent, Alek laughs. "I wasn't one to want to settle down until him either. I guess it was kismet."

I stare at him for several seconds before I plant another kiss on his lips. He's gonna make it hard to keep those three little words from slipping.

"You see?" I say to my friends, hoping they understand why I feel the way I do.

"What?" Alek asks, a grin on his face.

"Oh, yeah," Trevor answers, as a few of them nod along.

"I feel like I've been left out of something," he muses, not offended in the slightest.

I laugh. "Don't worry about it. Food is done, by the way. I don't have seven seats at my dining room table, so four of us can eat there while the other three eat at this little bar."

Dex, Dom, and Trevor sit at the bar while Ronan, Renzo, me and Alek sit at the table. Everyone is still in the same area, because it's not like the apartment is huge.

"You made this?" Alek asks.

"Well, kind of. Ronan and Zo came over early and helped."

"It's good," Alek says, taking another bite of the chicken parmesan pasta.

"Nothing fancy. Don't expect me to be Chef Boyardee."

He laughs. "I won't. I'm hardly a cook myself."

Conversation ebbs and flows, but it never feels awkward. We always find something to talk about, and the guys ask him questions about his work while he takes interest in what they're doing now that they've graduated. Well, Ronan's still in college, but he talks about his job and his future plans.

After a couple hours, once dinner is long gone, we hang

out in the living room, watching TV, but mostly just talking. I can't explain how good it feels that everyone seems to get along.

Eventually, my friends start getting up, giving us time alone. Alek shakes everyone's hand again, and once the door closes after they've gone, I let out a breath.

"I think they like you."

"Good," he says with a grin from the couch. "Now come show me how much you like me."

"Oh, it's a whole lot. I'm not sure I have the capability," I tease.

"I look forward to the effort then."

Before I get to the couch, my phone dings multiple times. I open it up and see the messages from our group chat. First from Zo, then Dom, followed by Dex.

> He seems like a good guy. I'm happy for you.

> Tell Mr. Missionary that I approve.

> You definitely seem to be in love. Congrats, bro.

"I can confirm that they like you," I say, flashing him the phone as I sit next to him.

He studies the screen, holding the phone in place so he can read them. His eyes linger longer than they should need to considering they're all short messages. I realize he's probably dissecting Dex's text.

His eyes flicker up to mine and he offers me a sexy smile.

"Hmm. I think I like them, too. Might need to talk to this Dom about my nickname."

I laugh, dropping the phone to the cushion. "You're probably stuck with that one."

"Then I guess the only thing to do is bend you over this couch and have my way with you. Can't do missionary now." He leans in and nips at my lip. "But about that other message."

"Hmm?" I murmur, scooting down, allowing him to settle between my legs.

"You know the one."

His lips skate across my neck before he bites down on my earlobe.

"Renzo's?" I ask, playing dumb as I rub his back with my hands. "He likes you."

"Mmhmm," he murmurs, kissing down to my collarbone. "The other one."

"Dex?" I ask breathily, lifting my hips in an attempt to get some friction.

"Does he know something I don't?" he questions, his tongue licking up the middle of my throat, over my Adam's apple, until he kisses my chin.

"What do you mean?"

I wrap my legs around him, wanting him closer.

"Don't play games with me, Jayden," he growls, sending a shiver up my spine.

"I didn't say anything definitive," I reply, kissing his lips. "Just thoughts."

"Any thoughts you want to share with me?"

"I don't know," I reply honestly.

"Well," he says, punctuating it with a kiss before easing back into a sitting position. "I have some thoughts."

My pulse spikes and my stomach clenches. I scramble up

to sit next to him, both nervous and excited. "What kind of thoughts?"

He holds my hand in his as we face each other. "As you know, I've never done the relationship thing, therefore I've never allowed myself the opportunity to know what true, deep feelings are like. However, during our separation this last time, through all the conversations, and knowing what it feels like to not have you, I started wondering if this was it. How do you know?" he muses, eyes vulnerable. "I kept asking myself that. How do you know? Well, I guess I knew when I came back for the festival. For you.

"You see, I spent that time talking to my therapist, warring with myself, and missing you. I didn't want to be without you. I loved who I was when I was with you. I loved that you made me challenge myself, and how I wanted to be better for you. I was happier when we were together and miserable when we were apart, and if that isn't love, then I guess I don't know what is."

My breath leaves my lungs in a rush. "You love me?"

He grins, squeezing my hand. "Was that not clear?" he says with a laugh.

I stutter, looking for words. "I mean, I guess I didn't think you...I don't know. I'm surprised. I didn't want to scare you. I wasn't sure where you were at, but if I'm being honest, I wondered if you did when we were in Chicago at my parents house. The things you said, and my mom reiterating everything you were doing and giving up for me. How could I not see it? But you have to know how much you mean to me. For the first time in my life, I felt content, and I know that seems like a mediocre word, but I never felt satisfied and fulfilled, you know? Until you. I was my happiest with you. I never felt more at home, even in a hotel."

"God, I love you," he says, hand going to my neck, bringing me in for a kiss.

I pull away. "I love you, Alek. More than I can properly explain, but I do."

We come together again, our mouths connecting, tongues tangling, souls entwining.

Tonight, we make love.

Epilogue

JAYDEN

WE MADE IT SIX MONTHS. That's all. Any longer than that and I might've lost my mind completely. We moved in together just last week. The past few months was him either staying the night here or me sleeping in his bed. It was clear we couldn't get enough of each other, and the constant back and forth to get more clothes just didn't seem worth it. We were living together part time, and we needed that full-time promotion.

I hadn't quite made it a year in my apartment, but Alek paid out the remainder of my lease because my only option was to stay there a few more months and he wouldn't have it. For now, we're in his condo, which is bigger and better than mine, and as time goes on, we may find an actual house, but this is all we need.

"Hey, babe," I greet when I push open the door to his office. "My parents will be here soon."

He looks up and grins, patting his desk. I stroll over and perch my ass on it, and he rolls up in his chair, grabbing my hips. "Think we have time for a little fun?"

I run my fingers through his hair as he buries his face in my lap. "I wish we did."

"Well, that's unfortunate," he says, his head coming up, but his hands finding their way under my shirt, caressing my skin.

"You better stop teasing me," I warn.

"Or what?" he asks with a grin, arching a brow.

"I'm not about to give away my revenge plots."

He stands, pushing his lips against mine. "Fine. No more teasing."

"Well, not forever."

He smirks. "Later then."

I stand up and wrap my arms around his neck. "Have I told you how much I love you?"

"Not today," he answers, his arms snaking around my waist.

"Mm. Guess I'm slippin'"

"Guess you need to make it up to me."

"I will."

He reaches into his desk drawer and pulls out an envelope, handing it to me. "Here."

"What's this?" I ask, flipping it over to open it up.

"You'll see."

I pull out several pieces of folded paper and read them over.

"We're going on a trip?" I ask, my eyes wide. "To The Bahamas?"

"We'll spend a couple days in Miami first, but yeah. I remember you talking about wanting to go to a proper beach. We'll be staying at Atlantis Bahamas."

My eyes scan the rest of the papers, looking at the photos printed, and all the details of what he's planned.

"Holy shit," I say with a laugh. "I can't believe it. When?"

He takes a paper and brings it to the top, pointing out the

dates. It's a couple months from now, but I recognize the time frame. "That's when we met. An anniversary trip?"

Alek nods, his smile wide. "I love you, Jay. It's been an incredible ten months, and I can't wait for everything we'll do in the future."

I squeeze him tight in my arms, kissing his neck. "Fuck, I'm so lucky. I have no idea how I managed to land you."

"You were relentless, and beyond tempting."

I chuckle. "True. I knew what I wanted." I step back and study the papers again. "So, we'll be in Miami for your birthday. Lots of celebrating to do."

I found out later that he had just turned forty-one before we met, so our anniversary and his birthday are only separated by a few days.

The doorbell rings, alerting us that my family has arrived. It's the first time they've been here since my graduation, but we've had a few conversations over the phone, and Dad has adjusted well to us being together.

I stuff the papers in the envelope and place it on his desk before giving him another kiss.

We make our way to the living room, and I open the door to reveal my parents' happy faces.

Mom hugs me first before saying, "Hey, Alek," and wrapping her arms around him. "How are you?"

"Happier than ever."

She beams. "Good."

Dad enters, hugging me before extending his hand to Alek and giving him a slight nod. "Hey."

"How've you been?" Alek asks.

"Pretty great." Dad looks around. "This is a nice place."

"Thanks. It'll do for now," Alek replies.

Janae enters, giving me a hug and saying hello to Alek before she starts touring the place. "This is the kind of apartment I want when I move out."

"Then you better start making some money now," Dad jokes.

She rolls her eyes and Mom laughs.

"Well, I'm starving," Mom announces. "What do you say we make some dinner?"

"If you're helping, I'm down," I answer with a laugh.

"Boy, you still haven't learned to cook for yourself?" she chides.

"I have a little, but your food will always be better. You're the chef."

She makes a face. "Mmhmm. Don't butter me up. Let me see what you got here," she says, heading for the kitchen.

Together, the four of us work in the kitchen, making a meal while talking and laughing, all while my sister hangs out in the living room, popping up from time to time to question my peeling or chopping skills.

Dad and Alek talk about work and they seem to be just like they were on that night in the bar in the hotel. They drink, talk about people I don't know, joke, and it makes me smile to know their friendship will be okay.

"You look happy, baby," Mom says, catching me staring at Alek.

"I am," I reply. "I didn't know I could be this happy. I thought I was before, but being with him has multiplied that."

She chuckles. "Love will do that."

Alek glances over at me, giving me a wink that makes my stomach do a flip.

"Yeah, I guess you're right."

"I always am," she teases, pushing her hair over her shoulder. "And you're cutting those wrong," she says, pointing her knife at my carrots. "I want them to be julienne, and that's more barot."

I look down at my chunky carrot slices. "I don't know what that means."

"Thinner, baby. Here, let me show you."

"I think I want to switch jobs. Dad and Alek aren't even doing anything but watching the water boil."

"Hey, it's a very important job," Dad says with a laugh.

Alek strides over, placing a kiss on my temple. "Okay, I'm here to learn from the chef."

Mom grins and the two of them start dicing up more vegetables while I join my dad. We talk about work a little before getting into our usual heated sports debate. He prefers basketball, and obviously, football is better.

All five of us join together at the table and enjoy our dinner with casual conversation and lighthearted jokes. When they call it a night, leaving to go back to their hotel until tomorrow afternoon when we plan to meet up again, Alek and I breathe a simultaneous sigh of relief.

"That went better than I imagined," he says.

"Definitely. I was afraid there would be awkward tension."

"Your friends love me, your family loves me, so I don't think we have anything to worry about now," he says with a grin, tugging me into him.

"Now let me show you how I love you the most," I say, unbuttoning his pants.

"You're the boss," he replies with a smirk.

"Mm. I love when I'm the boss."

His breath hitches when my hand skates over his cock. "I love how you love me."

Acknowledgments

Thank you for reading! I hope you enjoyed Jay and Alek's journey. I made a few announcements about this, but in case you didn't know, this story was supposed to be completely different. I had originally planned on it being a student/teacher romance that had some MFM action in the beginning. I got to about thirty thousand words and wasn't feeling it. I couldn't connect and didn't want to deliver a mediocre book. I scrapped it and came up with this. Even though I had to push the release date and create this new deadline that made me crazy, I'm so glad I did. I love these two! I hope you do, too. Please take a minute to leave a review if you can.

I want to thank my husband, because he reads every book I put out, and helps me polish them up. I'm glad I don't have to do this without you. Thanks for always being available to listen and help, and thanks for understanding when I can't make dinner or be present because I'm stuck in my fictional world. You're truly the best. I appreciate you so much. I love you.

To Robin from Wicked by Design for creating my covers, and always bringing what I have in mind to life. You're simply amazing.

Huge thanks to Cass Thomasson for all the work you put into my ARC team and helping me with my books. I adore you!

Thanks to every reader and blogger who takes the time to read my book and leave a review. You guys are the best.

To every author who lets me share my books in your group or who does NL swaps with me, I appreciate you so much!

About the Author

Isabel Lucero is a bestselling author, finding joy in giving readers books for every mood.
Born in a small town in New Mexico, Isabel was lucky enough to escape and travel the world thanks to her husband's career in the Air Force. She and her husband have three kids and two dogs together, and currently reside in Delaware. When Isabel isn't on mommy duty or writing her next book, she can be found reading, or in the nearest Target buying things she doesn't need. Isabel loves connecting with her readers and fans of books in general. Keep in touch!

Sign up for my newsletter.
Join my reading group.